EVERNIGHT

ROSS MACKENZIE

ANDERSEN PRESS

First published in Great Britain in 2020 by
Andersen Press Limited
20 Vauxhall Bridge Road
London SW1V 2SA
www.andersenpress.co.uk

2 4 6 8 10 9 7 5 3

British Library Cataloguing in Publication Data available.

ISBN 978 1 78344 831 9

Printed and bound in Great Britain by Clays Ltd, Elcograf S.p.A.

For Lorna,
and the childhood
adventures we shared

Shadow Jack

There was a man made of midnight, and his name was Shadow Jack.

The name suited him well; his clothes were dark and his hair was darker. His eyes were pools of shadow. As he slipped through the winding labyrinth of the slums on the night our story begins, his intentions were darkest of all.

He crossed a wooden bridge to a putrid lump of half-flooded land cut off from the rest of the slums. Filth lay thick on crowded, leaning dwellings and the rain-swollen river was black as tar and coated with a film of weed and scum. There were few streets or alleys or courts; mostly there were only waterways and flooded ditches, channels crossing this way and that, with houses built upon crazy-looking wooden stilts to escape the water, which seemed to swell every minute with the rain.

This was Devil's Island, and even at such a late hour there were huddles of coats gathered on wooden boats, shifting movements in the darkest corners. They left Shadow Jack to his business.

He took a deep sniff of the soaking air, searching through the many layers of death and filth and disease.

'There you are.'

Cutting down an alley, he came out at the bank of a canal, and sniffed again.

Somewhere nearby, over the rain, he heard an argument, and a fight, and then all was suddenly quiet. Across the waterway, the flicker of a lamp caught his sharp eyes, where a sorry figure stumbled to a glassless window and tipped a bucket of sewage out into the water.

Shadow Jack made a movement, quick, fluid, and at once he was gone from that spot in the alley and a black raven the size of an eagle was soaring into the wild night. The raven circled, looking down over the winding waterways and canals and crumbling buildings of Devil's Island, and then it swooped down, coming to rest on the ledge of a high window.

The raven hopped into the damp-ridden apartment within. With a sound like dark velvet it became a man once more, wrapped in his midnight coat. The room was bare, save for a simple bed and a wooden chair under the small window. It seemed, at first glance, that there was nobody there. But Shadow Jack heard a heartbeat, fast and frightened.

'We both know you're here, Jenny Winter,' he said in a low, dangerous voice. 'You know what I am. Your tricks won't cut it with me. I hear your heart, hear how *frightened* you are. And you should be fright—'

He stopped, because across the room there was a shimmer in the air, and a woman appeared before his eyes as if she had been wearing a cloak made of the very fabric of the world and had slipped it off. Jenny Winter raised a trembling hand. In her fingers she clutched a thin wooden stick, fitted, like a pistol, with a round of chambers; but instead of bullets these chambers held small bottles, and inside the bottles were coils of glowing coloured light.

Shadow Jack picked a speck off his coat sleeve, and examined it, before flicking it away.

'You can't kill me with magic, you know. Twelve of you have tried and failed already.' He took a small step towards her, and she raised her wand. The spells glowed fiercely in their bottles.

'One more step, and I'll send you through that wall!'

Shadow Jack turned his eyes skyward. 'Look . . . we both know this journey has come to an end. You're on your own, Jenny. Wherever you go, I'll find you. You've been running so long . . . you must be *exhausted*.' His voice had taken on a soothing tone. 'Imagine how wonderful it would feel to be free of the weight you've been carrying. Give me the Doomsday Spell, Jenny, and it'll all go away.'

Jenny's thoughts betrayed her; her hand made an involuntary movement to the place in her coat where she had stowed that most precious of objects.

Her eyes met his.

Shadow Jack lunged forward.

It happened in a fraction of a moment: Jenny Winter flicked her wand at him, and one of the magic bottles shone bright as a new coin in the sun. The tip of the wand glowed, and a bullet of blazing light hit Shadow Jack in the chest. It sent him crashing through the rotting brick wall, and he was falling, falling.

Jenny watched him. When he hit the water, *splash*, she seemed to wake from a daze, and she turned and ran, barging down the stairs and out into the driving rain. Out of the alley, across a narrow wooden footbridge, the river churning below, and along another short street, falling on her front in hurry and panic, staggering back up, continuing on. Then across Devil's Gate Bridge to the city proper.

There was no plan in Jenny's mind, no safe place to run to. The rain and wind pelted her, merciless and cold, and her hair stuck to her face. Around a corner, down a narrow winding path – she scattered a pack of drunks, and they yelled and cursed after her. She ran and ran and ran, until her lungs burned and her legs stiffened and every breath was a knife in her chest. At last she stopped in a dark, deserted lane branching off Milk Street, collapsing to her knees in a puddle, sucking in ragged gulps of air. But there was no time for rest. She struggled up, found a manhole cover and pointed her wand at the ground. One of the bottles in the round lit up, and a blazing spell shot out of the wand

and hit the metal cover, leaving a crumbling black hole in the street.

The sewer stream below was a foaming torrent. Jenny knew at once if she tried to escape through the tunnels she'd surely drown.

Something moved, up by the rooftops. A huge raven circled down through the storm, landed in the lane up ahead. It spread its wings, made a movement, and in a swirl of rain and mist, Shadow Jack was back.

Jenny raised her wand and shot a spell through the night towards him. He dodged it. Desperately she shot another, and another, until each of the spell bottles loaded in her wand was empty.

'No more,' said Shadow Jack. He held out an open hand, and to his amazement, Jenny reached into her coat and produced the small box made of polished wood. He stared at it, hardly able to believe that, after all these years, here it was – the Doomsday Spell, the key to his freedom.

He reached out.

But Jenny Winter spat at him, spun away and tossed the box into the coursing sewer water below.

'You Hag!'

Shadow Jack clubbed Jenny on the side of the head, knocking her down, and stared into the rushing stream. When he turned back, she was fiddling madly with the compartments in her belt. She pulled out a bottle, tried to load it into the wand's revolver chamber, but he kicked her hand, and both the wand and spell bottle went spinning.

As he stood over her, something on her glinted, and Shadow Jack reached down and grabbed the slender chain she wore around her neck. With a jerk he snapped it and a wooden pendant slid into his hand. The pendant was the shape of a teardrop, and something had been etched into it, a symbol so simplistic that it might have been the work of a child.

A bird in flight.

Shadow Jack gazed at it for a moment, then reached into one of the many pockets of his long black coat. When he brought his hand out, and opened his fist, there were eleven identical pendants nestling in his palm.

'Yours is the last,' he said, dropping the pendant he'd taken from her onto the pile. 'A shame one of the thirteen was destroyed. I would have liked the complete collection.' He closed his long fingers around the trinkets and tipped them back into his pocket. 'I want you to know, Jenny Winter, that some of your friends broke easily when I found them over the years – without much persuasion at all in fact. A few of them begged, and bargained, and names and locations spilled out of them, until only your name remained.'

Jenny stared up at him through her soaking red hair. Blood from her mouth mixed with the rain and tears on her face.

'In all the old legends, the Djinn are powerful beings,'

she said. 'But you're not powerful. You're weak. You're broken, and desperate, and all I feel is pity.'

Shadow Jack crouched down, and Jenny noticed for the first time that he cast no shadow.

'I don't care what you feel. I only care about finding that spell and claiming back my freedom.'

'You don't know what you're doing! If Hester gets the spell it'll change *everything*!'

'What happens in this world is of no concern to me. When I am free, there are other worlds waiting. In any case, you won't have to worry about the future.'

Shadow Jack leaned in, almost as though he were going to kiss her. He opened his mouth wide, the bones in his jaw clicking and snapping, revealing rows of sharp teeth, and a gaping, rotten darkness. Jenny could not move, could not breathe.

'Are you frightened of me now, Jenny Winter?'

Jenny screamed.

Beneath the Streets

Larabelle Fox was sheltering in the tunnels beneath the city when she heard a commotion.

She almost didn't notice, such was the great cacophony of rain and wind and rushing water barrelling through the darkened sewers. Rivers of rain had fed the stream, leaving many of the tunnels inaccessible. Fierce water rumbled past her feet, splashing her wax-coated boots, gurgling and foaming, carrying twigs and leaves and drowned rats and cats.

Lara's eyes were sharp and alert, and they flicked here and there and all about, watching the water as it passed through the golden light from the dragon-breath lamp tied around her neck. Her muddled reflection stared back at her from the rough surface, thirteen years old and brown-skinned and fiercely focussed. She was hoping to glimpse shining things in the waters: coins, or lost jewellery.

But it was not a treasure that caught her attention now.

It was the sound of an argument.

Lara extinguished her lamp at once, and crushing darkness folded in on top of her. A newcomer to those tunnels would have been instantly lost. Disoriented. Panic-stricken. Not Lara. Lara breathed deep and stayed calm. She knew every twist and turn and dip of the sewers in the same easy, natural way a small child might know the rhythms of a nursery rhyme.

Creeping forward, she followed the voices, the sound of her footsteps smothered by the stream. Around a bend she went, to an intersection where several sewers met. Light spilled from an adjacent tunnel, and Lara slowed, crouching low against the smooth cold brick. She peeked around the corner, tingling with curiosity.

There were five of them. Five boys. Each was dressed in a tosher's things: a wax-coated jacket and boots and gloves, with a dragon-breath lamp hanging around his neck. Four of the boys were large, almost men, but the fifth . . . the fifth was younger, and much smaller. The four larger boys had formed a circle of sorts around the smaller one. Lara knew him very well indeed, for she had taught him the ways of toshing herself. His name was Joe Littlefoot, and he was looking around at the others with fierce, frightened green eyes.

'It's mine!' His hand hovered protectively on the toshing bag slung over his shoulder. 'I found this stuff fair and square. I'm not even on your patch!'

'Well, we've decided to expand,' said one of the older

boys. His head was pale and shaved, his voice gravelly from all the pipes he smoked. Vin Cotton was his name, and Lara knew about him and his gang, and was wary of coming across them. 'I reckon the tunnel running under Milk Street belongs to us now. Which means the loot you find here is ours.' He pointed to the bag.

'You can't just claim tunnels!' cried Joe.

'And who's goin' to stop us? *You?*'

Lara bristled at this, felt her hackles rise. Toshing was not a noble profession, perhaps, but there had always been a sense of honour to it, an unspoken respect between the folks who risked their lives to find lost things beneath the world. To be a tosher took guts, and smarts, and bravery, and Lara thought that Cotton had none of these things. He was a coward. A bully.

'Last chance,' he said.

Joe shook his head.

'I need whatever I can get. My granny . . . she needs lookin' after . . .'

Cotton held up a finger to quiet him. Then he brought a knife out from his coat and pushed the point of the blade against Joe's throat; not enough to draw blood, but certainly enough to frighten Joe out of his wits. Lara almost cried out.

'I don't give a Hag's tongue about your granny. You need to learn a lesson in respect, sunshine.' He nodded to the others. 'Take everything he's got.'

They closed in. Thinking quick, Lara reached into her

own toshing bag, and brought out a bent metal spoon she'd found in the tunnels earlier. She stood up, reared back, and threw the spoon as far down the sewer as she could manage. It hit the wall with a *CLANG* and Cotton and his gang spun around and held up their lamps.

'Who's there?'

'Run, Joe! Run!'

Lara stepped into the light, and Joe's eyes grew wide. He broke into a sprint, his wax-coated boots splashing through the water towards her. Then they were away, twisting, turning through the tunnels, the stinking air filled with curses and threats from Cotton and his gang.

'Son of a Hag! Get them!'

'You're dead!'

'Put your light out!' Lara told Joe. He did as she said, and soon they were running almost blind through the tunnels, guided by memory and instinct.

'Nearest way out?' asked Joe.

Lara tried to calm her breathing, pictured the sewers in her mind. 'Needle Street!'

They tore along, to a spot where the tunnel forked in two, and they took the path to the left, Vin Cotton and his gang chasing . . . yelling . . . *gaining* . . .

Still they ran, gasping and panting, until something awfully wrong dawned in Lara's head, making her skid to a halt.

'Why've you stopped?'

'Sshh. You notice something?'

'Yeah. I've noticed we've stopped. C'mon!'

Lara didn't budge. The air had changed. She tapped her foot on the tunnel floor.

'The sewer stream. Where's it gone?'

The rushing sewer water had become a trickle.

'What does it matter? Come on!'

'No! Something's not right!'

Lara fumbled for the lamp around her neck, sparked it to life, and honey-coloured light pushed back the darkness.

Joe began to shout at her, but then he stopped, and stood by Lara's side. The two of them stared up the tunnel. A short distance ahead, the walls had collapsed inwards, and the way was completely blocked by brick and debris.

Back the way they had come, Cotton was sloshing up the sewer.

There was no way out.

THE RATS

'What do we do? Lara?'

Lara did not speak, because truthfully she did not know the answer. Before she could think properly, four lamps came bobbing around the corner. Their light shone upwards, casting strange shadows on the smiling faces of Cotton and his pals, making them look like goblins. They approached like a pack of wolves, and Lara and Joe retreated until their backs pressed against the collapsed debris of the tunnel.

Cotton came forward and held up his lamp.

'Lara, right?'

Lara did not answer. Fear was crashing around her insides, but she was determined not to let it show. Not to Cotton. She clenched her fists so tightly that her fingernails almost pierced the skin of her palms, and she stared into his cold eyes.

'Never known you to wander into our patch,' said Cotton.

'It is not your patch. None of these tunnels belong to you.'

Cotton smiled. 'That so? Well I say different.' He paused, nodded to her toshing bag. 'I hear you're one of the finest toshers in the city. What you got in there?'

Lara shrugged. 'Nothin'.'

Cotton flashed a sharp blade of a smile. 'Hand it over.'

Lara clutched the bag tight. A tosher's bag was a sacred thing, almost part of the tosher herself. Lara would no sooner hand it over than lose an arm, or a finger.

'Fine,' said Cotton. He looked to his mates and indicated Joe. 'Take the little man's stuff.'

They moved quick, and before Lara could react, they rushed forward, one of them folding Joe in half with a fist to the gut, another grabbing his bag, and the third throwing him to the floor. It was over in a moment. Joe lay crumpled in the trickling sewer stream, coughing and moaning.

'Joe!' Lara crouched beside him, her hand on his back. She pointed at Cotton. 'You touch him again and I'll . . . I'll—'

A hand grabbed her arm, dragged her up, and Cotton stuck his face in hers. He wrapped a lock of her dark, tightly curled hair around his finger, and brought out the knife again, brushing the edge of the blade down Lara's cheek. 'Would be a shame to have to rearrange these pretty features.' He stopped then, and his eyes were drawn to Lara's neck. 'Hello. What's this?'

Cold fingers of panic closed around Lara's heart as Cotton grabbed at the fine metal chain she wore around her neck. On the end of the chain, hidden beneath Lara's clothes, was a teardrop-shaped wooden pendant. Cotton pulled the pendant out and examined it.

'You leave that be,' said Lara.

'Looks like cheap junk to me,' said Cotton. His breath was rank with tobacco. 'But maybe I'll take it anyway, just to teach you a lesson.'

Lara could take no more. She was beyond frightened, but her blood was on fire with anger. She brought her knee up hard.

'Ooof!'

Cotton dropped the knife but managed to grab her arm and twisted it almost out of the socket. She fell on her face in the stream and banged her head on the sewer brick, blurring the edges of her vision. Her dragon-breath lamp smashed in the fall, and its light went out. The tunnel filled with harsh laughter, and she knew as she lay in the cold trickle of sewer water that there was no clever trick that would save her this time, no way out.

The fog in her head dispersed, and by the glow of Cotton's lamp she glimpsed her scared reflection in the water. The smooth, dark skin of her forehead was grazed and painful, and her large eyes glistened with tears.

If we're lucky, she thought, *Cotton and his boys'll take the toshing bags and go. But if they decide they want to make an example out of us, we're finished.*

In the darkness nearby, something moved.

15

A black rat crept from among the fallen bricks and rubble. It came close, right to her face; Lara stayed still as it stopped and sniffed at her, its cold nose brushing her skin, whiskers twitching against her. She blinked away the tears of anger and pain and fear, and stared into the rat's shining black eyes. She remembered some of the old tosher stories, tales about packs of rats so fierce they could kill the unlucky cove who came across them in the tunnels.

I wish that would happen to Cotton, she thought. *I wish you and your friends could teach him a lesson.*

And then something happened that made Lara's breath catch.

As Cotton and his pals laughed at her, the wooden locket began to vibrate against Lara's chest. And at the same time a soft, musical whisper filled her head, delicate and otherworldly.

The rat sat up, and stared at her, and twitched its head to one side. Then the sound died away, and the locket became still, and the rat scurried off into the dark.

Someone wrenched Lara's toshing bag away from her. Two pairs of hands dragged her up, held her in place as Cotton grabbed his knife and wiped the muck off on Lara's clothes. Light from his lamp shone on the blade as it came up towards Lara's throat . . . Then Cotton became very still. 'What's that sound?'

Lara half closed her eyes, straining to hear. There *was*

something . . . A layer of noise beyond the distant rush of the stream and the storm.

Something familiar.

'Rats! It's rats, Vin!'

They came quickly, dozens of them, hundreds, so many that the floor of the sewer was a carpet of twitching bodies and tails. The rats ignored Lara and Joe, went straight for Cotton and the others, swarmed on them, climbing and scratching and biting.

Cotton and his boys were yelling and screaming, batting rats away, shaking them from their hair and clothes. They turned and ran, the four of them, stumbling over the chasing rats, bouncing off the sewer walls. Lara watched, jaw agape, as they disappeared down the tunnel, until the light from their lamps was gone and the sound of their shouting had died away.

As Joe sparked his lamp, something brushed against Lara's foot. A single rat stared up at her, whiskers twitching. Her hand felt for the locket under her clothes.

I banged my head, she thought. *I banged my head and imagined my locket came to life. That's what happened.*

'Lara?'

'Yeah, Joe?'

'What in hell's teeth just happened?'

Lara shook her head. The sewer stream rumbled in the nearby tunnels. 'I haven't a clue.'

THE KING'S WITCH

In the centre of the great, sprawling city of King's Haven, Mrs Hester, the Silver King's Witch, entered her private tower in the palace and began the climb to the uppermost room. It was a long way up; by the time she had reached the summit of the staircase, her every breath was a gasping rattle. She stopped to compose herself at the heavy door, stooped and hidden under a white shawl. She was glad that her lungs would soon be young again.

'Sorry to keep you waiting,' she said upon entering the chamber, taking a heavy old key and locking the door. 'I'm afraid the life of the King's Witch is a hectic one.'

The room was a square of bare stone; there was no carpet on the floor, no paintings or hangings on the walls. In the centre of the room sat a single wooden chair, fitted with straps for the arms and ankles and waist, the sort of chair designed to hold a person who wants very badly to get away. In front of the chair a tall, thin object stood draped with a silk sheet.

Mrs Hester observed the person who was strapped into the chair.

'So lovely,' she said, reaching out and running a knotted old finger down the line of the young woman's jaw. The young woman trembled and tried to pull her head away. A cloth rag had been tied around her mouth so that she could not speak, but she uttered frightened, muffled sounds and her eyes were pleading and wide.

'Hush now,' Mrs Hester told her, stroking her hair. 'I'm not going to *hurt* you.' She stood beside the chair, and the young woman stared up, tried to see through the layers of material covering Mrs Hester's head and face. 'You want to see why I'm hiding?' Mrs Hester said. 'All right, my pet. But I warn you, it isn't pretty.'

Mrs Hester reached up and removed the shawl.

When the young woman saw what was hiding beneath, her eyes bugged almost out of her head, and the muffled sounds she made became high and desperate.

Mrs Hester's face was a horror, a mask of age and time and decay. It seemed that her features were made of wax, which had melted and begun to run and drip. Her eyes, hidden deep in their ancient sockets, were covered in a membranous white film. Her nose was sunken and shrivelled and came to a hideous gristly point. Her mouth was a narrow, dark pocket devoid of moisture. There were nightmarish folds of paper-thin skin hanging from her neck, and silver whiskers sprouting from her sagging cheeks. Most of her

19

bald pate was showing, covered only here and there with a scattering of straggly white hair.

Mrs Hester shuffled to the tall object in front of the chair and removed the silk sheet to reveal a full-length mirror, set in a wooden frame carved in the shapes of many birds: crows and sparrows and owls, blackbirds and starlings and eagles. The mirror was double-sided, so that the young woman in the chair could see her reflection, and Mrs Hester could see herself in the opposite side.

'My, I do look a state, don't I?' She shook her head, making the hanging skin on her neck swing back and forth. 'But that's what happens, you see, when you're as old as I am, when you've been around for as long as I have.' She touched her waxy features with twisted fingers. 'And the spell is unpredictable. I can never quite tell when it's going to fade. It happened very quickly this time. Which is why we're here, my pet. To sort it.' She glanced around the edge of the mirror at the young woman in the chair. 'I told you, my pet, that it won't hurt. You are doing your country a great service. You should be very proud.'

Mrs Hester reached into her white robes and brought out first her wand and then a tiny spell bottle filled with a few drops of dark, inky liquid. She walked round, so that she was standing behind the chair, and she said, 'Just one more thing, pet. Then we can begin.' She reached down and plucked an auburn hair from the young woman's head, then she took the stopper from the bottle and, with shaking hands, fed the hair into the bottle. As she replaced the stopper, the spell began to spark and fizz and turned the shimmering, streaked-silver of a pearl. 'There we go.'

Mrs Hester took her place on the other side of the mirror again and loaded the spell into her wand's chamber. She reached out and touched the tip of her wand to the mirror. The spell flared bright.

On the young woman's side of the mirror, the wooden birds carved into the frame all turned their heads towards her. The young woman stared wide-eyed around at them, half expecting the birds to break loose. But that is not what happened.

Instead, the young woman's gaze was drawn to her own reflection. At first she thought that her terrified mind was playing tricks. But then she looked closer, and she could see, with creeping horror, that it was real. Her reflection was changing.

It began with a series of deepening lines around her eyes and mouth, and then her hair began to thin and change colour, fade to dirty grey. Although her mouth was tied shut she could feel her teeth rotting away, her gums receding and drying out. Her shoulders became stooped, her hands painful and twisted, her fingers misshapen. The colour in her eyes faded, and her skin became a loose covering of rubbery folds. In less than a minute an entire lifetime had passed for the young woman's reflection. When she looked down at her hands and saw that it was real, that it was not

21

some trick and that she really was an old woman now, a dry, muffled sob escaped her, but she was too weak to struggle, too tired and racked with the pain of old age to do anything but sit slumped in her chair and stare at her new reflection.

On Mrs Hester's side of the mirror, the opposite was happening.

Where her reflection had been riddled with the decay of extreme old age, it was now becoming young. The hands of the clock were turned back as her skin flattened and smoothed, her eyes became large and deep brown, her hair became sleek and silver-blonde. Mrs Hester raised her hand, watching her fingers straighten and the age spots on her flesh fade until her complexion was silky smooth. When it was done, Mrs Hester was a much younger woman once more, and quite beautiful.

She turned this way and that, examining her reflection, a smile playing on her full lips. Only when the sobbing, mewing sound from the other side of the mirror became too much of an annoyance to ignore, did she walk around to the chair.

Only a minute ago a beautiful young woman had been sitting there. Now the unfortunate creature was hunched and ancient, barely able to hold up her own head. Mrs Hester observed her, stared at her baggy skin and empty mouth, at her milky eyes and mangled joints, and she almost felt sorry for her.

Almost.

But Mrs Hester was young again, and there were more important things to consider.

She stroked the old woman's hair.

'Hush now, my pet. I told you it wouldn't hurt, didn't I? You've done a great thing today, and that thought should comfort you in your final hours.'

The old woman tried to make a sound, but Mrs Hester was already out of the door.

THE DOOMSDAY SPELL

In a far-off part of the palace, King August Nightingale – supreme ruler of the Silver Kingdom – sat at a grand desk in a grand room and wrote a message. The only sounds as he worked were the scratching of the nib on witch paper, and the pop and crack of the fire.

When the king was satisfied he put down his pen. The chair creaked under his enormous weight as he leaned back and watched the witch paper arrange itself in a series of crisp folds, until it had become an angular paper bird. The paper bird hopped around the desk, spread its wings and circled the room as the king opened a tall window. The paper bird swooped through the open window and the king watched it flash out over the city.

The door to the chamber opened, and the king knew at once that Mrs Hester had joined him. She was the only person brave enough to enter his rooms without knocking first. He turned to her.

'I see you've sorted yourself out,' he said.

Mrs Hester moved her jaw around as if trying to loosen something tight. 'Yes, Your Majesty. Always takes a while to get used to my new skin. You sent for me?'

The king nodded, and Mrs Hester noted the troubled look in his eyes.

'More White Witches run away with the Hags, Your Majesty?'

The king's rage boiled over. He slammed the window shut, rattling the glass panes. 'It's unacceptable!'

Those damned Hags! A flicker of rage lit up in her chest, but Mrs Hester extinguished it, remained calm. The last thing she wanted to do was let the king know that her powers were weakening. There was a deep leather armchair by the fire, and she sat down and ran a hand through her hair. It felt good to have a full head of hair again. 'It's troubling, I'll admit . . .'

'Troubling? Your own people are turning against you and that's all you can say?'

Mrs Hester pressed the tips of her fingers together. 'What would you like me to say?'

The king's face darkened. 'I'd like you to tell me that it won't happen again!'

'If I said that, I'd be lying, Your Majesty. But I am working on something. And I'm close to finding a solution, I hope. True, the Hags from Westerly Witch have helped a small number of our White Witches escape, but what we must remember, I think, is that these cases are rare. Without souls, my White Witches don't have it in them to allow for such concepts as love or freedom. So most of them don't *want* to escape, see? They are born into servitude, just as their parents and their parents' parents were. They serve you. It is part of them. But extracting a soul is a complicated business, Your Majesty, and perhaps I might have made mistakes over time, maybe left a little of the soul in the body. That's what's caused this desire to leave in a tiny handful of them. But I don't reckon it can be many.'

Did she really believe that, though? How long, she wondered, had she been losing her grip? How many mistakes?

The Silver King scoffed. 'What if there's an army of them all plotting and waiting for the Hags to come along and help them escape? Every revolution begins with a whisper, Mrs Hester. What if the whispers from your Witches become a din we cannot silence?'

'Your Majesty, this problem can and will be solved. But it will take some time—'

'Just get it done!' said the king, bringing his fat fist down on the desk petulantly. He was thirty-five years old, still a relatively young man, and at times like this, when he was angered or troubled, he often resembled an overgrown toddler. He was spoilt, and selfish, and had no interest in his two young sons, whom he'd sent away to live in a castle in the south with their mother so that he could concentrate on the things he cared about, like hunting and eating and drinking fine wine. His thick, rubbery lips curled into a half sneer. 'If I can't trust my White Witches any more, Mrs Hester, if they all run off and leave me, remind me exactly why I will still need *you*?'

For a moment, Mrs Hester's eyes flared wide.

How dare you, she thought. *Hell's teeth, without me there might not even* be *a Silver Kingdom, at least not as great as it is today! And revolution? Don't talk to me about revolution, boy! I started my own revolution, and if things had worked out, if I had taken the throne in Westerly Witch all those hundreds of years ago . . . the world would be a very different place. I would not be answering to you for a start, you fat, slimy . . .*

Mrs Hester did not say any of this out loud, of course. She had seen many Silver Kings and Queens come and go, and she had learned how to play the game.

So she bowed to the king, her false deference a little over the top, and said, 'I hope, soon, Your Majesty, to show you I can still be useful. Will there be anything else?'

The Silver King grunted, sat back down and began once again to write at his desk.

Mrs Hester made a face to the back of his head and left the chamber.

Five minutes later she slammed the door of her own apartments with such force that the bottles on her shelves clinked and rattled. From one of these shelves she carefully lifted an ancient clay urn, its markings worn away by the ravages of time. Mrs Hester removed the lid, activating the ancient summoning spell binding Djinni to urn. An inky swirl of air appeared in the middle of the room, and when it was gone, Shadow Jack was standing before her.

In his hand he held a knife. The blade was wet with fresh blood.

Mrs Hester looked at the blade, and the blood, and raised an eyebrow.

'Did I interrupt something?'

'It can wait, Mistress,' Shadow Jack said, stowing the knife away. 'You have a new face.'

'I do.'

'It looks . . . upset.'

'No, it's just impatient.' She narrowed her eyes. 'How long until the spell is ours? You promised me we were close. More White Witches have escaped and the king is losing patience. I need to squash those Hags, once and for all.'

'Only a day or two. Jenny Winter is dead. The Coven is no more.'

'So what are you waiting for? Where is the spell?'

'There was a slight . . . problem. The Doomsday Spell is in the sewers. But fear not. I've already searched many of the tunnels, so I'm closing in. It will soon be yours.'

'And if someone else finds it before you do?'

'The only people down there are toshers and bandits. If one of them finds the spell, they won't have a clue what it is. They'll try to sell it, and I have every merchant and shopkeeper in the city on the lookout. Either way, it's imminent.'

Mrs Hester worried her bottom lip. The small dappling of freckles on her smooth forehead knitted. 'I can almost taste it. I'm so close.'

Shadow Jack's head dropped to one side. 'You are sure you want to do this, Mistress? You seem a little anxious.'

Mrs Hester glared. 'I'm about to set everlasting darkness loose on the world, and the only thing that can control it again is a spell, which you have promised to find me but failed to deliver! So it's you who should be anxious, because if you don't find me that spell, it'll be back in the urn for you. Or have you forgotten who's in charge here?'

'No, Mistress.'

'Good. Those Hags in Westerly Witch have made a fool of me for long enough. I want them gone, and I want that Mother Tree all to myself.' She stroked her hair. 'Show me again.'

Shadow Jack rolled his eyes. This all seemed so *small*. He was a Djinni, made by ancient Gods, forged in fire and shadow during a war that had left the universe a smoking ruin. It was a war between two factions of Gods: Light and Dark, and their armies were conjured from dust and flame and rock. Shadow Jack had been on the side of the Goddess Lady Light, but the war had been long, and he'd wanted it to end, and so he had betrayed his mistress and gone to the darkness. When the war was over, Shadow Jack had found himself on the losing side, and when the Gods had gone on to different realities, Shadow Jack had been left behind in an urn as punishment for his great betrayal. He was as old as this world, and there were only two things in it as ancient as he.

One was the great Mother Tree of Westerly Witch. It was said that when the last of the Gods, Mother Earth, left this reality, her tears had formed the oceans, and from the water sprouted the Mother Tree – whose enchanted Blossom charged the air, the source of all magic.

And the other . . .

A living weapon left over from the War of the Gods. A hateful, hungry darkness.

With a snap of Shadow Jack's fingers, Mrs Hester's chambers melted away, and the two conspirators stood inside a vision that seemed very real, on the banks of a great black lake under a night sky ablaze with stars. In the middle of the lake stood a small island of jutting rock. Mrs Hester stared over at it, looked down at her hands, and saw that she was trembling. It was in there, in that island, a darkness as old as Shadow Jack. She could feel it bubbling and writhing under the earth, trapped, starving, angry . . . the Evernight.

Another of Shadow Jack's finger snaps, and they were back in the reality of Mrs Hester's lamp-lit rooms.

'Get after that spell,' she told him, clasping her hands to try to hide the shaking. 'I've waited long enough.'

Without hesitation, Shadow Jack became an enormous raven and flew out of the open window. Mrs Hester watched him disappear over the city.

Her eyes turned to the West, and she thought of the Mother Tree and the city of Westerly Witch that she had once called home. She remembered clearly the great Blossom blooming every spring on the mountain-sized tree, its glowing flowers breathing magic into the world. The smell sweet as honey, and the sound crystalline and musical.

And it would all soon be hers.

With the help of the Evernight, she would wipe the Hags away like a stain. After that, she'd ride to the rescue, banish the darkness and be hailed a saviour. Every flower of the Blossom, every petal, every crystalline whisper of pure magic, would belong to her. And all she needed to complete her plan was an ancient spell hidden in the workings of a clockwork bird.

The Doomsday Spell.

RAIN AND IRON

The rain wasn't just falling, it was driving down from the heavens; trying, it seemed, to punch through the world. Despite the freakish weather, Thimble Road was filled with milling crowds, sellers and stalls and horses and carts, and the racket of the slums at work.

'Fresh fruit! Get your fresh fruit!'

'Here! Your horse tried to bite me!'

'Roasted chestnuts! Two bronze coins a bag!'

'Blueshell crab! Cockles! Mussels! Hot fish-eye soup!'

Among the bustle and commotion, a manhole cover in the middle of the uneven cobbled street jumped out of place and tipped over, and two scruffy, muck-covered children climbed out of the darkness, drawing gasps and murmurs from passers-by.

Lara and Joe slid the cover back into place and then hurried through the crowds, ducking under umbrellas, dodging puddles and piles of horse manure, until they came to shelter under the awning of a coffee house. The delicious aroma of roasting coffee overpowered the stench of the slums, of horses and chimney smoke and the great many people who might have benefitted enormously from an introduction to soap.

'You ever seen anythin' like that?' Joe asked, shaking the water from his messy blond hair. 'What them rats done in the sewer?'

Lara turned up the collar of her toshing coat against the rain. 'Never.' Her hands kept returning to the locket, making sure it was still. But that was daft, wasn't it? Of course it hadn't come to life! She'd been frightened, and had a bang on the head, and her imagination had done the rest.

'I've never in my life seen so many of 'em,' Joe went on. 'It was almost like they knew we was in trouble! Like they was *helping* us.'

'Don't be daft, Joe. They're rats! They got smaller brains than even you.'

He shrugged and looked up at her – Joe was eleven, two years younger than Lara, and very small and slight – and there was a sort of quiet awe in his expression. 'You *saved* me.'

'Don't be soft. Now you listen to me: don't go anywhere near the Milk Street tunnels again.'

'Lady Light save us! Don't fuss over me so much, Lara.'

'I mean it. It's dangerous enough down there at the best of times. I heard the coppers busted a Hag over in Crippleback Street yesterday – flushed a whole bunch of forbidden spells down the drain. Now all that wild Hag magic is a-runnin' through the sewer stream. You turn the wrong corner and you could end up as a piglet, or with flowers growin' out your nostrils or some such thing.' She suddenly stopped, and her mouth dropped open. 'I bet the rats that helped us were under the spell of some of that flushed-away magic!'

Joe's eyebrows knitted together. 'Would make sense I s'pose. They have been catching an awful lot of Hags recently, haven't they?'

Lara gave a grim nod. It wasn't something folks were supposed to talk about but there did seem to be a lot more Hags around these days. There had been whisperings that even some of Mrs Hester's White Witches had run away, brainwashed by the Hags. But how was that even possible? The White Witches were controlled by Mrs Hester and had no minds of their own. They lived only to serve the Silver King. Their spells were heavily regulated, produced in great factories to help the Silver Kingdom remain strong: spells to strengthen armour, or to grow gigantic crops to feed the army, or to give life to the metal horses that pulled the carts and carried the soldiers without ever growing tired. White Witch spells were numbered and labelled and never allowed to fall into the hands of everyday folk, for even sterile, unimaginative White Witch spells could be unstable in the hands of non-magical folk, resulting in the most unpredictable outcomes.

As for Hags . . . well, a more feared and despised race you would be hard pressed to find. Hags and White Witches had, as far as Lara could gather, been the same people, until the White Witches broke away many hundreds of years ago and moved across the sea to the Silver Kingdom. Hag magic was every bit as wild and imaginative and untamed as White Witch magic was colourless and sterile. Hags were outlaws, and whenever a Hag was caught, her spell bottles would be dumped into the sewers. Most of the spells made their way out to the Pewter Sea and sank to the ocean floor. But some bottles would become stuck, or damaged, and that is where the danger to toshers began . . .

'I'm sorry you got dragged into all that,' said Joe. He shook his head. 'It was my fault. I should've been more careful. I walked right into 'em.'

'Hell's teeth, don't be so glum, Joe! We escaped, didn't we? Just be careful from now on – we don't need to add Cotton and his pals to the list of things that might kill us.'

'I know, Lara.'

She ruffled his hair, which she knew he hated. Funny, when he'd first started hanging around, she'd thought of him as an annoyance. Like a scab. She'd tried to pick him off and flick him away, but he just kept growing back, didn't he? And then she'd found out about his poor granny and she'd helped him out here and there. And now it was two years later, and she'd grown quite fond of him – as fond as a person can be of a scab.

'I can look after myself, you know,' he said. 'I'd have given 'em a couple of sore 'uns, let 'em know they were in a fight . . .'

Lara chuckled. 'Course you would.'

He glanced at the remnants of the shattered dragon-breath lamp in Lara's hand. 'I'll get you a new one. I owe you.'

Lara poked a finger in his chest. 'Joe Littlefoot, if you get me a new lamp I'll be so mad, you'll wish you were back in the sewers with Cotton!'

'Least let me fix you some soup,' said Joe, looking at his boots. 'I've been on a lucky streak in the tunnels. I managed to buy some decent veg, and some chicken bones to make stock. It's tasty, it is.' He raised an eyebrow. 'There's potato in it.'

Lara's belly had been rumbling for days. She couldn't remember a time when the sewers had treated her so stingily. She hadn't found anything worth selling to Old Hans – who'd buy treasure from toshers to sell in his shop – for well over a week. 'Sure you got enough?'

'Positive. Granny would love to see you.'

Lara gave him a sad smile. That might have been true once. Not any more. 'Right. You're on.'

The wind picked up, howling through the narrow, crooked streets, and some poor woman's umbrella flew out of her hand and spun off through the air. Lara and Joe watched it tumble, head over handle, until it hit the body of an ironheart, a great metal horse made of iron and clockwork, enchanted into life by the king's White Witches. The umbrella landed on the puddled ground, and one of the ironheart's metal hooves came down upon it, crushing and shattering the umbrella as if it was made of fragile glass. The ironheart was pulling a cart loaded with barrels, and Lara and Joe ran to the back of the cart and hopped on, hitching a sneaky ride.

Tea Leaves and Trouble

The stink of the tenement building was thick. It pressed on Lara's skin as she followed Joe up the stairway. The bare floor was filthy, and all around were the sounds of arguments and raucous laughter and crying babies from overcrowded apartments.

Up and up they climbed, until there were no more stairs, only a very small door in a leaning, toadstool-infested wall. Joe fished a key from his coat, unlocked the door, and showed Lara inside.

The attic room was tiny and bare. There were two beds, and a stove, and that was about all, aside from a tatty armchair by a dirty window. In this armchair sat a frail-looking old woman. She did not seem to notice that Lara and Joe had come in. There was a threadbare patterned blanket over her legs, and her bony hands sat clasped on her lap.

'I'll get the soup on,' said Joe. 'You want tea?'

The rain had soaked them through, and Lara was shivering.

'Please.'

Joe busied himself at the stove.

'Watcha, Granny,' said Lara to the old dear.

Granny was staring out of the window, but her gaze did not appear to be fixed on anything. When Lara spoke, it seemed to take a minute or two for the words to reach her, then she looked up, and smiled, and for a moment Lara thought there might be a flicker of recognition in her eyes.

'Hello, my love. Oh my! You are a pretty one, aren't you? That lovely dark skin and those shining eyes! I bet all the boys is after you! Is this your house?'

Lara closed her eyes for a long moment, disappointment filling her up. She forced a smile. 'No, Granny. This is your house, remember? You live here with Joe.'

Granny gave her a blank stare, and then her old eyes lit up. 'I have a daughter you know. About your age. Do you know her?'

Lara didn't know what to say. Granny's daughter – Joe's mum – had died years ago when Joe was very little. Joe caught her eye and gave a sad shrug, and when the kettle began to whistle Lara was glad for the distraction.

The tea was hot and sweet, and it warmed their chilled bones.

'Does she ever remember things?' Lara whispered.

Joe sipped at his tea. 'Less and less. And she don't eat much . . .'

He stopped talking just then, because the old lady had

turned in her seat, and she seemed suddenly alert. She pointed a finger to Lara's cup. 'Finish that up, my love, and I'll read your leaves.'

Years ago, before she'd begun to forget, Granny had been well-known in this part of the slums as a gifted reader of tea leaves. She had predicted lots of things successfully, like whether an unborn baby was going to be a boy or a girl, or where and when a young woman might meet the man she would one day marry. She had once predicted a great flood and saved many hundreds of lives in the slums. But people were also suspicious of tea-leaf readers and Granny had learned it was best to keep her gift quiet.

Lara finished the last of the tea, leaving just a drop in the bottom. She gave the cup to Granny, who took it in her hands and sloshed the last drops around, gazing at the fragments of leftover leaves. She rolled her tongue around the inside of her mouth.

'You're leaving. Leaving King's Haven. Leaving the Silver Kingdom.'

Lara frowned. 'Leaving? No, Granny, I don't think that's right . . .'

Granny held up a finger, but she did not look up from the cup. 'I'm only tellin' you what the leaves say, love. Now, what else . . . Yes . . . Oh! I see you flying.'

'Flying?' Lara gave Joe a sideways look.

'On blazing wings, my love! Wings the colour of the sun!' She was becoming quite animated, sloshing the leaves around in the cup. 'The locket. Do you still have the locket?'

Lara's surprise was sharp and quick. She had never told anyone about the locket, not since she'd run away from the orphanage when she was small. 'How do you know about *that*?'

'It's not me, my love. It's the leaves. Now. *The locket.* Do you still have it?'

Lara nodded. All at once she was uncomfortable and troubled. The irrational feeling that something bad was coming swept over her.

'Good,' said Granny. 'That's important, that is. Keep it close. Keep it safe! Listen to it!' She really was becoming overly animated now, twitching around in the chair, trying to get to her feet. Joe placed a gentle hand on her thin arm.

'Granny. You need to calm down. Just sit, eh? Relax.'

She struggled against him, looked into the cup again, and her expression filled with darkness. She let go of the cup as if it had caused her pain, and it fell and smashed on the floor. 'Oh! Oh, I am sorry! I'm an old fool!'

'Don't worry, Granny. Just an accident is all.'

Joe went to fetch a broom.

'Are you all right, Granny?' Lara put a hand on the old woman's wrist. Her pulse was beating hard and fast.

Granny stared into Lara's dark eyes and said, slowly and deliberately, 'She's going to release it. Oh my heavens, she's going to do it!'

'Who, Granny? Who's going to release *what*?'

'The woman! The woman with the false face . . . she's going to release the Evernight.'

Evernight. The word sent Lara's thoughts rushing suddenly back to a time when she was very young, to the orphanage, and the stories the older kids told in the dark.

Without warning, Granny's hand clamped tight around Lara's wrist. 'They will come for you, girl. The woman with the false face and the man with no shadow.'

Lara's heart raced but a vacant smile had now washed over Granny's features and she'd returned to staring fixedly out of the window. The sound of the rain on the glass seemed very loud. The old lady's eyes moved from the window to Lara, and the expression on her face was one of surprise, as if she were seeing her for the first time. 'Oh. Hello, my love. Is this your house?'

Lara's fingers were touching the locket through her shirt. 'No, Granny,' she said. 'No it isn't.'

HOME

There were so many people in the slums of King's Haven it reminded Lara of the crates of crab she'd sometimes see down at the docks, all living and crawling and fighting on top of one another. Many got by in the poorhouses, slaving away in return for a bowl of sludge at the end of the day and a bed in a crowded, stinking dorm. Others, the lucky ones like Joe and Granny, lived in crumbling tenement buildings, entire families crammed in small, disease-ridden rooms.

Not Lara.

She'd already spent a chunk of her childhood living in other people's pockets, sharing dormitories and classrooms. When she'd run away she'd promised herself that she'd find something better.

And she'd kept that promise, just as sure as she'd kept the promise to be the best tosher in the city, and the promise to never rely on anyone else, because if you didn't give people the chance, then they couldn't let you down.

The Aurelian Opera House sat near the centre of the

city, away from the slums, on the banks of the great river Anchor. It was a huge old jewellery box of a building, the sort of place only real toffs could afford to visit; the Silver King himself had a private box there, among the red velvet and gold and the smells of caramel and slick polished mahogany.

Above the grand, cavernous opera hall there was an ancient attic. The attic was filled to bursting with countless trinkets and props and pieces of set gathered from many years' worth of performances and shows. It was so old, in fact, and the opera house had been built upon and extended so much, that people had forgotten that this attic existed. And so the jumble of sets there, the galleons and castle walls and painted hillsides, had gathered dust. It was a rambling, lost museum.

Lara had discovered the attic years ago and decided that it would do nicely.

Her bed was a sleigh made of wood. She had arranged sheets and blankets in such a way that it was comfortable and warm, and tonight she lay beneath those blankets, holding her wooden locket up to the light of a single dragon-breath lamp. Her finger traced the engravings on the polished casing. On one side, a simple bird in flight. On the other, a hurried scratching of letters forming a name. *Larabelle Fox.*

'That's important, that is,' Granny had said. 'Listen to it!'

Listen to it. What does that mean? It's a hagging lump of wood!

She turned the locket over in her fingers, every part of it familiar. Flashes of memory came to her: the disinfectant smell of Miss Wratchet's Home for Wretched Souls. The cold darkness of the dormitory and the echoing voices of the older children as they told stories . . . eerie stories of a night without end, and the ghastly, wild monsters who came with it. The Evernight, and the Painted Folk.

The thoughts made her shiver and she gripped the locket tightly. In all the world, the wooden locket was the only thread connecting her to the life she'd once lived, a life that had been stolen away on the night she'd been lifted from the wreckage of the terrible disaster on Crippleback Street: a tiny, miraculous survivor.

When she'd run away from the orphanage, Lara had tried to find things out, had gone to the neighbourhood where she had once lived, back to Crippleback Street. The people there – at least the ones who were not drunk – were friendly enough and had no trouble recalling the night of the incident.

'A great big explosion ripped right through one of the tenements,' a toothless old woman had told Lara. 'Tore through the brick like it was paper. And nobody could figure out what caused it.'

When Lara had broached the subject of her parents, though, neither the old woman nor anyone else she asked had been able to remember anything at all. It was as if Lara's family had been ghosts.

Presently, Lara wedged her fingernails into the tiny gap between the two halves of the locket, and she tried and tried to prise it open. What if there were pictures of her parents in there? People kept pictures in lockets, didn't they? She wondered if she looked like her mother or her father. Had they both been dark-skinned? Had her mum's hair grown outwards in tight black curls like her own? Sometimes she'd imagine that they were still alive, close her eyes and concentrate and almost *feel* them hugging her. But coming back from those imaginings was so painful that she had not tried it for a while.

The locket would not budge; it never did. Her fingernail bent back, and she swore and tossed the locket across the attic. It pinged and rattled its way to the floor among the many scattered things.

Panic flooded Lara's insides.

She stumbled across the attic, and began to toss objects out of the way, lumps of wood and lengths of rope, crates and boxes, her heart freezing up at the thought that the locket might be gone. Ah, but there it was, nestling in a pile of rags! Lara snatched it up and held it to her chest.

'I'm sorry,' she said. 'Never again.'

Tiredness took her then, and she climbed beneath her blankets and let sleep embrace her, the locket still clutched to her heart.

THE WHITE WITCH

Double Eight's heart beat furiously as he snuck out of bed in the still darkness of the dormitory. The room was long and narrow and bare, lined on either side with twenty-five identical metal bunks – fifty beds in total – and in forty-nine of these White Witches slumbered.

Double Eight stared around as best he could; the only light came from the tall arched window at the end of the dormitory. The silence was broken by the drum of his pulse and the gentle snores of the sleeping White Witches.

Wearing a plain white nightgown, Double Eight crept silently through the dormitory, casting wary glances. He had no doubt that the others would report him if they saw him out of bed, and the punishment would be brutal. Worse still, if anyone discovered the *reason* he was out of bed . . . well, then he'd have to face Mrs Hester – and everyone knew what she did to traitors.

Things were changing. Double Eight could feel it in his bones. Recently there had been rumours of runaways, mutterings that the Hags from Westerly Witch had finally found a way to rescue White Witches from slavery. As the rumours had grown, so had Double Eight's desire to listen to the voice inside him, the one that had always been there, that had begun as a seedling in his mind and grown and blossomed until he was fit to burst.

The voice told Double Eight that there was more to life than servitude.

And then, a moon or so back, there had been the strange incident with the beggar.

Double Eight had been trudging through the streets, a speck in a White Witch river heading towards the spell factories for another day's work in the heat of the cauldrons, when a commotion had startled him. As he came nearer, he discovered that an old crippled man – a beggar – had fallen on the wet cobbles and could not get up. He was moaning and pleading for assistance, and yet the White Witches were ignoring him, walking around him, over him, as if he did not exist. Double Eight could not simply leave the old man there to be trodden on, so he helped him up and fetched him his crutch.

'Oh, Lady Light bless you!' the beggar exclaimed as Double Eight helped him over to a ledge on which he could recover. 'Bless the White Witches! Bless the king!' When Double Eight tried to turn away, the old man had grabbed his hand with a tremendous grip. His eyes had been bright and quick. 'Do you wish to be free?'

Double Eight had been struck dumb by this sudden outburst, but the beggar smiled.

'Your eyes give you away,' he said. 'There's humanity in 'em. Life. Hester didn't get all your soul, boy – she left a little bit in there! You *do* want freedom, don't you?'

Double Eight glanced back at the joyless, stony faces of his fellow White Witches. 'More than anything.'

The beggar was still clutching his hand tight. 'We'll be in touch,' he said, and he spun Double Eight around and pushed him back towards the Witches. When Double Eight glanced back, the beggar was gone.

The first paper bird had arrived a few days later in the dead of night, turning to smoke as soon as he'd read its message.

You are not alone, Double Eight. We are watching. We are close by and we will help you when the time is right . . .

They began to arrive quite regularly, and he'd sit up in the dark and wait for the quiet sound of the flapping paper wings.

Westerly Witch can offer you a new life . . .

We can protect you . . .

The time is close . . .

Tonight, Double Eight was following the directions of the most recent message – only the second paper bird to have requested a reply. The first, last week, had prompted him to find a safe place to stow away an object roughly the size of a matchbox. Double Eight had taken a great risk by smuggling a butter knife out of the food hall and keeping it in his lumpy mattress. Over the course of several nights, he had used the knife to loosen one of the floorboards by his bed.

Tonight's risk, though, was far greater.

When he reached for the door handle, Double Eight's hand shook badly. He tightened his grip, clenched his jaw. Then, scouting around the sleeping dormitory, he turned the handle, opened the door and slipped out into the passageway.

The White Witch district was in the east of King's Haven, near the huge factories where the White Witches were put to work. The district comprised of a number of huge, institutional buildings, grand and stern and colourless, housing every White Witch in the city. White Witches were afforded no luxuries by the Silver Kingdom; their buildings contained no carpeting or decoration, no splashes of colour. Double Eight flinched at the sound of his bare feet on the floorboards, knowing any tiny creak was a danger. The building was in darkness; the dragon-breath lamps were all out, but Double Eight was glad of the cover of night, even if it made the shadows sometimes seem like living things.

Along the passage, out into a wider corridor, and then through another door to the huge entrance hall. This was where the most danger lay: streams of moon and lamplight gushed in through a huge arched window. In order to get to where he wanted to go, Double Eight would have to walk through that light.

Stooping low, he dashed to the top of the staircase, and then down the stairs.

He had reached the bottom step when footsteps came echoing towards him.

Double Eight's heart almost stopped.

For a few seconds he stood motionless, one foot on the floor, the other still planted on the stair. The steps were coming nearer, along the main corridor – any minute they'd walk through the double doors into the hallway and catch sight of him . . .

To the right of the staircase was the front desk – a counter where a receptionist would sit in the daytime. Double Eight made a smart dash for it, leaping over and landing on the floor on the other side just as two senior White Witches entered the hallway from the corridor.

Double Eight cupped a hand over his mouth, tried to breathe silent and slow. Through a gap at the bottom of the counter he could see the feet shuffling past the desk, the light from their wands reflecting on their white shoes, casting shadows on the bare wooden floor. They did not speak, but walked in the familiar, stony silence common among White Witches.

When the light died away Double Eight lay on the floor a while longer, until at last he gathered enough courage to peek over the desk. All clear. He came out slowly then dashed along the corridor. Soon he found the correct door and hurried down into the bowels of the building until at last he arrived in one of the large laundry rooms.

Roaring lamps always burned here to dry the newly washed clothes. The perimeter was lined with stone washing tubs, and drying ropes criss-crossed the place, hung with newly-washed gowns, making it impossible to see from one side of the room to the other. The smell of soap nipped at the nose.

Double Eight stood very still. A voice in his head was screaming at him: *Go back! Go back to bed, you idiot, and forget any of this ever happened!*

But Double Eight did not go back.

'Hello?' He spoke in a hushed tone, but his voice seemed very harsh in the silence, and he flinched at the sound of it. 'Are you there?'

Nothing. Double Eight gazed desperately around. In the gloom the hanging white clothes looked like ghosts.

And then, from among those ghosts came a voice.

'You've done well, Double Eight. You've been brave.'

Double Eight swung around, shaking with fright.

'Come out,' he said. 'Come out so I can see you.'

'Forgive me if I don't, love,' said the voice – a woman's voice. 'I reckon it's better, in my position, to keep out of sight. You understand?'

Double Eight nodded. 'I think so.'

'Good. Now before we go any further, my dear, before

I decide what happens next, I must ask a question. Why are you doing this?'

Double Eight frowned into the dark.

A hesitation.

'Because I want to be free.' It was the first time Double Eight had ever said those words, and he was shocked at the power of them, how they surged through him and lit his blood on fire. 'I want to feel properly alive. White Witches . . . we're not really allowed to be part of the world, you know? We're spectators. I don't want to be a spectator. I want to feel things and go places and tell my own story.'

There was a moment of quiet in the laundry room.

'Right,' said the voice. 'I reckon I can help you. But freedom isn't easy. Your problems won't vanish. And before we make this happen, there's something we must discuss . . .'

'My soul?' said Double Eight bitterly.

'Yes. Your soul. Mrs Hester has it, locked away in a secret place with the souls of all the other White Witches. If you come with us, you'll have to leave it behind.'

A terrible sickness rose in Double Eight's guts. 'But how can I be free without my soul?'

A pause.

'Have you ever wondered, love, what makes you different to the other White Witches? You ever considered why it might be that you have thoughts of freedom and magic and friendship while the others seem content to just exist the way they do?'

'Course I have. I've had to hide those thoughts every day!'

'Mrs Hester's powers are not what they were,' said the woman, and there was satisfaction in her tone. 'Her grip is loosening. When you were very young, she took away your soul, but she didn't get all of it. She missed a bit. There's enough of you left in there to wonder and dream and feel! And there's more like you. Some have come over to our side in recent months. We hope, one day, to find the place she keeps her stolen souls and set them all free, but until then, at least we can help White Witches like you.'

Double Eight stared into the dark, pressed a hand to his chest, felt his heart beating quick and clear. He had always known he was different, but he had never imagined there was some soul left in him, that a precious, shining part of him was hiding in plain sight. It was wonderful and frightening and terrible all at once.

The voice said, 'The choice is yours, Double Eight. If you feel leaving is too dangerous, you can go back to bed and forget this meeting ever happened.'

'No! I'd go mad. I want out.'

The sound of glass on the floor, something rolling, and Double Eight felt an object nudge his foot. He picked it up – a tiny spell bottle – and stared disbelievingly at the fizzing wisp of buttery-yellow magic inside. He had, of course, never seen a Hag spell, but he knew instantly that this was one, because it was colourful and warm and seemed full of wild imagination. And the sound of it was not the dreary, monotonous whisper of a White Witch spell. It was twinkling music that gladdened his heart. This was as different from the sterile, colourless magic of White Witches as fire from ice.

'What's this?'

'A spell. It'll help you travel far from the rest of your soul without great suffering.'

Double Eight reached for the stopper.

'Not now!' said the voice urgently. 'Getting you out will take planning. My team on the outside will need to prepare. And the spell takes time to work. A few drops on your skin every night until you hear word from us of the plan. The message I sent last week, the one askin' you to find a hiding place for something small . . . did you manage it?'

Double Eight nodded.

'Good lad. Keep the spell there. When it's time to go, I'll send a bird with instructions. Got it?'

'I suppose . . .'

'Stay out of trouble until then. Stay brave.'

Double Eight opened his mouth to speak, but he heard a swirling sound, saw some of the hanging clothes across the room sway in a breeze, and now he could feel that he was alone in the laundry room. With a shake of his hand, Double Eight sent the Hag magic in the bottle back to sleep. The yellow light died, and the musical whisper was silenced.

Then he began the journey back to the dorm, feeling as if he was carrying the greatest secret in all the world.

Back in the dormitory, Double Eight crouched beside his little bed, surrounded by the snores and sighs of the sleeping White Witches, and retrieved the butter knife from his mattress. When he'd levered the floorboard up he took the spell bottle and stuffed it into the gap, and then he clicked the board back into place.

'What are you doing?'

Double Eight almost yelled out in fright; the sound of a voice in the dormitory was unusual any time, never mind the middle of the night. He slid the butter knife up his sleeve and looked over his shoulder. One Hundred and Three stood at the foot of the bed, sleepily staring down at him. One Hundred and Three was twelve years old, a year younger than Double Eight, and Double Eight didn't think he'd ever heard him speak before.

'I couldn't sleep.'

'Why are you on the floor?' One Hundred and Three's voice was flat, faraway and emotionless. There was no spark of life in his eyes.

'A mouse,' said Double Eight. 'I thought I saw a mouse.'

One Hundred and Three's cold eyes lingered on Double Eight. 'Go back to bed or I'm telling. No one is supposed to be out of bed after dark.'

'You're right,' said Double Eight. 'I will.'

One Hundred and Three walked away. As Double Eight climbed under his sheets he shot a glance to the place in the floor where the spell was hidden. The floorboard *seemed* to be properly back in place. But had One Hundred and Three seen anything? No, Double Eight didn't think so.

His head was bursting with thoughts and plans and danger, his heart thudding.

He doubted sleep would come. It would be a long night.

WHISPERING BOOKS

The rain fell.

'It ain't natural! Weather like this in summer!'

'Lady Light save us! On Slipknot Road the water's up to your knees!'

'I reckon it's the Hags, you know! They've cursed us!'

'The king should do somethin'! What's the hagging point of havin' a squad of White Witches if he won't hagging use 'em!'

Gossip like this was spreading all around the slums. It was always the same, wasn't it? Whenever something happened that people could not explain, they would automatically blame the Hags from across the sea in Westerly Witch.

If there was a drought and the crops failed . . . *Oh, it must be the Hags!*

If the winter was especially cold and the river froze . . . *The Hags have cursed us!*

If a dog became rabid and foamed at the mouth . . . *It's been touched by a Hag!*

And so on.

Lara had always believed that this was stuff and nonsense, because the war had been over for hundreds of years, hadn't it? And if the Hags ever did see fit to attack, then they would do a lot worse than turn a few stupid dogs loopy or make some water fall from the bleedin' sky, wouldn't they?

Still, there was no denying the rain was a nuisance; she could not return to the sewers, because the underground streams had risen to dangerous levels. So she found herself out in the streets of King's Haven, sniffing around for food and opportunity – and in a city like this, with so many people and dark corners and twisting lanes, there was opportunity everywhere. Sometimes it came in the form of a freshly baked meat pie cooling on a window ledge, or the glisten of a coin in an unguarded pocket. Today it was an argument at a fruit stall.

'I'm tellin' you, these apples is rotten!'

'Rotten? How dare you, madam!'

'I want my money back!'

'Ha! Money back, she says!'

Lara slipped in unseen and, quick as a snake, snatched two shining red apples from the stall. She finished the first in seconds, core and seeds and all, and she smacked her lips and licked the juice from her fingers. The rain became a sheet of falling water, bouncing off the cobbles, and Lara ducked under the legs of a stationary ironheart to shelter beneath its metal belly, listening to the tick and whirl of the iron horse's enchanted clockwork insides.

'Oi! Get out of it!'

The driver aimed a kick at her, but she dodged it, tossed a few of her best curse words at him and ran away up the street, shielding her face from the sting of wind and rain. When her locket began suddenly to vibrate against her chest again, she stopped so sharply that an old lady barged into the back of her and pushed past, cursing.

Lara's hand clutched the locket through her clothes; it pulsed and buzzed with worrying ferocity. Lara heard a musical whisper drifting in the air – the shock of it was almost too much to bear. The sound, it seemed, was coming from a nearby store, and as Lara took a faltering step towards the door, the locket's vibration intensified. It was as if it was speaking to her, guiding her like a compass.

Listen to the locket, Granny had told her.

An impulsive need took a hold of Lara; she opened the door and ducked into the shop. The door closed, and the roar of the storm died away. She was met with a deep hush, and the smell of dust and old paper and leather.

It was a *book*shop.

It seemed she was in luck; there was nobody behind the counter, no uppity shopkeeper to chase her away. So she shook the worst of the water from her clothes and hair and began to look around the bookcases with great curiosity. All the while her locket buzzed and the sound of musical, fragile crystalline whispers filled her head. She had never been in a bookshop before. Why would she? She could not eat or drink *books*. Her fingers stroked the spines, and suddenly she was back in Miss Wratchet's orphanage classroom, drawing letters of the alphabet with chalk on a piece of slate . . .

A . . .

B . . .

C . . .

'*You call that a C, Fox? Hold out your hand!*'

SNAP!

'*If you cry, it'll be another lash of the cane! Now scrub that out and try again . . .*'

Lara chased the thoughts away and realised, as she wiped the sweat from her forehead, that she was shaking. She reached into her shirt, bringing the locket out into the dim shop light. It sat in the palm of her hand, vibrating as if there was an insect trapped inside.

Enchanted, Lara followed the melody, until she reached a bookcase and the locket gave a small leap in her hand. Lara let it drop, her gaze shifting to the bookcase, where one of the books was buzzing and trembling. She made a half-step towards the exit; part of her was frightened and wanted to leave. But her hand ached to reach out and touch the book . . .

Slowly, delicately, Lara's fingers closed around the vibrating book.

Clank.

She let go with a gasp, and the book snapped back into place. Then a quite extraordinary thing happened: with a low rumble, the bookcase lowered into the floor, until, *clank*, the top of it had become just another floorboard. Where the bookcase had been there was now an opening, and through the opening a darkened chamber filled with more bookcases, and columns of haphazardly balanced books. The whispering intensified, and Lara knew somehow that it was coming from these secret books. She stared around in frightened wonder. Was this *Hag* magic?

'Can I help you, love?'

Lara had been alone. She was sure of it. But now a woman stood beside her in the hidden doorway. She was apple-cheeked and had a thick head of tight-cropped chestnut hair all marbled with silver. She wore an itchy-looking knitted dress of many patchwork colours and held a cigar between her thin lips. To Lara's surprise she did not seem angry to discover a strange, soaking wet child in her shop. Curious, certainly, but not angry at all. Her smiling eyes went to the locket, and she tilted her head.

'That's a pretty thing. Where did you get it?'

'I . . . I'm sorry,' said Lara. 'I'm lost. I came in by mistake.'

The woman stared at her. 'You sure about that, love?'

'Yes. Sorry. I have to go. Sorry.'

Lara pushed past the woman, her hand pressing tight

against the locket, through the shop and out into the storm. The rain was still battering down, but the sting of the raindrops seemed distant now, because Lara's mind was somewhere else, filled with wonderings and confusion and thoughts of whispering books.

Turning a corner onto Needle Street, Lara almost tripped over a pure collector crouched in the road, shovelling horse manure into her bucket.

'Watch it!'

'Oh, shut your hagging mouth!'

On she went, head down, collar turned up to the driving rain, darting along an alley off Needle Street, under a railway arch, past a blacksmith and an ironworks, the whistle and rumble of a steam train shaking the ground. On the other side of the arch, Lara crossed Station Road, past one of the huge brick factories where the White Witches made their spells, dull grey smoke belching from the chimneys.

When two White Witches exited the spell factory, the sleeves of their robes scorched from working all day over hot cauldrons, Lara could not help staring at their blank, waxy faces in grim fascination. She'd heard White Witches were cursed at birth with powerful magic – and that the Kingdom took away their souls.

Children were taught from a very young age that magic was under no circumstances to be messed with, that if they ever came upon a bottle of magic, they were not to touch it. Doing so was dangerous, and if you survived the magic, you would not survive the punishment for messing with it.

Magic was something to be feared, then, and if that was the case, then White Witches, those strange, soulless creatures, should be feared too, shouldn't they? And yet.

And yet . . .

Lara wasn't frightened of them. Now, she had the unaccountable urge to speak to them, to ask them about magic, and her locket. Watching them, Lara felt for the first time that the world of magic was a glistening web and she was in danger of becoming ensnared.

When the witches were out of sight, Lara continued her journey, soon realising that, without thinking about it she had walked to the docks. The sounds of the place – the cursing and laughter of the men, the groans of the steam cranes, the thrumming engines and slow, deep horns – echoed all around her.

The rain had softened to a light drizzle, and Lara stretched and took in a big lungful of air.

Oh how she loved the smells here! A hundred different scents danced together, each more wonderful than the last. Wooden boats brought fragrant spices from the other side of the Silver Kingdom, pepper and cinnamon and powdered moonweed, and those aromas mingled with the perfume of the other vessels, the dry warmth of dragon breath in hulking metal boats from the North, and the burning heat of fire whisky from the South, and the salt-tang seaweed of the river Anchor itself.

As she walked between crates of coal and starfish and barrels of dragon breath, she felt that vibration against her chest again, a thrum like the wings of a bee. And among the sounds of the docks, the rumbles and clangs and yells, there was once more that delicate, crystalline melody.

Was she losing her marbles? Had she breathed in some gas in the sewers that didn't agree with her? Or had she maybe walked through some flushed-away forbidden Hag spell that had begun rotting away her mind?

Whatever this was, it was impossible to ignore. Some of the music was coming from her locket, and she looked around and wondered if anyone else could hear it, but the dock workers either could not, or were paying it no attention.

And part of the sound was coming from nearby.

Lara tried to block out the other noises, to concentrate, and she found that she was listening not just with her ears, but with something else inside of her, something she couldn't quite describe. It was as if the sound had reached into her chest and wrapped around her heart and was pulling at her. She went to the river, and stared along the rows of boats, breathing in the steam and smoke from their engines. Her gaze rested on a small, unremarkable vessel with the name *Dragonfly* painted on the side in gold. The vibration thrummed harder against her chest.

Inching towards the boat, she scouted around for the

crew, and waited, and watched, until she was certain that they were not around; it was perfectly ordinary for a boat's crew to unload their cargo and head straight for the taverns in the city.

Lara's hand was still pressing against the locket. She stared at the boat, walked to the gangplank, placed one foot on the metal walkway . . .

But this was mad! She could be caught at any moment.

The locket buzzed more intensely than ever against her skin, urging her on and the twinkling sound seemed to grow clearer. Granny's words echoed round her head.

'The locket. Do you still have it? Keep it safe! Listen to it!'

Listen to it . . .

Was it trying to speak to her now? Was it telling her that something important was on this boat? Had the locket somehow guided her into the bookshop too? But why? These were the thoughts of someone losing their mind, surely. And yet there it was again, that wonderful ache in her chest, pulling at a part of her she could not identify. She took one last look around the busy docks, checked that nobody was watching, and then she breathed deep and hurried across the gangplank.

THE SECRET CARGO

Lara had never been on a boat before. She hadn't thought about that until she stepped from the gangplank onto *Dragonfly's* deck. The sensation was strange, standing on the wooden boards, feeling the hulking weight of the boat sway and move underfoot.

The crystal sound rang clearer in her mind, and the din of the docks faded away. There was a strange charge in Lara's blood; her skin was all gooseflesh and it seemed that she was moving around in a dream.

She listened, letting the heart-tugging sound guide her, until she found a hatch on the decking, loosened the bolt, and opened it. At once the sound grew louder and the buzz of her locket became a hum, warmth spilling from it. The space below was dark, and her heart fluttered as she descended the creaking wooden steps and stood in the mouth of an empty cargo hold, squinting into the dark.

The place felt alive, like she was in the guts of a great creature. The air was flavoured with the ghosts of a thousand cargos. In the belly of the boat she followed the trace of the noise until her eyes came upon something in the darkness. A square patch of purple-blue light was shining through the boards from below.

A secret compartment!

Lara let out a long, slow breath, and gathered her senses. There was no handle, no gap wide enough to insert a lever. She crouched, and as her hands explored the rough wooden boards she found, just off centre, one section that felt a little different. She pressed on the board, felt it give a little under her pressure. A great wave of excitement crashed over her as she pressed again, this time more forcefully.

There was the sound of cogs and wheels, and she jumped back as the hatch door lowered and then slipped sideways to reveal a square hole in the floor, from which a bright glow spilled, dancing on the ceiling of the hold in swirls and shimmers.

She edged forward, her eyes widening, and her mouth falling open in wonder. There, hidden under the floor, were a great many little glass bottles. Inside each bottle was a wisp of glowing light. There were greens and blues, violets and reds, and they all swirled and winked inside their bottles like living things. All about the many blazing bottles the air crackled with energy and power, and Lara knew, deep in the same part of her that had been unable to resist coming aboard this boat, that she was in the presence of wild magic.

Hag magic.

I should be running, she thought. *Running far away from here. These spells could kill me! And if the coppers were to find me near Hag magic they'd have me swingin' from a noose.*

But Lara did not run. She could not. The sound of the spells had bewitched her and wrapped her in warmth and wonder. She longed to touch one of the bottles, and she found herself leaning over, reaching into the secret compartment, brushing the stoppers with her fingertips. She chose one of the smallest bottles, plucked it from among the packing hay, and held it in her hand. It was warm against her skin. The spell inside was the colour of the sea on a summer day. She held it close to her face, peered at it, and watched it swirl and shimmer and twine around the inside of the glass.

Suddenly the spell flared so bright that it dazzled Lara, and the bottle became white hot. She let it drop, and it smashed when it hit the wooden deck. Lara stood in the darkness, blinded, gasping. The air had changed, become sweet and cold, and there were popping and cracking sounds.

When her vision returned, Lara could not believe what she was seeing.

Trees and plants were growing *inside* the boat, bursting through the boards and sprouting up, branches twisting and reaching and filling the dark. These impossible plants became so thick and dense that it seemed to Lara she was standing in a forest. Panic filled her, and she came to her senses, climbing and scrambling and pushing her way up the wooden steps to the outside world once again.

There was a man on the gangplank.

He was mountainous, most of his face hidden behind a red beard, and he stopped with the shock of seeing this strange young girl on his boat.

The man stared at Lara, and she stared back, and it seemed for a moment that neither of them knew what to do. Then the deck between Lara's feet burst upward, and the branch of a great tree reached out into the daylight and sprouted yellow leaves.

The man's eyes grew wild and wide, and he swung around to check that nobody on the docks had noticed what was going on. Then he turned to Lara, rage and disbelief on his face. 'My *Dragonfly*! What. Have. You. Done?'

'Erm . . .' Lara searched through the great catalogue of excuses she'd accumulated through the years as a tosher and occasional thief. 'It weren't me, mister! I was walkin' past minding my own business when I saw a bunch of lads jumping on board this fine boat of yours. I said to myself, I said, "They're up to no good," and I chased 'em off. But not before they done some damage.'

He reached into his coat, pulled out a wooden stick fitted with a revolver chamber. Frozen, Lara watched him fumble in his coat, until he brought out a tiny bottle and loaded it into one of the chambers. He stepped onto the deck, raised the wand, and pointed it down into the cargo hold.

Lara took her chance. She rushed past him, avoiding his free arm as it reached for her, and sprinted over the gangplank and away through the docks, not daring to look back.

COTTON'S END

'Well done, boys. First day back at work after the floods and we've done pretty well for ourselves!'

Vin Cotton and his gang stood in a circle in the sewer under Milk Street. Cotton spat a brown wad of chewing tobacco into the stream. There was a hemp sack at his feet, and he reached in and began bringing out the things they'd taken from the toshers who'd stumbled into their patch that day.

'There you go, Davo. Here, John-John. You have this, Corky.'

The tunnel filled with the echoing sound of approaching feet, and Cotton stopped what he was doing. He nodded to the boys, and they readied their iron crowbars. Cotton put his hand in his pocket, closing it around the handle of his knife.

A man stepped from the darkness, tall, thin, dressed all in black. When he saw the gang, he stopped, and stared around them, and it seemed strange to Vin Cotton that the man did not seem to be afraid.

We'll soon change that, he thought.

'What kinda toshing gear is that?' he said with a snort, pointing at the man's black clothes.

The man ignored the question. 'I'm looking for something. A wooden box, about this size. I know it's down here. Have any of you seen it?'

Vin Cotton shared a smile with his pals. 'Wooden box you say? It valuable?'

The man didn't answer, only looked around their faces. He licked his lips. 'I'm *hungry*.'

Cotton was beginning to think this cove must have escaped from an asylum. 'I don't care if you're hungry. What I care about is gettin' rich. So you rest assured, guv'nor, if I do find that wooden box of yours in one of my tunnels, whatever's inside belongs to me. In the meantime, if you want to get back to the surface with all your limbs, you best empty your pockets.'

The man moved so fast he seemed to exist in many places at once. He drew out a large knife and spun between the gang, cutting their throats until only Cotton remained, staring around at his fallen pals, at their blood turning the sewer stream deep red. He brandished his knife with a shaking hand.

The light from Cotton's dragon-breath lamp flickered, and he realised that the man cast no shadow on the sewer walls.

Cotton leaped forward and stabbed him in the chest. It had no effect.

The man leaned in.

He opened his mouth, wider than should be possible, and wider still, revealing row after row of needle-sharp teeth, and a gaping darkness.

Cotton tried to scream, but he felt like he was being dragged from his body, that the part of him that thought and wondered and laughed, the part of him that was *him*, was being swallowed down. There was a ripping sound, and for Cotton the only thing left was coldness, and darkness, and never-ending pain.

Shadow Jack looked to the sewer floor, at what was left of his latest meal. Cotton's body was sprawled in an awkward position. His skin seemed baggy, as if his skeleton had shrunk, and his eyes were blank black marbles. Shadow Jack picked up the sack and looked through the contents. Then he checked Cotton's pockets, and the pockets of his gang. When he was satisfied the box was not in that tunnel, he moved on, leaving Cotton and his boys to become dinner for the rats.

THE SEWER STRANGLER

There was a pub on Indigo Lane called the Festering Stump, and it possessed all the charm that its name might suggest. Traditionally, the Stump was a favourite haunt of local toshers, and when Lara walked through the doors this evening, all the chat was about a horrifying incident in the sewers that had happened that very day.

'Really? The four of 'em?'

'Butchered, I heard, in a tunnel under Milk Street!'

'They say it's just one cove what's doing it too. Imagine that!'

'Well, I can't say they didn't have it coming!'

'I can't say I'm sorry neither!'

Lara searched around in the thick fog of tobacco smoke until she found Joe Littlefoot sitting with Albert Shiner and Les the Thumb near the back of the place. Joe was still flush, it seemed, for he insisted that he buy her a drink and wouldn't take no for an answer.

'Where you been?' he asked. 'Haven't seen hide nor hair of you for a couple days.'

It was true; after the incident on the boat, Lara had been lying low. Normally she'd broadcast such an adventure to anyone who'd listen, but if word was to get out about forbidden spells and Hags and smuggling, and her name was linked to it, she'd be in all sorts of trouble with the coppers.

She sloshed the thick, mud-coloured ale around in her glass.

'I been ill,' she lied. Then, changing the subject, 'What's happened in the sewers? What's everyone gabbin' about?'

Joe looked around at the others, and Albert and Les the Thumb raised their eyebrows.

'You haven't heard?'

'Obviously not, or I wouldn't be askin'.'

'Someone's killing toshers,' said Les. 'Down in the sewers. The Strangler, they're callin' him.'

Joe Littlefoot took a swig of ale. 'Seven dead and counting!'

Lara rolled a mouthful of soup-thick ale thoughtfully around her mouth. 'I'll bet it's Cotton and his gang,' she said bitterly. 'They've been getting worse and worse and now they've gone too far—' She stopped when she saw Joe's face. 'What is it? What's up?'

'It isn't Cotton.'

'And how d'you know?'

'Because,' said Albert Shiner, 'Cotton and his stooges are dead. The Strangler got 'em yesterday!'

Lara sat forward, the mug of ale forgotten in her hands. 'You *sure*?'

The others nodded.

'There's a couple of toshers already managed to escape this lunatic by playin' dead,' said Joe, 'and they both said the same thing: it was one man who did it. He comes from nowhere. They say he don't have a shadow! Can you believe that, Lara? And he asks all his victims about a wooden box.'

A bell rang somewhere in Lara's head. *A man with no shadow.* Where had she heard that before? 'Sounds like a ghost story,' she said, trying to sound convincing. But her insides were swirling and tumbling. She felt like the world she knew was slipping away, flying out of control. First her locket, then the bookshop and the spells on the boat and that strange noise in the air, and now this! The Sewer Strangler might just be the worst of it all, because the sewers had always been the place she felt safe, the place she could run to if she wanted to escape the world.

'Wonder what's in that box,' said Joe. 'What's he lookin' for?'

'Whatever it is,' said Les the Thumb, 'it must be valuable as a dragon egg.'

They sat in the smoky rabble of the pub considering this, until Joe gave them all a start by exclaiming, 'Blimey,

I almost forgot!' he reached under the table, brought out a brown paper bag and pushed it across to Lara.

She raised an eyebrow. 'What's this?'

'Open it and see.'

Lara ripped the paper bag open to discover a dragon-breath lamp fitted with a leather shoulder strap – the sort toshers used in the sewers. 'Joe Littlefoot! I warned you not to buy . . .'

'Oh give it a rest, Lara. You saved me down in the tunnels, and me a-feedin' you a bowl of soup is no repayment. Take it. There's a madman around here and maybe, just maybe, the light of this lamp will keep you safe.'

Lara scowled at him, but inwardly she was grateful and relieved; a tosher couldn't be a tosher without the light of a lamp. She turned the brass dial on the casing and a warm flame leaped to life within the glass. As it flickered, Lara thought for a heartbeat that she saw the shape of a bird in that flame. But when she looked closer it was gone.

Snared

A colourless scoop of porridge slapped into Double Eight's bowl in a steaming, lumpy glob. He looked at the porridge, and then up at the large, serious dinner man behind the counter in his white apron and hat. There was a huge, white-headed boil on the end of the dinner man's nose. Double Eight thought it looked like it might explode at any minute and shoot pus into the porridge pot.

'Thank you.'

He turned and sat alone at one of the long tables in the dinner hall. Hundreds of White Witches sat around him, mostly silent, eating their porridge and drinking their water. The meals were the same every day: porridge and water for breakfast, bread and cheese for lunch, and mutton stew for dinner.

Double Eight began to eat, forcing each slimy spoonful down his throat. The hall was hushed; White Witches did not form friendships, because friendship means opening the soul up to someone else. The only sounds were the scuff of chair legs on the floor, spoons scraping on bowls, chewing, sipping.

The familiar ring of the bell let everyone know that breakfast was over. Double Eight filed out of the hall, through the main corridor and out to the cobbled streets of the White Witch district. The rain was pouring down, and Double Eight pulled his white hood over his head and held it down against the wind as he hurried between the towering, gloomy buildings towards the gate.

There was only one way in and out of the White Witch district, a massive wrought-iron gate which opened twice a day, once in the morning and again late at night to let the White Witches come and go from the factories. The entire district was surrounded by a fifty-foot-high stone wall; no one could get in or out without using this gateway.

Double Eight joined the waiting crowd, the rain pelting him. Thousands of White Witches stood shoulder to shoulder, and yet it was as if they were unaware of each other. They did not speak, did not smile or look at each other. The giant gate screeched open and they flooded out into the streets of King's Haven.

It was early enough that most of the city was still asleep. The kingdom tried to keep the White Witches out of sight of the general population, and Double Eight was glad of this because any time he had walked the streets when people had been around, he had been met with cold, hateful stares and hurtful comments.

They don't think of us as people. To them, we're animals — less than animals.

The rain grew heavier. It almost seemed that nature had noticed the crust of filth on the city and was trying to wash it clean. But every layer of grime revealed another, and another, and the bubbling gutters ran with inky, sooty rainwater.

Through the factory gates the White Witches marched. Double Eight had spent every day for over a year – since his magic had matured and he had been transferred out of the school – working in the same building. Nothing ever changed. He could have walked the route with his eyes closed had he so wished: through the factory doors and along the corridor to his station, a heavy workbench in a row of hundreds of identical stations, all set to the sound of the dreary, lifeless whisper of White Witch magic. On the bench sat a cauldron, and in the cauldron, same as every other day, Double Eight lit a fire. He opened the cupboards in his bench, bringing out jars and bottles of ingredients, and he began to weigh and count them out.

He had only ever produced one type of spell.

He knew that there were countless spells in the world, that the Hags from Westerly Witch invented new, wild ones all the time. White Witches made the same spells day after day, moon after moon, year after year. Sometimes he would imagine new spells, picture glorious shafts of dazzling colour exploding from his cauldron. How sweet it would be if, just for once, he could use his imagination, create something wild that did not have to be numbered and inspected and drained of life and colour.

Of course, he had always known that he could not share these thoughts with anyone – even as a child he had sensed that the others did not feel the same way. The White Witch teachings said that emotions were weakness and all thoughts should be to serve Mrs Hester and the Silver King. This had made him hide his secret deep inside, made him feel like he was a freak, like there was something wrong with him. But maybe soon he'd be free of all that. Ever since his secret meeting with the Hag down in the laundry room, he'd been applying a few drops of the getaway spell each night, though there had been no obvious effects. He wondered how long he'd have to wait, how many more days until he was free, and if he'd be ready when the time came.

Double Eight's job – the same as every other White Witch in this workshop – was to produce the enchantment that turned everyday paper into witch paper. It was a relatively simple spell to produce. First Double Eight took a piece of paper and followed the instructions in the *Silver Kingdom Spell Book* (written by Mrs Hester), copying out a set of detailed symbols:

The bird, the heart, the compass and the cloud.

After the symbols were complete, Double Eight took the paper and put it in the cauldron, where it began to wilt and crumple and blacken in the flames. Next Double Eight took the other ingredients required to make the spell – a drop of distilled moonlight; a spoonful of powdered eagle feathers; the needle of a compass – and added them.

Then came the most important part of the entire spell-making process: the Witch's Prayer. Double Eight spoke the words softly, reverently:

'Born of mind, born of fire,
Born of Mother Earth's desire,
Use it wisely, use it well,
My heart, my blood, my gift, my spell.'

A spark of light. The cauldron vibrated and filled with swirling purple smoke. Quickly and efficiently, Double Eight brought out a set of identical spell bottles and filled each one with a little of the spell he'd created, until the cauldron was empty. He packed the bottles all in a box padded with straw, wrote the spell on the box and rang a bell on the end of his station. A minute later an old woman approached the work station pushing a trolley. She placed the box in her trolley to join the rest – all would have their colour removed. She left without glancing at Double Eight or speaking a word.

This is how every day had gone for over a year now. Make a spell then ring the bell.

Double Eight could not know it yet, but today would turn out to be very different.

Today would change everything.

Lunchtime was approaching, and Double Eight was satisfied with his work; he had managed to produce eight sets of spells – a full box up on his average. Wiping a hand over his brow, he felt his stomach rumble. And that is when he noticed the two White Witches approaching his bench.

They were big, big men, one with brown skin and a shaven head, the other with skin so pale it was almost blue and a head of messy grey hair.

They stopped at Double Eight's station, looked him up and down.

'Eight-Eight-Five-Four-Seven-Six?' said the man with the brown skin, using Double Eight's full name.

Double Eight nodded. His throat was drying up.

The pale man brought out his wand. Before Double Eight could react, the man pointed his wand at Double Eight, and one of the spell bottles in the revolver chamber flashed bright.

Ripping, searing pain tore through Double Eight's head. He tried to scream but found that he was falling into spinning darkness. He was unconscious before he hit the floor.

THE SOUL CAGE

'**W**ake up, my pet. That's it.'

Double Eight opened his eyes, moaning as the dazzling, blurry brightness of a cloudy sky came stabbing through a narrow window. He tried to move and became suddenly aware that he was strapped in a chair, bound at the wrists and waist and ankles. Panic grabbed him, wringing his guts. He spat out involuntary, frightened sounds.

A hand rested on his shoulder. Someone had been standing behind him, and now they walked around to face him. Double Eight's eyes opened wide and his fingernails scratched at the arms of the chair.

Every White Witch knew this face from posters and paintings and manuals. He was looking up at Mrs Hester, the King's Witch and leader of all the White Witches in the world.

'Don't speak,' she said, raising a finger to her red, full lips. 'Not a word, unless I ask you to.'

Double Eight managed to nod. His entire body was trembling; he'd never been so frightened.

'You might have heard,' Mrs Hester said, 'that we've been having a spot of bother. White Witches running away with the help of the Hags from Westerly Witch. I find this disgusting. Don't we feed you? Don't we give you a safe place to live? Shelter and work? *Don't* we?'

Again, Double Eight managed a nod. The fear in him was cold and grabbing.

Mrs Hester reached into her brilliant white robes, and she brought out something small and shining. Double Eight almost vomited. It was the Hag spell he'd hidden away under the floorboards.

'A loyal Witch in your dormitory reported you,' said Mrs Hester. She held the spell up, watched it curl around the inside of the bottle. Then she brought out her wand – a length of dark, polished wood with an angry green spell in one of the metal revolver chambers. 'Who gave you the Hag spell?'

Double Eight, shaking so much now that the chair was beginning to vibrate, shook his head. 'I don't . . . know. I nuh-never saw her f-face.'

Mrs Hester stepped closer, fixed Double Eight with such a frightening stare that he felt his throat lock up. She was intensely beautiful but somehow he could sense that her beauty was a mask, that there was something rotten underneath.

'You *nuh*-never saw?' she mocked. She raised her wand, flicked it, and the angry green spell flashed bright in the bottle before a coil of green poured from the tip of the wand and became a dazzling, smoky cobra. The snake reared back and thrashed forward in a blindingly quick movement, sinking its fangs into Double Eight's bound hand. He screamed in pain and terror as the spell snake's venom torched his insides. Every part of him was in agony, burning and turning to ash. He wanted to die, wanted to leave the pain far behind . . .

Mrs Hester pulled back and the snake let go.

'I'll ask again: who gave you the Hag spell? Who was trying to help you escape?'

Double Eight was blinded by tears. The pain was gone. He could see no puncture marks on his flesh. He sobbed. 'I swear on Mother Earth! I never saw her face! I don't know . . .'

The snake flashed down upon his hand again, and his insides were blazing, searing.

He heard himself scream.

Let me die, he thought. *Let it be done.*

Again, the snake broke away.

It struck five more times.

Mrs Hester watched with interest as Double Eight screamed and thrashed, as ugly veins and blood vessels stood out on his face and neck and hands.

Barely conscious, he heard her say, 'All right. I believe

you. No matter, I suppose. We will catch her.' The glowing snake spell vanished, and Double Eight wept, a strange mixture of relief and dread rising in him.

Mrs Hester walked into the shadows. She returned carrying what looked like a birdcage, but the bars were made of an otherworldly, silvery material, as if someone had taken threads of moonlight and twisted them together. Inside the cage was an object stranger still. At first glance Double Eight thought it a winged creature made of warm golden light. But the closer he looked the more unsure he became of what he was seeing. And the feeling it elicited in him, this ethereal thing, was at once happiness and longing and overpowering sorrow.

'You know what this is?'

Double Eight knew instantly. He knew, as he knew the sky was blue or the sea was wet, that the thing in the cage was not a creature at all. It was part of him.

Double Eight was looking at his soul.

'That's right,' said Mrs Hester as Double Eight's insides crashed, and a desperate longing pulled at his heart. 'You belong to me. Every White Witch does.' She tapped at her forehead and screwed up her eyes, and for only a flash of a moment he thought he saw her true face, ancient and rotting. She reached out and touched the tip of her wand to his chest.

Double Eight shut his eyes and tried to brace himself.

Mrs Hester, though, did not fire a spell.

'I think I might have left a tiny bit of your soul in there,' she said, tapping her wand against his breastbone. 'That's why you want to be free.' She leaned so close their noses almost touched, and when she breathed on him Double Eight could smell the faint whisper of death and disease. 'But you will never be free. I could take it now, you know. Take the rest of your soul. It would be easy – and how I would love to watch that light in your eyes fade, watch all your silly ideas of freedom wilt away.'

'Please,' said Double Eight, and the light from his soul became a kaleidoscope of colour through his tears.

Mrs Hester straightened up.

'But I'm not going to do that,' she said. 'I'm not going to take the rest of your soul. Do you want to know why?' She stroked at the strange glowing bars of the soul cage. 'When a White Witch dies, if that Witch has been a good servant, I release the soul. This means Grey Alyce can guide the Witch across the Desert of Bones to the next life. But a traitor . . . Well, a traitor does not *deserve* the freedom of death. I'm going to use you as an example. I'm going to show every White Witch what happens to traitors. I'm going to hang you in Reaper's Square. And when your legs have stopped twitching, I'm going to put your soul on display, and you, boy, will be for ever trapped between life and death. Ha! Let's see how many of your kind try to run away after that!'

She leaned forward and wiped the tears from Double

Eight's face, and he smelled that deep-set rot again. 'Look on the bright side. Most White Witches live and die without leaving a mark on the world. Tomorrow, Double Eight, you will become infamous.'

THE HANGMAN'S NOOSE

Lara's favourite thing about her forgotten attic in the opera house was the stillness. In a city like King's Haven, where people crawled over each other like an infestation of mites, quiet was rarer than stardust.

When Lara woke each morning, she could tell what sort of day it was going to be before she opened her eyes. The sound of birdsong from the roof was always a sign that it was clear and bright, while the distant calls of foghorns meant the world was blanketed in smog. Sometimes in winter she'd wake up to the padded hush of fresh snowfall.

For days now, Lara had been greeted upon waking by the steady patter of freakish summer rain. But this morning, when she stirred from fading dreams, the murmuring rain was absent and an unfamiliar sound filled the quiet.

Faraway voices.

Yelling.

Cursing.

As the last cobwebs of sleep fell away, Lara became

aware that there was structure to the noise. A rhythm, like a drumbeat.

A crowd was repeating the same word over and over . . .

HAG!

HAG!

HAG!

Lara dressed quickly, grabbing the locket from under her pillow and putting it on, tucking it beneath her shirt. She rushed down through the empty silence of the opera house to a side door and slipped through to the alleyway beyond. A few seconds later she was out into the Avenue of the Gods.

She had seen Hag hangings before, and she despised them, as she despised cruelty toward any living thing. There were Hag spies, or so she'd heard, scattered all over the Kingdom. According to the king's law, all Hags were dangerous killers, and yet Lara had never seen any actual evidence of this. People were urged to report anyone they suspected of practising Hag magic, and every Hag that was caught was offered the chance to convert, to become a White Witch. If they did not, the gallows would deal with them. A Hag hanging brought out the very worst in people. At the sight of a Hag seemingly normal people could transform into seething, wide-eyed lunatics.

There were hundreds of people on the street. Lara pushed her way through the crowd, shocked by some of the things they were yelling.

'Hang him!'

'Skin him!'

'He deserves to burn!'

'Slit him open! Spill his guts on the cobbles!'

Lara elbowed her way to the front of the mob walking towards Reaper's Square. It was the usual set-up: a shield of coppers in their stiff black uniforms leading the way, trailing two enormous ironhearts. The ironhearts pulled a trundling cage on four wheels, and inside that cage was the Hag.

Only this time it wasn't a Hag.

Lara stared in disbelief.

It was a White Witch! They had one of their own in a cage! Her brain could not make sense of it, so foreign was this sight. The Witch was still only a boy, perhaps fourteen or fifteen years old; he was skinny and pale as flour, and his straggly dark hair hung over his eyes . . . The bewildered, terrified prisoner gawped all about as the crowd threw rotten fruit and stones and filth from the street at him. One of the stones caught him above the left eye, and blood spouted from a deep gash.

Look at yourselves, Lara thought, staring about the crowd with a rising sickness in her throat. *You're like wild things.*

Into Reaper's Square they poured, chanting and shouting and swearing, until the gruesome parade stopped in the shadow of the palace, beside a raised stone platform on which a lonely set of gallows stood. The coppers swarmed upon the cart, bringing the Witch-boy out of the cage, dragging him up the steps all caked in muck and dung and rotted fish and vegetables.

'Turncoat!' yelled the crowd.

'Gut him!'

'Feed him to the dogs!'

Lara could not look away as the coppers pulled the Witch-boy to the gallows, slipping his head into the noose.

Movement at the grand palace gates, and Lara's attention turned to see a woman who was now marching to the gallows. Lara had only seen Mrs Hester, the King's Witch, a handful of times in her life, for she mostly stayed behind the palace walls and mixed with the toffs and high-ups. But the sight of her, with her beautiful white-gold hair and her flawless skin, was unforgettable – and so too was the strange charge in the air around her.

Behind the gates, in the palace grounds, Mrs Hester had gathered every White Witch in the city; they stood in straight, silent rows, gazing up at the gallows as she climbed the steps. She stared for a long moment at the poor Witch-boy in the noose, and then she brought out her wand and touched the tip of it to her lips. A spell blazed in its chamber, and when Mrs Hester spoke, her voice was magically enhanced, her every word booming out over the square.

'Friends! The role of a White Witch is a simple one: to serve the Silver Kingdom. To serve *you*. To produce, using only those spells deemed pure by the king's law, magic that will help you live full, rich, prosperous lives. Magic that helps the Kingdom keep a powerful grip on its many lands.' She paused here as another wave of words gathered in her head, preparing to crash over the masses. 'I brought my White Witches to the Silver Kingdom four hundred years ago. In that time, I have served your kings and queens, and together we have worked to build the greatest empire this world has ever seen. In every territory we conquered, we encountered Hags, and we drove them into hiding. But they are still out there. Still watching us.'

The crowd spat and hissed at the mention of Hags. Mrs Hester held up her hand and stillness fell upon the square. She nodded to a man who had appeared at the foot of the steps, and he climbed up to the platform, carrying something under a red silk cloth with great care. The King's Witch, clearly enjoying the moment, took the object from him. She pointed to the Witch-boy in the gallows, and then made a great drama of reaching out and removing the silk cover from the object in her hands . . .

. . . Double Eight blinked the blood from his eyes. The cut on his head was still pouring, and the noose was tight around his neck, wearing at the skin there. He was exhausted, beaten, bruised, and the stink of the filth on his clothes made him choke and gag.

He stood quite still, hands and ankles bound, looking down at his feet, refusing to glance up at the crowd; he had never seen so many people all in one place, and the thought that every person in the square was there to see him die, to cheer as the floor fell away and his neck snapped in the noose, made more stinging tears flood his eyes.

A ripple of frightened wonder passed through the Square, and he *did* look up now, and saw that Mrs Hester was holding that small cage with moonlight-bright bars, pointing at it with her wand.

'When a White Witch is born,' she said to the crowd, 'he gives his soul to us. Gives his soul to *you*. The Witch you see in the noose? He gave his soul, and here it is, in this cage. But he wants to leave us. He wants to run away. And so it is my . . . *sad* duty to make an example of him this morning. This is a message to you, friends: White Witches will never leave you. Never desert you.' She swivelled to face the palace, to address the assembled White Witches. 'And a message to you, my White Witches: if you turn your back on the Kingdom, I will find you, and you will hang. And when you die, I will keep your soul, and you will be for ever lost between life and death.'

The crowded square erupted at this. The roar was so fierce and deafening Double Eight felt it crash against him. A drumbeat began to sound, slow and steady, and the rabble faded to quiet expectation.

The hangman stepped forward, his face covered by a black hood.

Double Eight wanted more than anything to be brave, to hold his head up and breathe deep and look at the sky one last time. But he did not feel brave. He felt very afraid, and very much alone. He was crying again, his eyes smeared with blood and tears as he blinked and stared around the baying crowd, at face after screwed-up, hate-filled face.

And then, among that ocean of poison, his eyes came to rest upon a face that was not angry or hate-filled.

The girl's flawless brown skin seemed to glisten in the sunlight, and her large, dark, intelligent eyes were fixed upon him with such a gaze of shame and sadness that he could not look away. The cold loneliness in Double Eight's heart thawed a little, and then the girl did something unexpected and wonderful, something small that meant the world to him . . .

. . . Lara smiled at him.

She was not entirely sure why, or what good it could possibly do – she only knew that if it was her in the noose, she would rather the last face she saw was wearing a smile than a sneer.

Why did the boy have to die anyway? Because he wanted to be free? Lara thought that if she was trapped in a life of slavery and service, and she was offered a way out, she'd take it too. And if the Hags were the ones setting White Witches free, how terrible could they really be?

The drumbeat quickened.

Lara covered her eyes with her hands and peered through the gaps between her fingers. Any moment now the hangman would pull on the lever, and the floor would disappear beneath the Witch-boy. If he was lucky his neck would break straight away, but Lara had seen gruesome hangings where the poor cove on the end of the rope twisted and twitched this way and that, eyes popping with blood as they slowly choked to death.

The hangman reached for the lever.

A flash of light.

'Look! Up there!'

'There's folks on the roof!'

'What's that? What're they doin'?'

If Lara hadn't seen it for herself, she wouldn't have believed it: there were two people on a nearby rooftop holding wands aloft, and dark smoke was drifting up from the wand tips. The smoke twisted into the air, billowed and formed a cloud that hung over the square. The cloud tumbled and rolled and took shape. Here, wings unfolded from a smoke body, and there an armour-plated head formed, big as a carriage.

'Dragon!' came a voice from the crowd.

'Don't be daft! Ain't nothin' but smoke!'

'Hags!'

'Hag magic!'

'Run!'

An enormous bang, and a great shockwave cut through the crowd. The smoke exploded outwards, leaving in its place a dragon made of swirling red fire. The fire dragon beat its wings, sending blasts of scorching air towards the people.

Everything seemed to slow down. She watched what was happening like it was a dream, as if she was watching someone else's life from the outside. Panic. Screams. Chaos. There were people on the floor, ones who'd fallen in the rush, and others were standing on them, trampling them.

The dragon made of fire roared, and took to the air, swooping out over the palace and then arrowing down towards Reaper's Square. Lara fell to the ground with the crowd, certain it was going to crash into them, burn them, that this was how she would die. But at the last second it pulled up, its fiery belly screaming only a few feet overhead. The heat from it was searing and choking. Lara scrambled to her feet. She helped someone up – some toff lady.

'Run!' Lara told her. 'RUN!'

The fire dragon circled again, and swooped low over the crowd, scattering people like fallen leaves. Somewhere in Lara's head, a thought came to life.

It's not burning anyone.

This wasn't an attack. It was a *distraction*. She swung around to face the gallows, saw the rope swinging, the noose empty. The Witch-boy was gone. And beside the gallows, the King's Witch was fumbling with a spell bottle, loading it into the chamber of her wand and pointing it skyward.

The tongue of flame that leaped from her wand became a serpent, and the serpent met the fire dragon high above the streets, coiled around it, and the two fire creatures unravelled and faded, leaving ghostly shapes in the smoking sky.

The scattered crowd of people picked themselves up, helping others, looking up in awed wonder.

Lara decided that this was not a good place to be. The coppers would be looking to make someone, anyone, pay for this – and if you were from the slums then the odds of it being you were very likely.

So she cut through the square and away across Bone Bridge, towards the slums, and the sewers, and a place that still seemed real.

Mrs Hester stood panting at the gallows, staring wildly around the smoke-filled square. She stormed over to the empty noose, grabbed the rope, checked the rooftops. There was no sign of the Hags. A ripple of unease passed through the watching regiments of White Witches, for even though Mrs Hester had taken their souls and they could not dream of happiness or freedom, fear could still touch them. And there was nothing to be feared more than Mrs Hester's fury.

Crazy-eyed, she dashed across the platform and grabbed the soul cage, which had tipped over in the chaos. The boy's soul was still in there. They hadn't managed to free it. But they had used their damned escape spell on the boy, embarrassed her in front of the city, in front of her Witches. Mrs Hester looked to the sky, and screamed. Then she marched off towards the palace.

THE EVERNIGHT

Mrs Hester killed three of her White Witches on the way back to the palace, turning their insides to fire so that they died writhing and screaming. Her own insides were ablaze with fury and hatred. This morning was supposed to have been a show of strength, a way of frightening her White Witches away from any thoughts of freedom. Instead, the Hags had humiliated her and made her look weak. Worse than that, they had made Mrs Hester doubt herself – something she had never done before. How many mistakes had she made? How many White Witches had she left with traces of soul inside them? After the horror show earlier, she supposed that more of them than ever would now be dreaming of escape. She could not have that. Could not tolerate it. The king was already becoming agitated; if the oaf decided to get rid of her, she'd have no choice but to kill him – and that would make everything so much more complicated.

No. She would not let her plans – her life's

work – dissolve before her eyes. She needed to finish the Westerly Witches and control the Mother Tree so she could breathe magic straight from its Blossom.

She stormed up her tower, kicked open the doors and threw a few spell bottles shattering against the wall. Then she grabbed the urn and unstoppered it. When Shadow Jack appeared at Mrs Hester's side, he looked at her hate-filled face.

'Why do I get the feeling I've missed something?' he said.

'I want it done.'

'What?'

'I want the Evernight released. Now!'

'Now? Do you think that's a good idea? We don't have the Doomsday Spell yet.'

'Well, that won't be a problem for very much longer, according to you.'

'Even so, it would be better to wait. If you release the Evernight without the means to put it back in . . .'

'No, I'm sick of waiting. It has to be now!' She rounded on him, her face lit harshly by her wand, and he saw a strange, livid madness in her eyes. 'The Hags made a fool of me in front of the entire city! Made me look weak in the eyes of my own White Witches! I won't have it any more! I want them to die. All of them. And when the Evernight comes for them, I want them to know it was Mrs Hester who brought it to their door! Now take me to it.'

'Now? Don't you want to rest first? It's two days' flight.'

'No. I don't want to fly. I want you to get me there by other means. The Djinn way.'

Shadow Jack shook his head. 'It'll kill you.'

'A lot of things should have killed me long before now. I'm a tough old bird. Do it.'

Shadow Jack stepped close, wrapping his arms around her. They stood for a moment in an awkward embrace, and then a swirl of darkness cocooned them.

When the cocoon fell away, they stood on the edge of a black lake under a midnight sky bursting with stars. The air was freezing, the world twinkling under a coat of crystal frost. In the centre of the lake was a small rocky island. Mrs Hester knew this place well. Shadow Jack had brought her here many times, inside her mind.

Her head spun, and the stars danced and streaked through the sky. She dropped to her knees, gasping, threw up, and saw that her vomit was streaked with blood. Shadow Jack tried to help her up, but she pushed him away and climbed to her unsteady feet.

'I felt like . . . I was broken up in a billion little bits and then put back together again.'

Shadow Jack nodded.

Mrs Hester pointed at him. 'Well you better've put everything back in the right place. What is it? What're you looking at?'

'You're a little older,' said Shadow Jack.

Mrs Hester peered at her hands and saw that the youthful, milky skin had thinned. She went to the lake, loaded a light spell into her wand, and looked at her reflection in the still water; her eyes were framed with crow's feet, and there were lines on her forehead. Streaks of grey had crept through her hair. The youth she'd stolen from the young lady in the tower was already fading, no doubt due to the strength it had taken to survive the journey here. Years ago, she'd have handled it easily. But now . . . she was getting so damned old. And keeping all those White Witches' souls took up so much of her power.

She needed to set things in motion now, before it was too late for her. For the longest time she had lived so far from the Mother Tree, using only the magic that the Blossom flowers breathed into the air, magic that had been carried around the world and diluted. Imagine what she could do if she controlled the source of the magic. Imagine if she could walk among the Blossom again and feel it all around her . . .

Mrs Hester dug in her pockets, loaded another bottle into the revolver chamber of her wand and fired the spell at the lake. Where the spell hit the water a thin bridge of ice formed, cracking and popping. It stretched all the way out to the crag of rock in the centre. Mrs Hester ran out over the ice bridge and onto the tiny island, Shadow Jack at her heels, and began to climb the steep, jutting rock.

'Where is it?'

'I don't know exactly. Just that it's here.'

'This hagging coat!' Mrs Hester's long coat had snagged on the rock, sending several spell bottles clinking into the quiet darkness. 'Never mind that. Look!' They scrambled further up – the crag was much bigger than it had seemed from the ground and they were around halfway to the sharp summit – to a ledge, and a dark entrance.

Breathing heavily, Mrs Hester took her wand and loaded another light spell. The brightness of it stabbed at her eyes, but she did not care. She swept to the entrance, held out her wand, peered into the cave. 'Steps. C'mon.'

There were indeed steps. Lots of them, carved roughly into the rock, all different heights and awkward angles. The steps took Mrs Hester and Shadow Jack down into the earth, to a chamber far beneath the lake and the island. The air was stale and sour and damp, and when Mrs Hester put out a hand to lean on the cave walls, she recoiled at the slimy touch of them.

'What's that noise?'

From the blackness beyond the reach of Mrs Hester's light spell came the unmistakable rhythmic sound of breathing.

'Who's there?' She turned to Shadow Jack. 'Who's in here?'

'I don't know.'

Mrs Hester took a few spells from the remaining

pockets of her coat, loaded them into the chambers of her wand. Her eyes flicked around the place as she crept further into the chamber. Eventually she stopped, tilted her head and peered hard into the gloom as if making sure what she was seeing was real.

In the very corner of the chamber, sitting in a wooden chair, was an old man. Presently he was asleep – his beard was so wild and his hair so long that his face was barely visible. Somewhere in the matted tangle of his dirty whiskers, his mouth hung open. He was dressed in a long leather Witch's coat, and on his lap was a beautifully crafted wand with an ornate silver revolver chamber.

Mrs Hester looked at Shadow Jack. Shadow Jack shrugged. Mrs Hester motioned for him to step aside, and he melted away into the shadows. Then Mrs Hester moved forward, quickly swiping the wand from the old man's lap, and kicked him in the shin.

He started awake, looking around in a bewildered sort of way, then saw Mrs Hester standing over him and tried to jump up. But he was so old that he could only climb slowly from the chair and by the time he was on his feet he seemed quite exhausted.

'Who are you?' Mrs Hester asked him.

He opened his mouth and said, 'Flaahrghensht fwooop.'

Mrs Hester stared blankly at him. 'What?'

'Lonky-yopdoodlepip!'

'Come again?' said Mrs Hester.

The old man shook his head violently. He put a finger in his ear, wiggled it around and made the sort of noise a person can only make when they are trying to scratch an itch somewhere in the middle of their brain. 'Fwaaaa. Hhhnnnggggg.' He blinked. 'I'm s-sorry. I haven't . . . spoken for . . . oh, it must be coming on for nine hundred years now. I'd rather forgotten how.' He straightened up as best he could and said, in a surprisingly deep and commanding voice, 'Why have you come?'

Mrs Hester tried to be calm, though her heart was thundering. 'For the Evernight, of course.'

The old man looked very grave. 'Who are you?'

'My name is Mrs Hester. I am the leader of all White Witches.'

'White Witch? What's a White Witch?'

'The world has changed since you came here,' said Mrs Hester. 'There was a civil war between two factions of Witches. Now there are the Hags, who claim Westerly Witch, and the White Witches, who wish to possess it.'

'Well I'm not concerned about Hags or White Witches,' said the old man. 'I'm only worried about the Evernight.' His expression became haunted, and his eyes seemed to sink further into their deep sockets. 'You can't imagine how strong it is. They say Lady Light herself locked it away in the underworld during the War of the Gods. Then, when we Witches unwittingly let it out a thousand years ago, it was up to Sam Hawk, the greatest High Witch there ever was, to put it back. Well, after that he sent me to keep watch, to make sure the Evernight stayed trapped beneath the earth. That's what I've done – and what I'll do until I take my last breath.'

Shadow Jack stepped into the spell light. The old Witch stared up at him, and then at the floor, where he cast no shadow.

'Djinni,' he said in a harsh whisper. 'A *real* Djinni?'

Mrs Hester took the old man's wand and snapped it over her knee. He put his hand to his chest and wailed. 'Don't do this. If you let the Evernight out it'll eat up all the goodness and light and happiness in existence. You have no idea how strong it is, what it can do. You won't be able to take it back!'

Mrs Hester leaned over and planted a kiss on his forehead.

'You've earned a rest, I think. Sleep tight.'

She nodded to Shadow Jack, who took out his blade. A moment later the old man, the Witch who had once been the strongest of his kind, who had stayed faithfully at his post for almost a thousand years, was dead.

At the final beat of the old man's heart, a deep rumble shook the island. Mrs Hester and Shadow Jack stumbled around as chunks of rock fell from the ceiling and shattered. Beneath their feet the dust of a thousand years scattered to reveal a circular seal on the ground, a ring of interlocking branches, and in the centre, a bird in flight.

When the rumbling died away Mrs Hester stood at the edge of the great seal.

'Are you sure?' said Shadow Jack.

Mrs Hester tried to still her hands. She could feel the coursing power of something ancient beneath her feet and for the first time she could remember, she was frightened. But a greater fear spurred her on: the fear of losing power. Her hatred for the Hags, for the king, her embarrassment at being made to look weak in front of her White Witches, had lit a fire in her mind, burning away the last traces of reason. She only wanted the Hags to suffer, only wanted to have the Mother Tree all to herself, only wanted to watch the Evernight strangle the last breath of life from the High Witch.

She took her wand and touched the tip to the seal. At once the etchings glowed bright, and the cavern rumbled and shook, but the power was white-hot and stabbing in Mrs Hester's veins, and she screamed. The enchantment took her up and tossed her away.

'Oooof!' She landed heavily, losing the grip on her wand. Shadow Jack's hurrying footsteps approached, and he helped her up and guided her wand back into her hand. She lit the place and looked at her scorched fingertips, noticing the smooth skin of her hands had become thin and wrinkled. 'It's too strong,' she managed to say, hardly believing her own words. 'I'm too old.'

A pause.

'Stand back,' said Shadow Jack.

He walked to the centre of the seal. He stamped his foot, and crouched down, and ran his finger across some of the inscriptions Sam Hawk had made so long ago. He tasted his finger, tasted the magic, and he nodded, and stood up, and became the raven, soaring up to the roof of the great chamber. Mrs Hester held up her wand, and at the edges of her spell light she saw him tuck in his wings and dive. In a short distance he picked up incredible speed, and when he hit the ground he went crashing through the centre of the seal, leaving a rough hole from which viscous, smoking black liquid began to spit.

Mrs Hester stepped back, her eyes full moons. A rumbling growl shook the land, passed through her body and made her knees buckle. The seal exploded fully open from beneath, depositing Shadow Jack on the ground. He was a man once more, and he stumbled up, covered in the black liquid, wiping it from his eyes, spitting and hacking it from his throat.

'We have to go.'

Mrs Hester did not argue. They rushed out of the chamber, the walls crumbling around them, up the staircase and out into the clear night of the dark side of the world. Half falling, they stumbled down the crag, and as they ran across the ice bridge, the top of the island exploded, raining hot rubble and ash down upon them, making the ice melt and crack at their feet. When they made it back to the land, they turned to see fire coming from the open rock, livid orange flames licking up from a place Mrs Hester could only imagine.

A thin, spidery crack crept down the island of rock. As the crack reached the lake, a thunderous roar filled the darkness, and the ground deep beneath the surface of the lake tore open, causing the water to churn and bubble as it drained away. Soon the lake was dry, and on its exposed bed strange, dark-dwelling fish flipped and flopped, suffocating.

From the crack in the lake bed came another screaming roar.

An inky, smoky substance geysered up towards the stars, where it gathered and tumbled and snaked in the air, growing, blooming, a nightmarish mixture of substantial and insubstantial matter, of shadow and putrid, stinking gas, of fear and death and hatred, lit from within by flashes of crackling lightning.

The Evernight had awakened.

Deep in the mountains and corners of these Midnight Lands, tribes of dark creatures had slept for almost a thousand years. Now, as the Evernight began to stir, so too did its people, rising from slumber, the markings on their skin glowing with the crackling power of reborn dark magic. They began the trek towards the lake. The Painted were on the move.

INTO THE SEWERS

'Here! Is it true what happened in Reaper's Square?'

'There was a dragon, so they say!'

'Nah! I were there. It was *two* dragons!'

'One of 'em ate a White Witch!'

'It was Hags! Musta bin! I reckon we're all done for!'

The narrow, twisting streets of the slums were crawling with gossip and chatter. It was always amazing to Lara how quick news passed among the slum folk. It was said, if a cove farted, by the time word of it reached the other side of the slums, people would have decided what he'd had for dinner the night before. Great flocks of paper birds were flying this way and that, darting through the streets, carrying messages and notes and hearsay about the incredible event.

'I seen it with my own eyes,' Lara said, approaching a group of gossip merchants. 'I was there, I was. In the square.'

'Tell us!' they cried. 'We have to know! Are we under attack? Was it Hags?'

Lara stroked her chin thoughtfully.

'Hmm. My memory's suddenly gone a bit hazy. Must be the fright that's done it. I reckon a couple of coins might help bring it back . . .'

She gave them an innocent smile, and they grumbled and clubbed together to hand her a few bronze coins.

'Ah. *Now* I remember . . .'

Lara wedged the end of her crowbar into the gap between the drain cover and the street, and she leaned, and leaned, until *clank*, the manhole cover popped out of place. She manoeuvred it to one side, sat at the edge of the hole, her legs dangling down into the dark, and listened with great concentration. She could tell by the sound of it that the stream was still moving rapidly, still bubbling and foaming, but the level had dropped. It was nothing she couldn't handle, so long as she kept her head in the game, made sure to watch every step.

She stared down into the darkness, and her heart fluttered in her chest. Thoughts of the Sewer Strangler came into her mind, of a man with no shadow creeping in the tunnels, waiting to pounce. For the briefest of moments, she wondered if she should hold off from entering the sewers until the attacks had stopped. But she swatted the notion away like a fly, angry with herself for ever thinking it.

With a final look around, she climbed into the hole, her feet steady on the rungs of the ladder, and began her descent.

Before she disappeared from the world above ground,

Lara reached up with her metal bar and levered the cover back over the sewer entrance. She had done this countless times, and on each occasion there was a moment, right before the cover dropped into place, when the last of the daylight would flare like a diamond on a ring, and the sight of it would make Lara's heart race, and she would ask the question: *Will that be the last time I ever see the sun?*

After that, there was the clunk of the cover dropping into place, and darkness.

At the foot of the ladder, deep beneath the streets, Lara reached into her toshing bag and brought out the new dragon-breath lamp Joe had bought her. She turned the dial on the bottom of the brass lamp, and a bright flicker of flame jumped to life behind the glass, casting golden light around the sewer tunnels.

Most people shivered at the thought of going down into the guts of the city, among the filth and the stench, the rats and sewer creatures, the bodies. But Lara looked around now, at the light shining on the smooth tunnel bricks, catching the rippling surface of the water. She listened to the gurgling song of the sewer stream, and she smiled. Because this was her world. Her patch. And who knew what treasures it might give up today.

The smell isn't so bad today, Lara thought as she sloshed through the splendid gloom. Some days, usually during the heat of the summer when the river was low and the sewers didn't get flushed through with rain as often, the stench was so thick you could almost see it, and it was slick and oily on your skin. But today, after the downpour and the high tides, the tunnels seemed shiny and new. In fact, Lara would wager they were a great deal cleaner than some of the streets above.

Every tosher had their favourite spots – parts of the sewer where they knew the brick was cracked and worn, or the channel was shaped in such a way that small, heavy things could gather and become wedged. Lara had several of these spots. Snapleg Corner had been a corker, because there was a sweet section that nobody else seemed to know, a join beneath the water where she'd frequently find coins. Problem was, half a moon back Snapleg Corner had filled with noxious gas, and along had come a tosher with his dragon-breath lamp, and the naked flame had met the gas and BOOM! No more Snapleg Corner. No more tosher either.

So Lara settled today on Blood River.

Blood River was a short passage of sewer on the south side of the river. It was known by that name because it was directly under a slaughterhouse, and when they hosed the blood off the ground it would flow down the drain and empty into the sewer stream, dyeing it red.

As Lara walked, she kept her ears and eyes on full alert. Gas pockets were only the beginning of the dangers that lurked beneath the city. There were places where the current could wash you clean away. Every tosher knew the times of the high tides like clockwork, and they'd scurry back to the streets before the river gates were opened and the sewers flushed. There were stories of strange sewer dwellers too – creatures that hid out of sight and would see a tosher and take the chance of a good meal.

Somewhere nearby, a scurry of rats crossed the stream and scratched and sniffed away down another sewer, causing Lara's thoughts to drift back a few days to her confrontation with Cotton and the way the rats had helped her escape. She took out her locket, holding it in her palm, allowing the light from her lamp to slide around the smooth edge and catch the etching of the bird. She gave the locket a shake, but it remained still. She was becoming convinced now that she had unwittingly stumbled into spilled magic in the sewers, and her locket had come to life for a short time because of it. Now the magic must have worn off, so all was back to normal.

There was plenty of flushed-away magic in the sewers, after all. Alfie Button, they said, had been toshing when a cocktail of spells had rushed past, engulfing him in a cloud of magic and shrinking him until he was no bigger than a field mouse. Poor Alfie had met his end when his neighbour's cat had spotted him one day and decided he looked quite tasty. Then there was Peg Leggot, who'd fallen into a glowing pool and turned to stone. She was still down there, under Admiral Street, and any tosher who passed her would pat her head for good luck.

Yessir, danger was everywhere down here.

And don't forget the Sewer Strangler, Lara's brain told her.

Least I have the advantage, she argued back. *Down here, this is my world, not his.*

But she could not quite shake away the fear, and she was cross at herself for that.

The sound of sloshing feet up ahead slowed her. She extinguished her lamp and ducked into the shadow, straining to listen. Reaching into her wax bag, she brought out her crowbar, and raised it above her head, ready to bring it crashing down.

'Lara? That you?'

The glow of another lamp emerged from the darkness, and with it the friendly, freckled face of Joe Littlefoot. Lara breathed again, lowered the bar, and laughed at herself for panicking so.

'It's me right enough, Joe! How're you going? Any luck?'

Joe flashed a smile. 'I should say so!' He brought the toshing bag down from his shoulder, opened it, and Lara looked inside and saw two silver coins, three copper ones, a shining earring with the stone missing, and a glass eye.

'Hell's teeth, Joe! Leave something for the rest of us!'

'Ha! I'll tell you, Lara, I've never known a spell of good luck such as this! I'm heading down Old Hans' shop now. I reckon I'll eat for a week off this catch!' He turned serious then. 'You haven't seen anyone lurkin' around in the shadows, have you? I keep imagining the Strangler will jump out at me any second!'

'I do too! But I haven't seen nothin' yet.' Lara gripped the crowbar and swung it a few times. 'I'm ready for him though.'

Joe stared up at her with a sparkling sort of awe in his eyes, as if he was gazing at an otherworldly being. 'I reckon it's the Strangler who has to watch out, with you in these tunnels! Happy toshing, Lara!'

And off he went, whistling at his good fortune.

When Lara reached Blood River, the water was the murky brown of cloudy ale, but the air was free of the iron smell of slaughterhouse blood. She went right to work, checking her favourite spots, her slim fingers probing cracks in the brickwork under the stream. The first try turned up nothing. The second, too. But when her fingers felt around on the third, she touched something hard and cold and small, and her heart gave a leap. She worked the object loose, brought it out from the stream, and held it up to the light from her lamp. A coin! Copper, but better than nothing. A fine start to the day!

It turned out there was nothing more to be found in Blood River, so Lara set off for the tunnels deeper below the earth, trudging through the rushing stream in her wax-coated boots towards other lucky locations she'd filed away in her memory.

Alas, today was not to be her day. She found nothing

else; after several hours her fingers were sore and raw, and it was almost time for high tide anyway, so she circled around and made her way back to the entrance beneath Bone Alley, a lonely copper coin in her toshing bag. She had hoped for more, for sure, but that coin would help feed her for a day or two.

Lara was ready to climb to the surface when her eyes made a grim discovery. At the edge of the lamplight a pair of small, awkwardly sprawled tosher's feet came into view. The sight stopped Lara dead. She held the lamp up, squinting into the gloom, her heart picking up pace and her breathing hushed and ragged.

She crept closer, the light from the lamp uncovering more of the little body. Most of him was soaked with sewer water, as if he'd been in the stream and dragged himself out. As the lamplight fell on the tosher's face, Lara gasped. 'Joe!' She dashed to his side and leaned over him, sliding her hand behind his head, trying to shake him awake. His face was swollen badly, one eye puffed shut, his nose covered in dried blood. She listened close. He was breathing steadily. 'Joe! Wake up, Joe!'

A groan started deep in his chest, rumbling up his throat, and he opened his mouth and let it out, sending it echoing through the tunnel. He opened his good eye. 'Lara?'

'It's me, Joe. You're all right. You'll be all right, Joe.'

It appeared that Joe was in a dream of sorts, and then he seemed to waken, for he became agitated, and he sat up and winced in pain, and began feeling around on the sewer floor.

'Take it easy, Joe.'

'My stuff,' he managed to say. 'My toshing bag . . .'

Lara helped him over to the sewer wall, where he leaned against the smooth bricks. 'What happened, Joe? Who did this to you?'

Joe looked up at her, and fear was spilling from his eyes. 'The Sewer Strangler, Lara! It's true what they say – he don't have no shadow! At first I thought he was after my haul – he took my toshing bag and he rummaged through it, but he wasn't interested in any of it. He chucked it all in the stream! Then he came towards me again and, oh, Lara, he started a-layin' into me! "Where's the box?" he said, again and again, every time he hit me. "Where's the box?"'

Lara's veins were on fire with anger, and with fear for Joe. 'How'd you get away, Joe?'

A tear trickled down Joe's face, mixed with the fresh blood from his nose. 'I just lay still,' he said, his eyes far away. 'Tried to go limp, like I was dead. He threw me about for a while, and then a look of surprise crossed his face. It was the strangest thing. His eyes went all wide, and the air around him swirled and blurred, and he disappeared!'

Lara looked at Joe from head to foot. As bloody and battered as he was, there didn't seem to be anything immediately life-threatening about his injuries. He tried to get up again.

'My stuff. I need to find my stuff. I need to look after Granny!'

Lara pushed him back down. 'Sit tight, Joe. Keep still. I'll look for your catch.'

She found Joe's dragon-breath lamp nearby, and she lit it and placed it at his side, and then she went off into the stream. His toshing bag wasn't far away, weighed down by the metal crowbar. She opened the drawstring and looked inside, finding no trace of the treasure Joe had uncovered on his toshing route that morning. So she took to the stream and began the search, combing every part of it with her fingers. She found nothing.

'Sorry, Joe. Looks like it's long gone.' She saw the disappointment in his face, and she felt so sorry for him that she reached into her own toshing bag and brought out the copper coin she'd found, and then into her pocket for the coins the coves on the street had given her for recounting the events in Reaper's Square. She slipped the coins into Joe's bag, then pretended to have one last rummage. 'Hold up, Joe, I was wrong. Looks like he missed something!' She brought out her copper coins and handed them over. 'It's not much, but it's better than a kick in the teeth. So to speak.'

Joe took the coins and gave her a wincing smile. 'You've always looked after me, Lara. Always.'

'Don't get soft now,' she said, helping him to his feet. All the time she was looking about, checking the shadows, listening. She was ablaze with anger now, shaking, and as they staggered through the sewer together, Lara felt the locket buzz against her chest again, felt the warmth spill from it, and her head was filled with the sound of crystal voices, and with the visions of the Witch-boy in the gallows in Reaper's Square, and the Hags on the roof, and the dragon made of fire.

The Coming Dark

Away to the east of Lara and the great city of King's Haven, farther even than the Weeping Isles, a fishing boat steamed along on the white-tipped waves of the Border Sea. *Mary's Light* was a crab boat, and her skipper was one of the few willing to fish in the waters so far east and away from home. It had been a good day; they'd pulled trap after trap from the depths, all filled with fat blue-shelled crab – blue gold they called them – and so the skipper was in a jolly mood as her men worked.

Presently, they dropped anchor to check more traps. The first trap here was fit to burst with huge blue-shells – the biggest catch of the day so far – and there were whistles and whoops of delight. More traps came up, all full, and the crew sang and laughed and danced.

Then a sudden darkness fell upon the boat.

The banter of the crew died away. They stood still, rising and falling gently with the boat, staring disbelievingly up at a vast, clear night sky bursting with bright burning stars, and a full silver moon. The air grew biting and cold. The breeze brought with it the faintest scent of rot, sweet at the edges.

'What's happening?'

'We must've drifted out of the Silver Kingdom, Skip!' suggested Big Matts, the first mate.

Skip shook her head, pushing past his huge bulk.

'Impossible!'

Big Matts pointed a fat finger westward, where the night sky became dusk and then daylight out towards the horizon.

'Skip?'

The voice was distant.

'Skip!'

She tore her eyes from the dark sky, looking at the disbelieving faces of her crew, and then out at the water. Somewhere in the nearby night, the flickering light of an oil lamp blinked into life. Then another, and another. Hundreds of lamps, thousands. *Mary's Light* was surrounded by hulking black ships. They'd been invisible under the cover of darkness. Standing on the decks of those ships were creatures straight out of storybooks and nightmares.

Somewhere in the back of her mind, Skip remembered the stories her brothers had told her when she was a tot. Stories of the folk with dark magic etched into their skin.

The Painted.

'The sky!' yelled Frank Calder, another of the crew. 'Look at the sky!'

Skip did look. She wished she hadn't. One by one, the stars were blinking out.

In her mind Skip was six years old again, frightened, shivering. She recalled staring in grim fascination at a watercolour in one of her books, a detailed illustration of a vast being in the east, reaching out across the world with tendrils of darkness, turning day to night.

'We're done for!' wailed Frank Calder. 'It's the Evernight! Lady Light help us!'

The rest of the crew began to pray, their low muttering punctuated with sobs.

The black boats came nearer.

A Painted jumped onto the deck of *Mary's Light*. When he stood straight he was far taller than any man on the boat and, like all the Painted, it seemed that his muscular arms were too long, his hands hanging down level almost with his knees. He was wrapped in ragged clothes and furs, and he stared around at the crew with glistening black eyes. Every inch of his thick grey skin was covered in the tattoos and markings of dark flesh magic.

'Don't move,' Skip told her crew. 'Don't do anything stupid!'

Big Matts was a damned good crabber, and strong enough to crack a dragon egg, but he wasn't too clever. He seemed to think that 'Don't do anything stupid' meant something entirely different, because he stepped forward and swung a big, wild fist at the Painted.

The Painted caught Matts' fist. One of the tattoos on his neck glowed bright. The Painted squeezed, and the skipper heard the bones in Big Matts' hand crack and splinter. Big Matts screamed as if he was four years old. Then the Painted let go, and Matts slumped to the deck, clutching what was left of his hand.

Nobody else moved.

The Painted took two steps forward, so that he was standing close enough for Skip to smell him. It was a wet, musky smell, and it stuck in her throat.

'Get off my boat,' she managed to say.

He did not move, did not smile or laugh or frown. He stared down at Skip, his dark eyes soaking up the light from the lamps.

The Painted reached a large tattooed hand into the depths of his animal-hide clothes. When he brought it back out, he was holding a curved blade with a handle made of bone. He took the knife and pressed the point of it into his own hand, on the fleshy mound of skin below his thumb. Blood seeped from the cut, and Skip was amazed that his blood was red, just like her own.

The Painted held his hand out, palm up, so that the blood began pooling in the centre, and he took the knife and held it in his teeth. Then, with his free hand, he dipped a finger into the pool of blood, and pressed it against the skipper's forehead.

The blood was warm on her skin. His fingers traced a

shape, and he returned to the pool of blood for more, like a painter dipping his brush in a paint pot. When he was satisfied, the Painted took the knife from between his teeth and raised the blade to the skipper's forehead.

She felt the point of the blade break her skin, and the searing pain burst across her forehead, through her skull. If she had been able to move, she would have screamed out and cursed and spat. As the blade carved a shape into her, the pain spread out from the roots, infecting every part of her, her blood and her bones and her flesh, until it became so unbearable she wished for her heart to stop. Skip's eyes rolled upward, and she saw that the stars were completely gone. The sky was black, empty. It swallowed her up.

And then the blade left Skip's skin, and the pain shrank and withered.

I'm not dead. I might make it through this. Oh, Lady Light, let me see my home again!

But the darkness in the sky flooded her brain, her every thought, unlocking the doors in her mind, finding her memories, killing them one by one . . .

The first time she'd held a fishing rod.

The smile on her daddy's face as she cradled that first, slippery, cold fish in her arms.

The smell of fresh bread in her grandma's kitchen ('Keep your fingers to yourself or you'll lose 'em!').

Skip clung to these, fighting the darkness, holding on . . .

But the people in her memories were faceless now. The places blurred.

Her brothers became strangers, and soon even the stories were gone, and the memory of her family and their laughter was sucked into the blank abyss, and she no longer knew who she was, or where she was, or what colour the sky ought to be.

She only saw the Evernight. It had become her world, filling her every heartbeat with the instinct to protect it. Skip watched the Painted mark her crew with their blades and blood, and felt nothing.

When the marking was done, the Evernight's coiling darkness crept towards the west, and the ships began to sail.

Old Hans

Tingalingaling!

This was the voice of the bell on the door of Old Hans' shop. It was a cheerful sound, Lara thought, as she shook the afternoon drizzle from her clothes, and this was a cheerful place, a haven where toshers were welcome and made to feel like people worth the air they breathed.

Dark and dusty and filled with curiosities and cobwebbed corners, Old Hans' shop was a treasure trove of artefacts from life in the slums: everything from books and lamps to pet snakes and pistols, from taxidermy to bowls of dolls' eyes.

Lara approached the counter with a smile on her face, because for the first time in ages she'd had a decent day's toshing. The Strangler may have struck again in the night, but what was Lara to do, give up toshing and starve out of fear? The tunnels might seem darker than normal, the shadows threatening to come alive around every corner, but the sewers were Lara's territory, and she would not hand them over.

Old Hans sat hunched behind his counter, as crooked and tatty as the crumbling shop around him. Currently, he was writing in a ledger, concentration etched in every wrinkle on his rubbery face. As the pen moved across the columns of numbers, Old Hans' tongue followed it, licking his lips from one side of his mouth and back again.

Lara waited patiently, listening to the scratch of Old Hans' pen on the ledger, breathing the jumbled perfume of the shop, the dust and rotting wood, and the smell of other people's lives.

At last, Old Hans seemed satisfied. His tongue disappeared back into his thin mouth, and he placed his pen on the desk and closed the ledger. Because of his age, Old Hans always had the shakes; it affected his hands, and his head was always moving up and down in little nods, like he was agreeing with the thoughts in his own head.

'Larabelle Fox! Why, I haven't seen you in weeks!'

'Were you worried about me, Old Hans?'

'Hard not to be worried about a young girl when there's a killer on the loose,' he said. Then, in a grandfatherly sort of tone, he added, 'You bein' careful, Larabelle? Lookin' after yourself?' Before she had the chance to answer, he held up a crooked finger. 'You wait there.' He stood up and shuffled through the door behind the counter to the back of the shop. A few minutes later he was back, and he placed a plate of bread and cheese on the counter. 'Tuck in, gal. You look half starved!'

Lara was so hungry she almost swallowed it with her eyes. She ripped off a hunk of bread and stuffed it in her mouth, followed by the creamy cheese. How wonderful it tasted! She cleared the plate in hardly any time at all, and when she was done she licked the crumbs from the plate, and the last of the taste from her fingers. The warm, full feeling of food in her belly radiated through her, and she sighed happily.

'Lady Light! You must've been famished, girl!'

'I've been going through a bit of a dry run. The sewers can be a right git when they want to.'

Old Hans nodded. 'Happens to the best of 'em. But I assume, since you're here, that your dry run has come to an end? Eh?'

Lara smiled. Her dry run had indeed come to an end. She reached into her pocket, brought out a closed fist, and opened it over the counter, dropping a golden ring onto the scratched wood. She watched Old Hans, excitement fluttering in her chest.

'Well, well. What do we have here, eh?' He adjusted his glasses, and reached under his counter, producing a brass magnifying glass. Then, with gnarled, shaking fingers, he picked up the ring (it took him a couple of attempts) and held it in the palm of his hand, and examined it closely. 'Hmm.'

'Hmm?' said Lara.

'Hmm,' said Old Hans.

He put the brass spyglass down, popped the edge of the ring between his teeth, and bit down. Then he returned it to the counter and leaned on his elbows.

'Well?' Lara was full of nervous excitement.

'It's pretty,' said Old Hans. 'But I'm sorry to tell you, Lara, that it isn't real gold. Nor is that sparkler a real diamond.'

Lara had been buoyant, but now she deflated a little. 'You sure? It's heavy enough.'

'Lara, I've been doing this for a long, long time. Believe me, nobody wants to see you fishing a gold ring out of them sewers more than I do – it means more coins for both of us! But this isn't it. Not today.' He gave her an appraising sort of look. 'Of course, you're more'n welcome to go elsewhere for a second opinion. My old eyes are not what they used to be.'

Old Hans had kept his shop in Bone Alley for as long as anyone could remember. Parts of the slums had grown up around it. Every tosher had done business with him at some point, and nobody had a bad word to say about him, which was a rare thing among toshers, who spoke almost exclusively in bad words. Lady Light knew he'd helped Lara out of a scrape or two over the years. Even so, she'd been *sure* this ring was going to feed her for a while. Maybe it wouldn't do any harm to have someone else take a look. But this was *Old Hans* . . .

'No,' she said, trying to force a smile. 'No, Old Hans.

Whatever you say is fine by me. What can you give me for it?'

He rubbed the silvery stubble on his old chin. 'I reckon I'll shift it to some young fool in love who wants to impress his girl. I can't ask more than a silver coin for it, so I'll give you half of that. Eight coppers.'

'Ten,' said Lara.

Old Hans screwed up his face. 'Nine.'

'Done.'

Tingalingaling!

Old Hans watched the girl go out of sight, then came out from behind the counter and shuffled to the door and bolted and locked the many locks. After this, he went back behind the counter and reached for the ring he'd just bought from Lara, and he made his way to the storeroom in the back.

The storeroom was packed with shelving and boxes and crates. Half-repaired puppets hung from the ceiling on their strings, and the floor was hidden under piles of bicycle wheels, pots of paint, bird cages and stacks of old, damp newspapers. Old Hans went to a spot on the bare brick wall where the mortar was worn and crumbling. He wedged his old fingers into a gap in the mortar, and manoeuvred three bricks out of the wall, leaving a hole. Within was a safe. Old Hans smiled at the sight of it. He turned the dial on the safe this way and that, until it unlocked with a click, and he pulled the door open, and stared at what lay inside.

Treasure.

It paid to be in with the toshers, paid to put up with their stench and to greet them all with a 'How do you do?' and a 'Look after yourself in them sewers'. And it was wise to give them a fair price for most of the loot they brought up from the tunnels, because if you did that, if you convinced them you were *Good Old Hans* for long enough, then they'd trust you when they found something *really* valuable.

And that's when the money was made.

Inside the safe Old Hans kept a large pile of fine jewellery: tangled threads of silver and gold, brooches set with smooth precious stones, glimmering watches, strings of pearls.

Every one of these pieces had come from a tosher. And in each and every case the tosher had no idea of the real value of what they were selling.

Selling! Ha! More like giving *away!*

Old Hans looked at the ring. Real gold, it was, with a real gem to boot! A couple more pieces like this and he'd finally have enough to retire, far away from the stink of the slums and the toshers. He breathed on the ring, buffed the stone on his sleeve, and placed it on top of the pile of treasures in the safe. Then he locked the safe door, put the bricks back, and returned to the shop, smiling at his own cleverness.

The Clockwork Bird

It was late that afternoon when Lara discovered the object that would change her life for ever.

Her mood was black, because the ring she'd been so pleased about had proved worthless and she'd been forced to go back into the sewers and look for more. But even her most reliable toshing spots now seemed empty.

Curse all that rain! she thought. *And curse the swollen sewer streams for washing away anything good!*

With the tide almost in, she sloshed back towards the surface, muttering under her breath.

And that is when her foot caught on something hard and square in the water.

Lara's dark mood evaporated at once, and she put her toshing head back on and held her lamp to the surface. The water was milky brown, with no hint of clarity, so she hung her lamp around her neck and leaned over, reaching her hands into the murky stream. Her fingertips traced the sewer bricks down there, leaving channels in the film of scum that covered the underwater bricks. And then she touched something smooth and square.

The box – that's what it felt like – was stuck good and proper, wedged into some crack or hole that she had never encountered before. As she worked, she took a mental note of the place. A hole like this was bound to be a trap for all sorts of good stuff. Her nimble fingers worked around the box, gently probing and pushing and pulling, until it loosened and broke free. Lara brought it out from under the sewer stream. Water had filled the box, and she turned it sideways, letting it empty through the crack along the hinges.

She held the box up to the warm light of her lamp. It was made of dark, polished wood. There was nothing fancy about it, no carvings or decoration, save for a tiny pair of golden wings clasping the lid shut.

As Lara examined the box her heart began to thump. There was nothing quite like the sparkling, intoxicating feeling of discovery, of fishing something unexpected and unusual out of the dark waters. Her fingers trembled as she reached for the clasp, and unfastened it. She opened the lid.

Her imagination had already run away, filled with thoughts of jewels and gold and glittering treasure. But when the lid opened, and the warm light of her lamp poured into the box, what was waiting inside made Lara's breath catch in her chest.

It was a bird!

Not a real bird, of course. But one made of wood and gold and clockwork. It was the size of a sparrow, with golden wings, every feather a sliver of metal as fine as a moonbeam. Metal cogs and gears whirred within the open cavity of its wooden chest, like the inside of a complicated clock. Its head was carved wood, with a golden beak and perfect, sparkling sapphires for eyes.

'Hello,' whispered Lara. 'Where have you come from, my little friend?'

She lifted the clockwork creature out of the box; it was light and delicate, and she handled it with great care, stroking the cold metal of its wings and the jewels of its eyes. Her heart was giddy and light. This was a wondrous object, a shining, magical treasure. Never in her life had the sewers rewarded her with anything like it.

A voice in her head said, *I think I might be rich.*

Then another thought barged its way into her mind.

The Strangler. What had Joe said again? What was it the Strangler had been looking for?

A box.

Lara stared at the objects in her hands, the bird and the box, and suddenly she was aware of how alone she was, how small and fragile in those tunnels. As quickly and gently as she could, she stowed the bird back in place, closed the clasp, and slipped the box into her toshing bag before escaping back above ground.

*

Later that night, as Lara slept in the quiet of her old opera-house attic, something inside her toshing bag began to move.

The box that Lara had discovered was still in there, but in all the jostling of getting out of the sewer, the golden clasp had come undone, and the box had fallen open. The little bird, the one made of wood and clockwork and shining gold, lay beneath the box, under Lara's crowbar.

In the dark of the bag, the bird's sapphire eyes sparked to life, blazing blue. The clockwork bird moved its head this way and that. Then it wriggled out of the tight spot, causing the metal bar to bump to the floor. The bird probed the toshing bag with its beak, looking for a way out. When it could not find one, it thrust its head forward, cutting through the dirty, damp material, and squeezed out of the hole.

The bird hopped around the labyrinth of props, feet click-clacking on the boards, giving the odd object an exploratory peck. Then it took to the air, swooping through the dark, eyes scattering blue light around the place as it ducked and spun, coming to rest from time to time on high perches.

When it landed on Lara's chest, she let out a sleepy sigh, but did not wake. The bird stood twitching its head, seemingly watching the girl, rising and falling with her every breath. Through her nightshirt, Lara's wooden locket thrummed. After a while the mechanical creature walked around in a little circle, settled down, and tucked its head under its wing. Then, almost as if it was drifting off to sleep, the light in its eyes went out.

DARK DREAMS

Double Eight woke with a scream, clawing at the night, momentarily stuck in that place between sleep and wake where the dark visions of his dream still gripped him. He felt rough hands on his shoulders shaking him, and the dream disintegrated, leaving him wide-eyed and confused, looking up at a broad, red-bearded face lit starkly by a dragon-breath lamp.

'Quiet, boy!' said the man. His eyes were wild and harsh. 'You tryin' to let the whole world know you're here?'

Slowly, Double Eight's senses returned. He was hiding out in the belly of a boat at the docks, waiting for the Hags to secret him away to Westerly Witch.

'I had a dream,' he said. 'I think something's happening. Something terrible.'

The man – Rob Nielsen was his name – looked fearful. 'Tell me.'

'I don't know . . .' said Double Eight. He tried to put it into words. 'Something came out of the earth. Darkness.

And there were people with marks all over their skin. The darkness was . . . it was *alive*. It could see me and I knew it was coming to get me . . .'

Rob Nielsen stared at the boy. He was only a White Witch, and of course White Witches weren't taught their history. The boy didn't know what he had seen. But Rob . . . Rob had just awakened from the same dream, and he was willing to bet that Witches all over the world had seen the same thing. The Evernight and the Painted.

Rob was correct. Witches everywhere, White and Hags alike, had the same dream that night, the dream of a great disturbance in the world, of a darkness of unimaginable power.

Mrs Hester, like Double Eight, had woken in the middle of the night with a start. With her hand pressed to her chest to feel the rapid thrum of her heart, she'd gone to the window of her palace tower and looked out towards the White Witch district. Lamps were blinking on in the institutional buildings, in the dormitories and hallways.

Mrs Hester felt a tightening in her throat and her chest. It struck her for the first time that she had done something incredibly foolish. The Evernight was loose. Soon it would reach the city, and with it would come the Painted. The reality of what she'd done made her shiver. But this was no time for second thoughts. It was too late for that. The plan must go ahead, and for it to work, she needed the Doomsday

Spell. That was the key to everything. With the spell in her pocket she could wait until the Hags were ruined and then send the Evernight back to where it had come from. What was left of the world would be hers.

So come on, Evernight. Do your thing.

A KNIFE IN
THE BACK

Lara jerked awake, sitting up in bed gasping, panting, from the terrible nightmare she'd just had of darkening skies and tattooed monsters. Something fell off her chest, rolling with a clunk to the floor.

The clockwork bird.

She squinted at it.

'How did you get *there*?'

She tried to remember, but everything was hazy and dreamlike. If this bird really was the object that the Strangler had been searching for, then it wasn't safe to hold onto it for very long.

Tingalingaling!

The rain had stopped and the skies cleared, but despite the morning sunshine Old Hans' shop was still cast in shadow and gloom.

He was hard at work polishing a collection of small

brass ornaments, madly scrubbing at them with an old rag. The smell of cleaning spirit stuck in Lara's throat.

'Lara!' He was wearing a pair of magnifying spectacles, and his old eyes filled the lenses completely, making him look like a strange owl. 'Back again so soon, gal?'

'Yes, Old Hans. I've found something.'

She noticed Old Hans' eyes wandering to the toshing bag, to where the weight of the box was pressing against the waxy material. She leaned on the counter. 'The Strangler. They say he's a-lookin' for something down in the sewers. Have you heard?'

Old Hans stared at her with milky grey eyes. 'I've *heard* he's searching for a box.'

Lara pulled open the drawstring of her wax toshing bag, and gently lifted out the wooden box. She placed it on the counter, and the lamplight gleamed on its smooth edges. Old Hans looked at it, and then at Lara.

She gave a nod. 'Open it.'

Old Hans' fingers were shaky and stiff. He struggled with the golden clasp. As he lifted the bird gently from the box, a strange look flashed across his face, but it was gone in half a blink. 'This came from the *sewers*?'

'It's what the Strangler is after, Old Hans. It must be! And if he's willing to kill for it, then it's gotta be valuable. Look how fine it is!'

Old Hans did not answer right away. As he examined

the bird, turning it over in his hands, lifting its delicate wings, it seemed to Lara that he had fallen into a trance, bewitched by its beauty and shining splendour. 'It's a fine thing indeed,' he said at last.

'Can you shift it?'

He looked up from the bird and smiled.

'Oh I knew you could! That's why I brought it to you, Old Hans. You're the best! You're a good cove!'

'I appreciate that, Lara. I appreciate it very much. Does anybody else know about this?'

'Nope. Just you.'

'Good girl.' He came out from behind the counter, went to the door and locked the many locks. 'We want to keep this to ourselves. Don't want word getting out that we have it, do we? Don't want the Strangler a-knockin' on the door.'

'Course,' said Lara. She stared at him. His fingers were all twitchy, and he didn't seem to know what to do with himself. 'You all right?'

'Mmm? Oh. Dandy, Lara. Just dandy. Here, what say me and you head to the back, out of sight, eh? I'll make a nice cup of tea and we'll decide what to do next.'

He placed the bird back in its box and held it under his arm. Then he opened the hatch on the counter, let Lara through, and guided her to the back of the shop.

'You got a buyer in mind?' she asked, her thoughts bursting with gold coins.

'Oh I think I know someone who'll be very interested.

And if he is, well, let's just say there'll be no more mucking about in the sewers for you, my girl. Ever again.'

'You know,' said Lara, 'I reckon I will still go down there from time to time. It's too much a part of me to stop for ever. Like you collecting things, I suppose.'

Old Hans opened a door to a small, square room so crammed with jumbled stock and boxes that there was barely space to stand. 'That's right. In here. Ladies first, ahaha. There's a desk near the back. You sit there and I'll go and make us a nice cuppa . . .'

The door closed with a bang.

Lara spun around.

'Old Hans?'

A key rattled on the other side of the door. Lara tried to open it, but it was locked.

'Old Hans! Is this a joke? Let me out!' She was banging on the door now, a horrible feeling of dread creeping over her. 'I'm warning you! You let me outta here right this hagging minute!'

There was nothing on the other side of the door but silence. Lara stopped struggling and turned around and leaned her back on the door. She put her face in her hands and shook her head, anger and confusion ripping her thoughts all to pieces.

He wouldn't do this, would he? Wouldn't steal from me? But how can I be so sure? That bird is probably worth a fortune and—Oh, how could I be so soft-headed?

Whatever Old Hans was up to, it was unexpected, and frightening, and on top of everything else that had happened in the last few days, it was almost enough to break her.

But no. She reached for the locket around her neck. The feel of it in her hand calmed her, clearing her mind. She closed her eyes, breathing deep. Then, when she was recovered enough, she began to explore the room, looking for a way out.

THE PAPER BIRD

Old Hans stood on the other side of the door, his guts squirming like a bag of snakes and his hands trembling as they clutched the box. The girl had quietened down now, stopped banging and shouting. He could hear her scratching around for a way out. There was none.

He moved away, up the stairs to the little flat he kept above his shop, his knees popping and cracking as he climbed. He went to his desk and poured himself a large fire whisky. Then another. This helped the trembling a little.

Old Hans opened the wooden box and lifted the clockwork bird gently out. He turned it over in his hands, examining every bit of it. It was the finest piece of craftsmanship he'd ever seen. Clockwork horses were common enough in the Silver Kingdom of course, but a clockwork *bird* . . . he'd never heard of such a thing. In places the metal was so thin you could almost see through it. It was, indeed, worth a fortune . . .

He wondered for a second what might happen if he decided to sell it, to ignore the wishes of the gentleman who had come to his shop a few days before. The man with no shadow. He shuddered. If he did sell the bird, he suspected that he would not live long enough to spend even a few coins of his new wealth.

No. He would do as he had been asked.

Old Hans put the bird down, opened a drawer in his desk, bringing out a small piece of card he'd been keeping there. The card was black on both sides. The shadowless man had slipped it into Old Hans' hand with fingers as cold as ice. As soon as the man had come through the door, Old Hans had felt uneasy. There had been something about the way he moved, about the way he carried himself, that made Old Hans think that under the surface, under the calm exterior and the black clothes, there was something else, something old, and dark, and very dangerous.

'An object was stolen from me,' he had said in his oily voice. 'Something I'd like back very much. A wooden box. And inside the box, a bird.'

This is when he had given Old Hans the black card.

'If you come across this box, let me know at once. Write my name on this card and it will find me. You'll be well rewarded.'

And he had told Old Hans his name.

Then, as he had left, the stranger had looked back, and

said, 'If you discover the box and do not tell me, I will find out, and I will come for you.'

Now Old Hans sat at his desk and stared first at the card and then at the clockwork bird.

A bang echoed up through the floor from the stockroom below. It was a shame that the girl had become involved. She was one of the best toshers in the city, and loyal too – always bringing the treasures she'd found to Old Hans first. He'd miss that. But as soon as she'd taken that box out of her bag he'd known that there was no other way. It was up to the man with no shadow to decide what would happen to her, and that was nothing to do with Old Hans.

He picked up his pen, and in black ink that was invisible on the black card, he wrote down the name the man had given him.

Shadow Jack.

The card – witch paper – folded itself up until it was a tiny, black, angular bird, and he watched it fly to the window, hovering there expectantly. Old Hans stumbled out of his seat, shuffled to the window and threw it open. The black paper bird soared out into the sunshine, disappearing over the city to find the shadowless man.

Away across King's Haven, in a small wooded area within the rambling palace gardens, among the roots of an ancient oak tree, there was a hole in the ground. The hole was deep, and narrow, and led to a small, roughly cut hollow in the earth.

Inside this hollow, away from the urn that had been his prison for so long, Shadow Jack slept. He dreamed of the war, of crumbling planets and flaming galaxies and safe, quiet places like this, and in his dream he was a hero. The Gods rewarded him with his own worlds, with freedom.

A bird made of black paper swooped into his dream, and he woke up, and sniffed the warm, earthy air.

Shadow Jack crawled out of his resting place beneath the earth.

The paper bird was waiting for him in the branches of the oak tree above his hollow, and when he saw it, Shadow Jack held out a hand, and the black paper bird swooped down and landed on his pale palm. Shadow Jack unfolded the bird and sniffed the paper. Then he smiled and put the paper in the pocket of his coat.

There was a sound on the breeze, soft as dark silk, and Shadow Jack became a raven, and took to the sky, heading for the old man's shop.

The First
Rescue

Old Hans poured another fire whisky (was it the fourth or the fifth? Oh, what did it matter!) and tipped it down his neck. He was beginning to feel a little more relaxed about the whole situation. Soon Shadow Jack would come and clean it all up, and when he was gone again, Old Hans' pockets would be full of coins.

The clockwork bird was lying on his desk, and he picked it up and stroked the cold, shining gold of its wing feathers. It really was a shame that he couldn't keep it for himself. Such a rare and wondrous object . . .

When the bird's sapphire eyes began to glow, Old Hans thought at first it was the whisky playing tricks on his mind. But he squinted at it, and adjusted his specs, and still the eyes glowed.

The bird moved.

It jerked its wings awkwardly. Old Hans let out a squeak of fright. He jumped in his chair, the legs screeching on the floor. The clockwork bird stood up. It shook itself down.

It snapped its head around to face him, and it seemed to look him up and down. When it launched itself at Old Hans, he let out half a scream and pushed backwards, crashing his chair to the floor.

The bird was all over him, pecking at his face, his eyes, scratching with sharp feet. Old Hans tried to hide beneath one arm, swatting at the bird with the other, but it was unstoppable.

'Gerroff! Gerroff me!'

He stumbled to his feet, barging blindly around the room, knocking over lamps and ornaments, finding the door at last. Away to the landing he fled, feeling for the bannister, the bird still pecking at him. His foot missed the first step, and he fell, feet and arms and legs tangled, banging and bouncing, until he came to rest at the foot of the stairs.

He was aware that the bird had landed on his face, and it gave him one last peck on the forehead for good measure.

Then Old Hans passed out.

Down in the storeroom, Lara's fingers traced the place on the wall where the mortar between the bricks had been removed. She dug her fingers into the gap, the way she might do in the sewers when she found a plum toshing spot, removed the loose bricks and stepped back, peering into the space in the wall and hoping desperately for a way out.

There was a safe nestling in the gap.

What you got in there, you old rat?

She fiddled with the dial, clicking it this way and that, but the combination could have been anything, and the safe stayed locked.

Lara went back to the door.

'I found your safe!' she yelled. 'I got it open! I've filled my pockets with your stuff! You better come in here and stop me!'

When he did not reply, she got angry again, and banged on the door.

'Let me out! Let me—'

A series of sounds echoed through from the rooms above, first a yell, then a bang, then some awkward scrapes and shuffling footsteps. Lara leaned close to the door, listening. It sounded like some sort of struggle. The racket ended with a cacophony of tumbling bangs.

Breathless, she stayed silent. There were no more sounds, no trace of footsteps or creaking boards. Had the Strangler somehow found out about the bird? Had he come for it?

'Old Hans?'

The words had barely escaped her mouth when that familiar, delicate sound began to spill from her locket. She pulled it free, held it up, and watched in dumbfounded amazement as the etching of the bird glowed dazzlingly bright.

The sound of rattling in the lock made her jump. She reached for the nearest object, a candlestick, and raised it over her head as the door unlocked and creaked slowly open.

The doorway was empty.

The hallway was in darkness, the glow from Lara's locket casting a spooky light on the walls. She edged out of the storeroom, keeping the candlestick above her head, ready to strike, but as she moved into the hall, all was quiet and eerily still.

Old Hans' crumpled body lay at the foot of the stairs. She dashed to his side, crouched down, put her ear to his chest, and found a heartbeat. The old fart was still breathing, and Lara was relieved about that, not least because she had no desire to be wanted by the coppers in connection with a dead body.

Tap.

Clack.

Rattle-rattle!

The sounds startled Lara, and she spun around and followed her ears, creeping to the open door of the storeroom, peering around the edge to the other side. What she saw there made her stop, blink, and look again.

The clockwork bird was moving around as if it were alive. Not only that, but it seemed to have managed to get its beak jammed in the keyhole, and it was flapping its wings and shaking its head madly, trying to break free.

Lara reached out a trembling hand.

'Easy. Hush now.'

Her fingers closed around the cool metal of the bird's wings, and she took its head gently between her thumb and forefinger and managed to manoeuvre it free. She opened her hand. The bird sat in her palm, staring up at her, its head twitching this way and that.

The soft whispering came from her locket again, and she felt a ripple pass through her entire body. The locket erupted with light, filling the whole shop.

'Hell's teeth!'

She staggered back, covering her eyes, and then the light died away, and her vision took a few moments to adjust to the dim hallway again. The bird was standing by her feet, looking up at her. It gave one of her shoes a peck, then leaped gracefully into the air and landed on her shoulder. It seemed quite at home there.

Slowly, very slowly, Lara raised her hand to stroke the golden feathers of its wings.

'What *are* you, mister bird?'

There was a groan from the floor. Old Hans' voice said, 'Hag!' His eyes were open wide, his face a twisted mask of fear and disgust. 'Hag!' he repeated, the strength coming back to his tongue. He pointed a shaking finger at Lara and at the locket around her neck. 'Hag magic!'

'Now, Old Hans, this is not what it looks like.'

Lara knew *exactly* what this looked like. There was an enchanted clockwork bird on her shoulder and a magic locket around her neck. It couldn't have been any more obvious if someone had written *HAG* across her forehead.

'Hag! Murderer! You tried to finish me off!'

'I never did!'

He was on his knees now, and Lara tried to help him up, but he swatted her away.

'Gerroff! Someone call the coppers! Help!'

Lara knew there would be no reasoning with him. Thick, choking panic clogged her throat. Everyone was going to think she *was* a Hag. They'd hunt her. Try her. Hang her!

She reached down and took the keys from Old Hans' pocket, and ran through the shop to the door, trying the different keys in the locks until, click, they began to open.

'Lara!' Old Hans was at his counter now.

Click.

'Give me the bird and I won't tell anyone your secret.'

Click.

'Lara! Larabelle Fox!'

Click.

The door opened. Lara dropped the keys, and grabbed the clockwork bird and stuffed it into her pocket. Then she ran out into Bone Alley, Old Hans shouting after her.

'Help! Thief!'

The yell brought a murmur from the crowds. But this was King's Haven, and thieves were as numerous as raindrops.

'HAG!'

That word, spoken in the open, was as powerful as a pistol shot. It stopped Lara in her tracks, and the murmurs all around her turned to gasps and shrieks. She looked back at Old Hans, and for a moment she thought he looked sorry, and that he'd decided to let her go. But his face hardened, and he pointed at her.

'Hag! Hag, there! She tried to kill me!'

Others on the street had stopped now too, and they were gawking at her, pointing, whispering.

'Keep back!' yelled someone.

'Somebody get the coppers!'

'She's only a girl! I say we take care of her ourselves!'

'Yeah! Hag children aren't so dangerous, I heard.'

Lara turned on the spot, her heart frozen, her body shivering. There were people all around her now, closing in.

'She'd have done somethin' by now if she could!'

'Here! There'll be a reward if we catch her!'

'Is it less if she's dead?'

Everything seemed to slow down. Lara looked at their faces. These were normal people, mothers and fathers with children and families, but it was as if they had been possessed by a devil. They were hissing and spitting and jeering, and their eyes were full of malice and blood-lust. Some were almost close enough to touch her now . . .

'Stay back!'

There were hands on her, on her shoulders, her arms.

157

She struggled free, but more hands grabbed at her hair and face, and she smelled the stink of sweat and alcohol, and her eyes were blurred with tears, the street a spinning tangle of fear.

A hand clamped over her face, and another reached into her coat, fumbling around. Lara realised it was Old Hans trying to get the bird. She bit down hard on his finger, heard a scream, and the hand let go.

'She bit me!'

'Get her!'

'Look! Coppers! Oi, boys, do your job won't you? Get this Hag off our streets!'

The Second Rescue

Lara did not want to give the watching crowd the satisfaction of seeing her cry, so she closed her eyes as the coppers roughly bound her hands behind her back, the metal cuffs jamming into her flesh. The coppers led her, pushing and jostling, through the streets, where crowds were gathering. Insults and curses rained down on her, making her wince. Other things fell on her too, rotten food, handfuls of muck from the street, even the steaming contents of a pure collector's bucket. Her hands were bound, so she couldn't protect her face, and the muck caked her mouth and nose, reeking, making her gag.

She was surrounded by people on all sides, yet she had never been so alone. Lara knew they'd march her to the cells and lock her up. She'd be tried as a Hag, of course, and what chance would she have, a girl from the streets – a tosher? Old Hans would probably testify, and most of the people on the street would make up stories and swear they'd seen Lara do magic, because even a mere mention of the word Hag got their blood boiling these days, thanks to Mrs Hester and the king. Who'd believe Lara's word against all of that?

Nobody, she bet. Nobody at all.

So it would be off to Reaper's Square. To the gallows.

Lara's tears mixed with the muck; it was in her hair and her eyes and she could barely see.

Suddenly, a sound like thunder shook the street, and before she knew what was happening, Lara's eyes were blinded by black smoke. She was in the centre of a cloud of screams and confused yells and coppers' whistles. Someone barged into her, knocking her to the ground. The crowd was stampeding now, driven by blind fear, and they trod on her, on her hair and her arms and legs, on her stomach, winding her.

Rough hands dragged her up, and she felt herself being thrown over someone's shoulder, carried through the smoke and screams and confusion.

The last thing she thought, before she passed out, was that the person who was carrying her, whoever that might be, had changed direction. They were heading away from the jailhouse, weren't they? But she could not be sure, and soon the darkness wrapped around her, and took her away.

Picking Up
the Scent

Old Hans poured himself another fire whisky with trembling hands, swallowed it down, and clenched his teeth as the amber liquid warmed his throat and chest.

Curse that girl! And curse the bird too! If *she* hadn't turned up he wouldn't have found himself in this predicament. And he knew that he *was* in a predicament. The man with no shadow was on his way, expecting Old Hans to have the bird, and all he'd find would be empty hands and hollow words.

A huge raven swooped in through the window, making Old Hans cry out. The air around the raven swirled black, and at once Shadow Jack stood in the room.

Old Hans' eyes grew huge. 'Djinni,' he whispered.

Tall and thin, dressed in a ragged black suit and coat, black eyes shining from under the rim of his black hat, Shadow Jack moved forward and stood over Old Hans. Old Hans looked up into Shadow Jack's face, and he shivered.

'Where is the bird?'

Before Old Hans could answer, Shadow Jack spotted the wooden box on the desk, and he picked it up and turned it in his hands.

'Now wait a minute. There's somethin' I have to tell you before you go openin' it . . .'

Too late. Shadow Jack opened the box. He looked at the empty place inside where the clockwork bird should be, and then he looked at Old Hans. In the time it took to blink, Shadow Jack threw out a foot and tipped the chair backwards, sending Old Hans crashing painfully to the floor. He put his foot on Old Hans' throat, and leaned.

'Where is the bird?' he said again. 'Give it to me. It is Mrs Hester's property.'

He released the pressure. Old Hans gasped and wheezed. 'It were here! I swear it. A girl brought it in – a tosher. Found it in the sewers. She wanted to sell it. I did just what you said, sir, I kept the bird here, and the gal too in case she went a-shoutin' about it. We were all set. But then something happened. That bird . . . it came alive! It set about me, nearly put out my eyes! And I fell down those stairs and when I woke up the girl was gone. She took the bird!'

Shadow Jack's face did not change. 'The bird . . . it *moved*?'

'Didn't you hear me? It more than moved, it tried to kill me!'

Shadow Jack considered this. 'Who's the girl?'

'Lara.'

'Lara?'

'Yes, Larabelle Fox. A Hag, I'm sure of it. She has some sort of magical locket thing round her neck.'

Shadow Jack's eyes widened and he sniffed at the air, and followed his nose downstairs, to the storeroom. When he had been tracking the members of the Doomsday Coven, he had been dealing with powerful Witches trained in the art of misdirection and concealment, individuals who, until he had exhausted them with the chase, had the ability to make themselves almost invisible and untraceable. But this . . . this was just a little girl. Finding her would be child's play.

He took one last sniff of the dusty air in Old Hans' storeroom.

'Got her.'

He made a move, and then paused. A magical locket? His hand went to his pocket, jangled the lockets he'd collected from the Coven. It couldn't be . . . could it? The Doomsday Coven was gone.

There were strange forces at work. He could feel them gathering like clouds. Perhaps, before he acted, it would be wise to speak with Mrs Hester. He could not afford another misstep.

When Shadow Jack was gone, Old Hans went back upstairs to his flat, his heart all aflutter, and began a frantic search through his bookshelves. When he finally found the correct volume, he slammed it down on his desk, his thoughts spinning with strange excitement, and flicked through the pages until he found the section he'd been looking for.

As he read the passage, the leftover fear from his encounter with Shadow Jack faded, and the corners of his old mouth twitched upwards into a slight, greedy smile.

Old Hans closed the book. He sat back in his chair, arms folded.

He was quite sure he'd just met a Djinni. A real Djinni! But they were supposed to be long gone, weren't they? If it *was* a Djinni, just imagine the riches something like that could bring him. Shadow Jack was being controlled by Mrs Hester, so it appeared, but that could be fixed. The cogs and wheels of Old Hans' sharp little mind were already beginning to formulate an idea.

THE WEEPING
ISLES FALL

Four days' sailing from the mainland of the Silver Kingdom, away to the east, lay the Weeping Isles, five mounds of jutting grey rock covered for the most part in dense redwood forest. The Weeping Islanders lived in towns and villages scattered along the coastline of the islands. They were a fishing people, and they were as upright and sturdy and tough as the redwood trees that provided them with the wood for their ships.

As Lara was having her troubles far away in King's Haven, the Weeping Islanders faced a danger of their own. When the afternoon sky turned suddenly to night, they gathered in the streets, and stared up at the infinite stars in wonderment and confusion and fear. Families held each other in the streets, mothers and fathers keeping their children close, and the children laughed in innocent delight.

'Look, Mama! Stars!'

'So many!'

'How come it's dark, Papa? Is it time for bed?'

At first, when the stars began to go out, the spectacle was met with only hushed silence. But when the last star disappeared, and the moon faded to nothingness, leaving a gaping, endless black hole above the world, the panic began, and the first anybody knew about the intruders was when they walked into the streets, wrapped in animal skins, and drew their bows.

Agata Olofsson was on the main street with her son when the Painted came around the corner. Agata knew that the Silver Kingdom had once been many different countries, before the great Argent Army had rolled over the world, backed by the magic of the White Witches, and claimed everything in the name of the king. Each of these countries had had their own cultures, religions, gods. But whatever their differences, a single story was common in every tongue. The tale of an ancient darkness in the east.

The Evernight.

Agata started awake from her daze. She looked down at her little boy, Joshua, who was tugging at her dress.

'Mama. Mama!'

Agata swept him up in her arms, and she turned and ran up the hill, to the family's cottage. She went to the store, unlocked the cupboard and brought out her hunting bow and quiver. She slung her bow over her shoulder and went back to the door.

When she opened it, there was a Painted only a few steps away. Agata did not hesitate. She drew her bow, aimed, and loosed the arrow. The shot was true, she knew as much as it left the bow. It hit the Painted in the heart (if he had a heart). But he only looked down and wrenched the arrow from his chest.

Agata scooped her wide-eyed little boy into her arms, and she ran up the dark street, round the winding hill, through screams and yells, clangs of metal and the firing of pistols. The coppers had arrived, but there were not so many on the island, and their guns seemed to be as useless against the Painted as her arrows.

There was a stone wall bordering the edge of town, and beyond that a small grassy meadow, and then the forest. Agata held her son tight in her arms as she ran. When she reached the border of the forest, Agata put down her son, and she stared into his large blue eyes. She kissed him, and held him tight, breathing in the scent of him. 'Now, you listen,' she said, wiping the tears from her eyes. 'Be a good boy. Run through the forest to the next village, to Aunt Rebecca. You remember the way? Good. Tell her that I sent you, that you need to leave. She'll look after you.'

'Mama. I want to go with you!'

An arrow ploughed into the nearest tree.

'I'll be there soon enough,' she told him, running a hand through his blond hair. 'I promise. Now go. Go!'

'Mama!'

She pushed him away into the trees, her heart cracking in two.

His big eyes glistened in the dark for a moment, and then he turned and ran.

A twig snapped nearby.

Agata spun, and found herself face to face with one of the Painted.

A minute later, when she had been marked, and when the searing pain was gone, Agata was not Agata any more.

She was no one. She had no past, no family, and the only thought in her mind was the Evernight, and that she must give her life to protect it.

THE WHITECROWS

The heat of fire whisky grabbed Lara by the guts, dragging her towards consciousness. She coughed and hacked and started awake, spraying whisky out of her mouth and nose, tastebuds and nostrils ablaze.

'Easy,' said a woman's voice. 'Be still, child.'

Two faces were looking down at her with concerned eyes. A grey-haired man with craggy features and a woman with an apple-cheeked complexion who wore a patchwork dress of many colours. Lara had seen the woman before, and she recognised the smell of the place, the mix of leather and paper and dust. She sat up and found that she was in a bookshop – the very one in which she'd encountered the whispering books.

A muddle of memories came back – Old Hans and the bird and the baying mob. The coppers . . . the smoke . . .

She tried to get up, but a firm hand held her down.

'Hush, girl,' said the woman. 'You're safe now. You're with friends.'

Lara's hands went to her pocket – empty. The clockwork bird was gone! Then, alarmed and confused and frightened, she felt her neck. Her locket was gone too! She struggled up, and this time they let her go, and she backed away. Her body ached from being stamped on by the crowd.

'It's all right,' the woman told her in a gentle voice. 'The coppers can't get you here.'

'My stuff,' said Lara, clawing at the empty place around her neck. 'My stuff is gone!'

'It ain't gone.' The woman slipped behind the shop counter and came back holding Lara's necklace and the clockwork bird. Lara snatched the necklace and put it on, feeling better at once. The bird was not moving. It sat in the woman's hand like something dead, or asleep, until Lara touched it, and its sapphire eyes blazed.

The woman and the man exchanged a look of great surprise.

'What's your name, girl?' the man asked urgently.

'Lara.'

'Well, Lara, I'm Magnus Whitecrow, and this here is my wife, Bernie.'

'You saved me? How come?'

'Because they were most probably going to send you to the gallows!' said Bernie. 'What a business, wanting to hang a young girl!'

'But who would save someone accused of bein' a Hag?

170

Everyone hates Hags. Unless . . . unless *you're* Hags! Oh, but I can't be here. I'm in enough trouble as it is!'

The woman, Bernie, reached into her pocket and brought out a fat cigar. She lit it, and took a slow, calm puff. 'I'll thank you not to use the word Hag in my company. It's a dirty expression invented by White Witches after they broke away and joined the Silver Kingdom.' She took another puff from the cigar and then used it to point at Lara. 'I have been around for quite a long time you know, love. I've seen a thing or two. But in all my years I've never met a Witch who don't *know* she's a Witch.'

'Me?' said Lara, putting her hands to her chest. The bird fluttered from one shoulder to the other, pecking at the frizzy ends of her black hair. 'I'm not a Haaaa— a Witch! I'm a girl from the streets, that's all!'

'Pfft! And I'm a fairy godmother! You're a Witch, love, you mark my words. Listen . . . you hear that in the air? That sound like crystal and starlight and glass dreams? That's magic that is.'

Lara listened, and at once she became aware of a whisper, familiar and spooky. 'Magic? How can you *hear* magic?'

Bernie Whitecrow looked to the heavens, as if pleading for patience. 'Because you are a *Witch*!'

'What I'd like to know,' said Magnus, 'is how you came to grow up not knowing what you are. Where are your parents?'

'Dead.'

'How? When?'

'An accident. When I was a baby. I spent a few years in an orphanage, till I couldn't take it any more. Ran away. Been toshing ever since. I'm good at it.' Lara raised a finger. 'Explain this to me: if I'm a Witch, how come I only just began hearing that strange sound *you* say is magic a few days ago? Why haven't I heard it all my life, eh?'

She felt sure she had them beaten with this, but Bernie Whitecrow did not seem worried.

'What age are you?' she asked Lara.

'I dunno exactly. Thirteen I'd guess.'

'Well there you are, see! A Witch's magic don't begin to show until the Witch starts to change from a child into an adult. Your magic is only just waking up, love!'

Lara stared defiantly back at the old woman, but she had been shaken by doubt. Could it be true? Had she been a witch all this time without knowing it? It would make sense of so much . . . the strange sounds . . . the rat in the sewers . . . the boat packed with spells calling to her. She did not want it to be true. Being a tosher was a fine thing, it was freedom. But being a Witch – on either side – could only bring trouble.

'Let me show you something, Lara.' Bernie led her to the back of the shop, and the sound of magic twinkled louder. They came to the bookcase Lara had been drawn to on her last visit, and sure enough Bernie reached for that same book, pulled, and the bookcase lowered into the floor, leaving the open doorway to the secret room. As before, musical, glass-fragile voices spilled from the books on the shelves here. Lara breathed in the smell of old pages, and the scent of forgotten stories. 'Books are magic objects,' Bernie told her. 'Not the sort that needs a wand or a cauldron. A different type of magic. It's in the pages, the words. A good story burrows its way inside you, becomes part of you, changes who you are. That's why I opened this shop. I still deal in magic here, just not the kind they can arrest me for. At least, not for the most part.' She lifted one of the books from the shelf in the secret chamber and blew the dust from it. 'Take a look.'

Lara fanned through the pages. The dust got inside her nose and made her sneeze.

'Now,' said Bernie, 'I want you to close the book and run your finger down the spine, from top to bottom.'

Lara did as she was asked.

'Open it again.'

This time, the book fell open in two halves, and the pages – the very same pages Lara had been leafing through only moments ago – had been hollowed out to create a small chamber. Inside the chamber was a glass bottle. Bernie reached out and touched the bottle, and at once a silver coil of smoke sparked inside.

'A spell?' Lara's eyes followed the light around the inside of the bottle. 'But this is against the law. I can't be here. You're *Hags*.'

'Listen, child, this talk of Hags has got to stop. Mrs Hester goes on about Hags bein' evil, Hags wantin' to kill, Hags wantin' to rule. It's nonsense. If anyone's evil, it's her. How else would you describe a woman who takes away the souls of her people and locks 'em in cages?'

Lara's thoughts jumped back to the White Witch she'd seen almost hanged in Reaper's Square, to the sorrow and fear in his face, and to that strange glowing thing in the cage . . . his soul. It did seem evil to break a person into pieces like that. She leaned closer and tapped the bottle. 'So what does this spell do?'

Bernie Whitecrow smiled. 'It's a healing potion. A wondrous thing. Could heal so much of the disease and sickness in this city if only it were recognised. As it is, it's only available on the black market and every day poor people are dying unnecessarily.'

As Bernie spoke, Lara noticed her old eyes fell many times upon the clockwork bird, and when they did, they filled with wonder. Lara let the bird hop onto her finger. 'Why do you keep looking at it, Mrs Whitecrow?'

Bernie Whitecrow's eyes reflected the blue glow from the clockwork bird's own sapphire eyes. 'Have you ever heard of the Doomsday Spell, Lara?'

'No. I don't know anything about magic at all. I keep telling you!'

'But surely you've heard of Westerly Witch?'

This was familiar. 'That's where the Hag— the other Witches live, I think.'

'Bingo. Westerly Witch is the historic home of all Witches in the world. It is a magnificent place, an entire city built upon the branches of a giant tree that reaches the sky. Every year, Lara, the Mother Tree blooms with great glowing flowers – the Blossom – and those flowers breathe magic into the world. This is where all magic comes from. Where Witches get their power.'

'And what's that to do with me?'

'Just listen, girl! Hundreds of years ago, Sam Hawk, the greatest Witch who ever lived, created a spell to protect us from the dangers left behind long ago by the Gods. The most powerful spell ever made. He called it the Doomsday Spell and it was kept safe in Westerly Witch for centuries – until the civil war. Mrs Hester led a faction who wanted to use the Doomsday Spell to conquer the world. They stormed Westerly Witch, and a bloody fight unfolded. Witch against Witch. Eventually, Hester's crew was beaten and scattered. And in their desperation for sanctuary they made a deal with the Silver Kingdom and became the White Witches you know today.'

'So what happened to the spell?'

'This is where things get really intriguing,' said Bernie. 'According to legend, during the civil war the spell was entrusted to a secret coven of Witches, taken far from Westerly Witch and hidden away from Hester.'

Magnus Whitecrow joined them, clutching a large cobweb-covered book. He nodded towards the clockwork bird. 'Birds are sacred creatures to Witches. We believe that when we die, and Grey Alyce has led us across the Desert of Bones, a bird will carry our soul to the next life. So it makes sense, I suppose, that Sam Hawk chose to contain his Doomsday Spell in the body of a bird.' He opened the book, sending a plume of old dust into the chamber.

Lara studied the page, a fine drawing of a group of people in long robes – the Witches of long ago, she supposed – gathered around an ornate plinth. On the plinth sat . . .

A *bird*.

Lara squinted at the page, moved closer, her pulse quickening. The drawing of the bird was recognisable at once. It was made of wood and gold and clockwork. Lara looked up from the page, turned her head *very* slowly, and stared at the clockwork bird on her shoulder. It pecked gently at her nose. 'But that's . . . is that . . . it can't be . . .'

Bernie's face lit up. 'I think that the birdie perched on your shoulder, Lara, might just be the Doomsday Spell – the most powerful piece of magic left in all the world.'

And as she spoke those words, the sun went out.

A BARGAIN

Lara stood by the door of the Whitecrows' bookshop, her hand on her chest, making sure her terrified heart was still beating. The locket buzzed against her skin like the wings of a dragonfly, and the sound of the spells, the magic from the locket and the bird and the books, intensified and reached a shattering, painful level before it died away to nothing.

'The sun. Where did the sun go?'

Through the window she could see part of the sky, clear and impossibly black and bursting with stars.

In the dark of the shop, Bernie and Magnus Whitecrow were rummaging in their coats. Lara heard the clink of glass, and two flares of dazzling light appeared at the tips of their wands.

Lara's body was shaking, trembling, her legs weak. The screaming out on the streets, the shouting and confusion, was growing, and Lara wanted to scream too, to run to the sewers and hide in the deepest tunnel she could find.

Bernie touched her arm, and she jumped.

'Lara. You must listen. I know you are frightened. We all are, love. But you must keep a clear head.'

'But the sun has gone.' She stared up into Bernie's face and saw the colour had drained from her cheeks, that she was shaking too. The old Witch closed her eyes and took a few slow breaths.

'Think, Bernie,' she said to herself. Then, 'The docks! Rob will be there!'

'But he won't be ready,' said Magnus. 'He isn't due to sail for two days.'

'Mother Earth's knobbly knees, Magnus! I think in the circumstances Rob will be ready any damned time we say!'

Lara's brain was slowly beginning to work again.

'Is this Witch magic?'

Bernie shook her head.

'No. This isn't Witches.' She was breathless, touching at her throat. 'It's the Evernight.'

Magnus shook his head and screwed up his face like he'd tasted something very bitter. 'Now, Bernie, we don't know that.'

'Don't be a fool! Of course it is! Somehow it's got out. And the Painted won't be far behind.'

Lara stared at the dark sky again, thinking back to those nights in the dormitory when she'd huddled under her blankets as the older kids told frightening stories of the

178

Evernight, and of the Painted who'd come and slit your throat in the darkness.

'It's real? It's really real?'

Bernie suddenly looked old and frightened. She reached out for the clockwork bird, but it flew from one of Lara's shoulders to the other. 'There's a boat at the docks. We must travel to Westerly Witch, and hope that we can get there before the Evernight does; the High Witch must be told about this bird.'

'I don't want to leave!'

'You *must*, child. It's already been set in motion. The bird, I think, only responds to you. There is a connection. Will you really be so selfish as to deny us your help?'

Lara looked out of the shop window at the shadows of fleeing people and heard the coppers' whistles all over the city. It was as if she were a twig caught in the rushing sewer stream, helpless to control where she was headed. A picture appeared in her mind's eye, of little Joe all alone in his tiny flat, confused and scared and trying to look after Granny.

'Course not. I'll come with you. But only if there's room on the boat for two friends of mine.'

Bernie and Magnus Whitecrow exchanged a long look.

'Fine,' said Bernie. 'We have a bargain.'

A JOURNEY BEGINS

'You had a bang on the head or something?' Joe Littlefoot stood in the doorway of his tiny attic flat looking up at Lara as if she'd grown another nose. The only light in the passageway was the warm glow from Joe's toshing lamp, which he'd lit in a hurry when the sun had disappeared. His face was covered in blossoms of yellow-blue bruising from the Strangler attack. 'All this talk of Painted folk and leaving King's Haven . . . this isn't like you, Lara.'

'Look outside, Joe! The place is in a panic. It's not safe.' Lara nodded towards Bernie, who stood down in the gloom. 'There's a boat waiting. Come with us, you and Granny. Just until things calm down a bi—'

'Are you deaf? We're not leaving!' It was the first time Joe had ever raised his voice to Lara, and it was so unexpected that she was unsure what to do. Even Joe seemed surprised, and his face softened, and he looked to the ground. 'We can't.'

There was a sound from the dim flat, a gurgling, rasping hack, and Joe spun away inside.

Lara followed, finding him by the side of Granny's bed. She was buried in dirty blankets and in the grip of a fever. Lara could not hide her shock – she had seen Granny only a few days ago, but it seemed the old woman had shrunk since then, becoming little more than a bag of bones.

Joe took a damp rag and dabbed at Granny's forehead. 'I think it's bad. Really bad.'

'Hold on!' Lara dashed back out to the stairway and led Bernie Whitecrow into the flat. 'Can you do something, Bernie? Please? One of your healing potions.'

'I don't have one with me and we don't have time for this,' muttered Bernie, but Lara gave her the pleading eyes and Bernie scoffed and reached into her coat for her wand. One of the spell bottles in the revolver chamber flared and a bright warm light burst to life at the wand's tip, illuminating the small flat so that she could get a better look.

Joe's mouth fell open, and he dropped the rag. 'You're a Hag! I can't have a Hag in here!'

'Hush, boy.' Bernie leaned over Granny, pressed her free hand to the old woman's slick forehead, and then she looked at Lara and gave a small shake of the head. 'She's very sick. Best I can do without a proper healing potion is make her comfortable. It's up to her body to do the rest.' Again her hand disappeared into her coat, and Lara thought that there must be more pockets in that thing than was surely possible. Bernie offered a tiny vial of liquid to Joe, who backed away from it like it was a stick of live dynamite.

'Hell's teeth, boy, if I had meant to do you harm you'd know it by now. It'll help with her pain.'

Joe gingerly took the vial in his hand, pulled out the stopper and tapped a few drops of the liquid into Granny's mouth. The effect was instant; where she had been twitching and uneasy, she was now still. Joe looked at Bernie with a mixture of surprise and gratitude.

'We're going,' said Bernie. 'Now.'

Lara pulled away. 'No. Not without them.'

'The old woman is too sick to travel. The journey will kill her.'

'Then I'll stay and help Joe. *You* take the bird!'

'Stop it!' Joe Littlefoot stood between them, looking taller than Lara had ever seen him. 'Lara, I don't know what you've gotten tangled up in, but I can't have any part in it, you hear? Granny needs me, and I'll be no use to her if I'm swinging from the end of a rope because I've been mixing around with Hags – no offence. You're putting Granny in more danger just by being here, so . . . I think you should go.'

Lara stared in disbelief. 'But, Joe . . .'

'Please go.'

Bernie's hand was on Lara's arm, pulling her away, and this time she did not fight it. She allowed Bernie to lead her through the door and, as they went out into the dark hallway, Lara glanced back into the little flat where Joe was staring after her.

'I'll come back for you, Joe! I promise!'

Joe did not answer, and when Bernie extinguished the light at the tip of her wand, his face disappeared in the black of the unnatural midnight.

Lara did not have any time to ponder Joe's situation, because as soon as they were back on the streets she realised that she'd need all her wits just to make it to the docks alive. The dark of the sewer tunnels had never frightened her – but it was *supposed* to be dark down there, wasn't it? *This* darkness was freakish; as she struggled through the midnight streets with Bernie, her eyes were drawn to the sky, and the sight of it, endless and black and star-filled where only an hour ago it had been clear and blue, caused prickles of fear to run through her body. She clutched at her pocket, felt the bird nestled in there, and the warmth of him helped to make her brave.

The dark had come mid-morning, when every part of King's Haven was bustling and alive, and now those same crowds, the ones who had been buying and selling and drinking and chattering, were rushing around all in a panic, trying to get back to loved ones or simply find somewhere to hunker down.

'It's the end!' yelled one man, pushing past Lara, almost knocking her over. It seemed every time she blinked the noises and smells intensified, and the atmosphere was thick with fear.

183

'Lady Light save us!'

'Mummy? Mummy, where are you?'

'Oi! Gerroff! Take that! I'll teach you to try to pick a lady's pocket!'

A driverless ironheart thundered past, pulling a cart heavy with barrels of dragon breath. Without a driver to guide it in the dark, the great clockwork horse ran into a building, and the dragon breath exploded.

BOOM!

The sound hit Lara first, a wave of it, and then a punch of fierce hot air lifted her from her feet, rag-dolled her across the street. She landed heavily on the cobbles, the air whooshing out of her, pieces of debris raining down.

Screaming.

Crying.

Wails of pain all around.

Belching thick smoke rolled into the street, filling Lara's lungs and eyes. She scrambled up, staying close to Bernie as they fought through the crowded chaos of the slums. Bernie had stowed her wand safely away and was using a lamp for light: frightened people usually looked for someone to blame, and a Hag holding a wand would be an easy target.

Under the railway bridge to the docks, where the tide was almost full. It seemed to Lara that the danger had heightened her senses, because the smell of fire whisky, pepper-stem and moonweed was stronger than she ever remembered.

Bernie pointed the way. 'We got a boat, smuggles spells and supplies from Westerly Witch and takes newly-freed White Witches in the other direction. Captain knows his stuff. He's a great smuggler, but he isn't half a pain in the . . . ah, here we are!'

Lara took one look at the boat in question, and her stomach twisted. It was *Dragonfly*, the boat she had snuck aboard – the one in which she had discovered the Hag spells all hidden away.

'Bernie!' Magnus came running down the gangplank and wrapped his arms round his wife. 'Thank Mother Earth! Rob's done a grand job. We're almost set to leave.'

Lara watched the captain at work, a mountain with a beard, hauling crates and thick ropes around with ease under the flickering warmth of dragon-breath torches.

'That's it, lads! Be smart about it!' The captain came striding over, and Lara ducked behind Magnus and Bernie. He pointed to the sky. 'What d'you make of this, Bernie? A trick? White Witches?'

'Not a chance. They ain't clever enough – and there isn't enough magic in the world even if they were. This is the Evernight, Rob. It's back. And all that panic you hear, all that fear . . . the Evernight will be a-gobbling it up.'

Rob folded his great arms, almost hugging himself. 'You think it's reached Westerly Witch?'

'No. I reckon we'd all feel it if it had. Maybe it's not strong enough yet. Maybe it's holding back. Who knows.'

Rob looked around the heavens. 'Well, I'll feel a whole lot better when we get home. This city is fit to rip itself to rags.'

'Agreed,' said Bernie. 'And we've one more passenger, Rob.'

Lara's eyes widened as Magnus Whitecrow shepherded her out of his shadow. She gave Rob a fierce, defiant stare. His face became a tangle of recognition and rage. He stepped forward, almost tipping over.

'You!'

'Steady there, Rob! What's the matter?'

'The matter, Magnus Whitecrow, is this street rat almost cost me my cargo and my boat!'

'What? Oh. No, Rob, this is Lara. She's with us.'

'She's a thief, is what she is! She snuck aboard *Dragonfly* and woke up every spell in the hold! It took me hours to get rid of all them trees all a-sproutin' from the deck! I could've been found out! Hanged!'

Lara puffed out her chest. 'I never took nothin' from you! It was an accident!'

Rob's face was turning a dangerous shade of red in the lamplight. 'You two,' he said to Magnus and Bernie, 'are welcome. But this . . . this *sewer rat* is not gettin' on my boat!'

Bernie Whitecrow, it seemed, had had enough. She stepped forward, facing up to Rob, the top of her head barely grazing his chin. In a voice so sharp it could have punctured the hull of the boat, the old Witch said, 'You listen to me, Rob Nielsen. Whatever's happened in the past, I don't care. Somehow the Evernight is back, and the Painted won't be far off. We need to get this gal to Westerly Witch! Now you quit behavin' like an overinflated ninny and let Lara on this boat or I'll make sure to let the High Witch know you interfered with her plans!'

A wave of anger crashed over Rob's face. But he put a stopper in that, and swallowed it down. 'I swear if she steals anything, I'll feed her to the sea wolves myself.'

He turned away and slammed his fist on the side of the boat. 'Lads! We're leavin'! Now!'

Dragonfly's steam engines rumbled, and the paddles churned up the river as the boat carried Lara and her friends away from the panic of the darkened city, up the river Anchor and out into Bad Mouth Bay.

Lamps were blinking on all over King's Haven like firebugs, and as the boat steamed beyond the bay and into the Pewter Sea, Lara felt a pang in her chest for the streets. This was the first time she had ever travelled beyond the borders of King's Haven. The alleys and sewers had been her home, her cocoon. She had wrapped herself in the fabric of the place. But now she was emerging, becoming something else.

She stood at the bow of the boat and stared up at a sky so clear and black and filled with stars it seemed like it went on for ever. Bernie had been deep in conversation with Magnus Whitecrow and Rob Nielsen, but now she broke away and joined Lara. The air had become cold enough that foggy breath danced out of their mouths.

Lara continued to gaze skyward. 'I remember bein' little . . . I was scared stiff in the dormitory while the older kids told those stories about the Evernight. They said the Painted come out of the darkness and eat people's flesh and drink their blood. And the ones they don't eat they cast a spell on, turn 'em into slaves. Is that true?' Lara thought of the people she knew, the ones she'd left back in King's Haven, and horrible, bloody imaginings filled her head.

Bernie put an arm around Lara, but didn't answer.

'What are we going to do, Bernie?'

Bernie stared down at the water breaking on the bow. 'We're goin' to see the High Witch – the leader of all the free Witches in the world. And we can only hope that bird of yours is the Doomsday Spell. And if it is, you might just be the most important Witch there is, right now.'

Bernie let her words hang in the air, and Lara could feel the old Witch's eyes on her. 'I don't know if I believe that I *am* a Witch, Bernie.' As she spoke, the clockwork bird flew out of her coat pocket and landed on her shoulder.

'I believe it,' said a timid voice.

To Lara's great surprise, a boy had joined them. There was a haunted sort of emptiness in his eyes, and he was pale as milk. She breathed in sharply.

'I know you! You're the White Witch-boy they were going to hang in Reaper's Square! I saw you in the noose.'

The Witch-boy nodded. By the look on his face he was experiencing a similar rush of memory. 'And I saw you in the crowd.'

Lara stared at Bernie, open-mouthed. 'But that would mean . . . you're the ones who saved him too? You made that . . . that fire-dragon appear?'

Bernie gave Lara a wink, and her eyes twinkled.

'You don't know the half of it,' said the Witch-boy. 'Magnus found me weeks ago, and Bernie snuck into the White Witch district to help me. They could have been killed!'

'Pah!' said Bernie. 'I'd like to see 'em try.'

'So you've run away from Mrs Hester and the king?' said Lara.

'I suppose I have, yeah. My name's Double Eight.'

'Double Eight?'

'Actually, my full name is Eight-Eight-Five-Four-Seven-Six. But that doesn't really roll off the tongue.'

A clang from somewhere in the belly of the boat made him jump, and he looked to the unnatural night sky. Lara thought he seemed very fragile and small.

Bernie went to put an arm around his shoulder, but he flinched away, as if expecting her to strike him. She slowly let her hand drop. 'We're all frightened, love. But you're among friends. And you two have a lot in common. You're both starting over.'

189

She explained about Lara, how she was only coming to realise her past, and about the clockwork bird. When she was done, Double Eight looked Lara right in the eye and said, 'How can you not know you're a Witch? I can *feel* the magic spilling out of you.'

'I don't know,' said Lara, feeling annoyed. 'I wasn't born into it like you . . .'

'Born into slavery, you mean?'

'No need to go all funny. You aren't the only one who's had it tough, you know.'

Bernie stepped between them.

'I'm sure when you two get to know one another, you'll be great friends. But right now, Lara, I suppose I'll have to prove you're a Witch once and for all, won't I?'

'Oh? And how will you do that?'

But Bernie only smiled and said, 'You'll see.'

Blood on the Table

Mrs Hester stood at the window of her tower and stared up at the Evernight. She was wrapped in furs, and a roaring fire burned in the hearth, but still she was shivering.

'In the time of the Gods it was called the Bodach.'

She turned away from the window, back to the fire-lit room, and there he was, leaning on the wall, arms folded. Shadow Jack.

'What are you talking about?'

'The Evernight. During the war, it was a living weapon. Lady Light defeated it and trapped it deep in the underworld, and it would have stayed there had your people not opened the door a thousand years ago.'

Mrs Hester cocked her head to one side.

'*My* people?'

'Long after the war was over and the Gods were gone, a large exploratory party of Witches travelled to the dark side of the world,' said Shadow Jack. 'They found the Bodach's prison and let it out, not realising what it was. It marked them with dark magic and made them its army.'

'The first Painted,' breathed Mrs Hester. She imagined them out there now, travelling with the night, coming towards King's Haven, an army of monsters. Her breathing was shallow and short. 'You have the spell, I presume? I can think of no other reason why you would be here.'

'Not quite,' said Shadow Jack.

Mrs Hester brushed past him, to the display shelves where she kept the ancient urn made of clay, upon which there were many faded symbols. The sight of it made him shiver.

Mrs Hester looked at Shadow Jack, and then she looked at the urn. She lifted it down, turning it in her hands. 'You know, the day I walked into that antique store in the south and saw this urn sitting among a pile of worthless junk, I couldn't believe my eyes. They didn't know what they had of course, didn't have a clue there was a Djinni inside – I wasn't even entirely sure myself – and a single silver coin was enough to seal the deal.' She glared up from the urn. 'When I let you out, you promised to bring me the Doomsday Spell. Yet here we are, more than ten years later. I'm. Still. Waiting.'

'I *know* where the spell is,' said Shadow Jack.

'Yes. In the sewers. You've told me that. But why don't you have it yet?'

'It's not in the sewers any more. There has been a complication. A girl.'

'A girl?'

'Yes. It seems she has a necklace. It's . . . troubling me.'

Mrs Hester screwed up her face in puzzlement. 'You think she's in the *Coven*?'

'Maybe. I don't know.'

'But there were only thirteen,' said Hester. 'Thirteen protectors of the Doomsday Spell, and you've done away with all of them.'

'Look.' From his pocket Shadow Jack brought out a handful of wooden lockets and placed them on a table.

'There are only twelve,' said Mrs Hester.

'Right. The missing one was destroyed the night I killed Bella Fox. The Crippleback Street explosion. At least that's what I assumed.'

Mrs Hester considered this. Then she rushed across the room, to a wall packed with shelves stocked with many bottles and jars. She reached for a large jar, took off the lid and brought out the carcass of a rat.

At a desk by the window, she dropped the rat down and slit along its belly with a small knife, letting its guts and innards spill out. The hot coppery smell of blood filled the room. Mrs Hester took her finger and mixed and moved the pile of remains on the desk, the heart and lungs and intestines, and when she seemed satisfied, she studied the mess, her eyes searching, narrowing and widening, and her lips moving silently as if she were reading some fantastic story. Suddenly she brought her fist down on the bloody desk and glared up at Shadow Jack with a murderous expression.

'The thirteenth necklace was *not* destroyed.'

Shadow Jack growled and balled his fists tight.

Mrs Hester's finger traced through the rat guts. Her expression flickered with rage. 'The girl you speak of – the one who has the necklace now – she's Bella Fox's daughter. She was there in Crippleback Street.'

'But she would only have been a baby! She'd never have survived.'

'Unless the Hag hid her away. Protected her.'

'So . . . you are saying Fox passed the necklace on to her child? And with it her duty . . . her link to the bird?'

Mrs Hester nodded. 'Which means you've let me down. The Coven has not been destroyed. While the girl lives, her soul is linked to the Spell, and only she can use it. I can't control this thing we've released.'

'*We've* released? I think—'

'Your job isn't to think! Your job is to do exactly what I say! You handed the Coven a second chance when you let this child live all those years ago, and if she figures out who she is – what the spell is – all my plans will be for nothing! What if she tries to use the Doomsday Spell? At best she won't use it right. At worst she won't be able to handle all that power – it'll probably kill her. Then where will we be, eh, with no way to control the Evernight? There'll be no more Hags, no more White Witches, no more magic! The

Mother Tree will die . . .' Mrs Hester's breath was growing shallow and fearful. 'We'll be finished.'

Shadow Jack examined his fingernails. 'Perhaps,' he said, 'you should not have decided to play with something so powerful. I tried to warn you . . .'

Mrs Hester drew up close to him, her face twisting and twitching with panic and hatred and fury.

'Find the girl. Kill her. Bring me the spell. Last chance. If you fail this time, you go back in the urn, and I'll make sure nobody else ever finds you.'

FLIGHT OF THE WITCHES

In the highest branches of the Westerly Witch's Mother Tree, Leora Twigg, High Witch, stood on a platform with her council and looked to the east. They could all see it: the monstrous, living darkness in the sky, and feel its power. There was fear in their hearts.

'How did it get out?' said John Bearclaw, a huge man with dark brown skin and only one arm – the result of a run-in with an angry mob of Hag hunters many years before.

'Does it matter?' said Becca Stone. 'It's free. What we have to find is a way to put it back in.'

'Why hasn't it come here?' asked Emmet Feather, indicating the sky above Westerly Witch, which was still the clear sapphire blue of a sunny afternoon. 'It's torn across most of the world but stopped some way short of us. Why?'

'It's waiting,' said the High Witch.

'For what, ma'am?' said John Bearclaw.

'I think it's sending the Painted to King's Haven to build an army. And then it will come here and destroy us.'

'Those poor people!' said Becca Stone. 'Shouldn't we help them?'

'Those poor people,' said John Bearclaw, who was cunning and clever, 'would hang you as soon as look at you. Why should we rush to their aid? They have their precious White Witches, do they not? Let Mrs Hester fight this. In the meantime, the Doomsday Coven will come to our aid, I'm sure of it. That's what it was set up for, after all.'

'The Evernight is growing stronger. I see no evidence of the Doomsday Coven controlling it,' said Leora Twigg. Her hair tumbled over her shoulders in dark red ribbons, and her large green eyes seemed to glow in the sunlight. 'It's feeding on all the fear. We have no way of knowing who the Doomsday Coven are, or where they are, or how to communicate with them; by the time they turn up – *if* they turn up – it might be too late.'

'Aye, ma'am,' said Becca Stone. 'It's been hundreds of years since the Coven was formed. Time has surely scattered them around the world. We can't be sure that they're even still out there at all! What if Sam Hawk's Doomsday Spell is lost?'

A murmur passed through the circle.

'I say we fly today,' said Emmet Feather. 'Now. We meet this darkness head on! Fight it before it has fully formed its army, before it plunges us and Westerly Witch into darkness. That's what Bernie Whitecrow'd say if she were here, ma'am.'

Leora nodded. Bernie was her most trusted friend;

but with Bernie Whitecrow it was always about the next adventure; she had insisted on going off to King's Haven to smuggle White Witches out of the city, and the High Witch had agreed to let her go. But how she could have used Bernie's wisdom now.

Birds rustled the surrounding branches, and sunlight fell through the canopy of leaves, dappling the wooden platform.

'If we fly,' said Leora, 'there is a strong chance we won't be coming back.'

'But if we don't fly, ma'am,' said Emmet, 'the sun will soon set for the last time over the Mother Tree.'

The High Witch fiddled with a strand of her long red hair. 'A vote. We shall have a vote. All in favour of flying?'

Five hands went up, including Leora Twigg's.

'Against?'

John Bearclaw raised his hand.

'It's settled, then,' said Leora. 'We fly.'

A cauldron sat over a spitting firepit in the centre of the platform. The High Witch and her council sat around it. She brought out a most unusual bottle then; its glass body was shaped like a hawk. The wooden stopper was a hawk's head. Leora took the bottle and tossed it into the cauldron in the centre of the circle. At once the flames leaped high, and then exploded outwards in six fingers of light. The light hit every member of the council in the chest, and they each fell into a deep trance. From the Witches' mouths came coils of golden, cloudy light, and the light drifted up into the air above the circle, forming six huge, winged, bird-like creatures, dazzling and burning bright.

The souls of Leora Twigg and her council were not like the souls of White Witches. White Witches' souls were small, fluttering things, made weak by imprisonment, starved of hope and freedom. The souls of the High Witch and her council were enormous, wild, thundering things, and they soared up over the Mother Tree, swooping and calling, and blazed out across the Pewter Sea to meet the Evernight.

SPELL WRITING

'Wake up, Lara.'

She had been asleep and warm and comfortable in a bed of packing hay in the hold of the boat, until a familiar voice disturbed her. Opening her eyes dreamily, she saw the warm glow of a dragon-breath lamp.

'Bernie? What's wrong?'

'Come with me, love. And put your coat on. It's freezing up there.'

The air on deck was bitingly cold; the Evernight sky stretched endlessly as Rob Nielsen's boat steamed through the foam-peaked waves. Lara pulled her coat tight and shivered as she followed Bernie to a spot near the bow. Double Eight was sitting on the deck beside a small, heavy-looking metal cauldron with a fire alive inside it. Lara breathed the scent of burning twigs and leaves.

'What's this?'

Bernie set her lamp down, reached into one of the many pockets of her Witch's coat and brought out a cigar. She lit the cigar in the fire, took a puff, went back into her pockets and produced a leather wallet, a bottle of ink and a quill. Opening the wallet, she took out a square of paper, which she slid across the deck to Lara, and offered her the quill.

'I . . . I don't understand.'

'I said I'd prove you're a Witch,' said Bernie, blowing smoke rings. 'And this is how. You're going to write a spell.'

Lara leaned back. 'A spell? I can't do that!'

'Take the pen, love.' Bernie put the quill in Lara's hand. 'Writing spells isn't about how many textbooks you've read. It's about feeling, Lara. It's about listening to what's inside you. But only a true witch can do it. Now, I'd like you to try making a light spell. It's a good one to start with in these circumstances.'

Lara looked at the quill in her hand, and then at Double Eight. 'But how?'

Double Eight shrugged. 'I've only ever written one spell, and that came out of a book. I wasn't allowed to try anything else. I'm learning, same as you.'

Bernie motioned to the cauldron. 'The thing about spells, my loves, is they're different for everyone. A spell is like . . . well I suppose it's like the recipe for a chocolate cake – everyone has their own version of what it might be, their own flourishes and ingredients, and no two will ever be the same. Think about light. Think about what it means to you. How it makes you feel. What's the first thing light makes you think of?'

Lara considered this.

'Warmth.'

'Good. Put that down on paper as best you can – but use symbols instead of words.'

Slowly, Lara lowered the quill to the paper and drew a simple, unmistakable image. The sun.

'What else does light make you feel?' asked Bernie.

Lara's mind travelled back to the sewers under King's Haven, to the moment she would climb back to the surface and open the manhole cover, and she'd feel the relief at being back in the daylight. 'Safe,' she said. 'Light makes me feel safe.' Again she touched the nib to the paper, this time drawing a simple little house, and a stick person inside that house.

'Good. Now try a couple more. When it's done, you'll feel it.'

What else does light mean to me? thought Lara. *Life. It means life.*

She drew a flower.

And colour. But how do I draw that? Oh, I know . . .

She drew an eye, and then she looked at the paper, at the symbols she'd drawn. They made perfect sense to her.

'I think I'm done.'

'All right, love. Now I want you to take that paper and put it in the cauldron.'

'Into the fire?' said Lara, 'Why?'

'You'll see.'

Lara lifted the paper and dropped it into the flames. She watched it catch.

Bernie leaned in. 'Now I want you to say these words.' She whispered in Lara's ear, then sat back as Lara began to speak.

'Born of mind, born of fire,
Born of Mother Earth's desire,
Use it wisely, use it well,
My heart, my blood, my gift, my spell.'

And then . . .

As the paper blackened and turned to ash, the flames in the metal cauldron changed colour, from orange to dazzling new-coin-in-the-sun gold, and coils of glowing smoke drifted from the bowl. At the same time, Lara's head filled with the tinkling, musical sound she'd heard in Bernie's shop.

Lara snapped her head up, staring in amazement at Bernie. The older Witch stared back, wide-eyed, let out a triumphant laugh and punched the air. 'Ha! I told you, girl!' Hurriedly she brought out a tiny glass bottle, pulled the stopper, and held it up to the smoke. Whispers of the glowing smoke drifted into the bottle, and when it was full Bernie popped the stopper back in and grabbed her wand, loading Lara's spell into the revolver chamber. She stood up, held out the wand and gave Lara a hopeful look. Then she squeezed the trigger on her wand.

A flare of warm golden light erupted at the tip.

'Haha! It worked. Look, Lara! Haha! Look, love!'

Lara was so stunned, so utterly flabbergasted, that she could do nothing but stare as Bernie waved the wand around while dancing a jig. Then the old Witch put the spell out and hugged Lara tight.

'Told you,' said Double Eight with a smile.

'I did it!' said Lara. 'I actually did it! I made magic!'

'You did, girl, you did!'

Lara felt her locket buzzing hard against her chest, and she reached into her clothes and brought it out, holding it in her open palm. 'I'm a Witch,' she whispered. The clockwork bird had been nestling in her pocket as usual, and now he popped up, hopping onto Lara's palm, and gave the locket a peck as it buzzed more intensely than ever. 'Bernie, if I'm a Witch, does that mean that my mum and dad . . . were they Witches too?'

'Your mother was, for sure, Lara. Magic's always passed down from mother to child, see.'

Lara tucked the necklace back under her shirt, and the clockwork bird took off and flew a few times around the boat before landing on her shoulder. She barely noticed him; her mind was far away, wondering about her parents, knowing that the magic in her blood had come from her mum.

It was Double Eight's turn to try the spell now, and Lara watched with great interest as the Witch-boy drew his own symbols with trembling hands. It was amazing to her – and sad too – to think that he had not been allowed to explore magic, to test his gift. Here he was, no better off in his knowledge than she, and it showed in his nerves and the shaky, clumsy drawings he made.

'Don't we have to add anything else?' Double Eight asked when he'd completed his sketches.

'How d'you mean?' said Bernie.

'Well, in the factories, there's always ingredients to add to the drawings.'

'Oh,' said Bernie, 'yes, of course you'd be used to that. Mrs Hester has her White Witches use ingredients because they don't have souls. The soul y'see . . . well, I suppose it acts as a lightning rod for magic, attracting it, focusing it in one place. Without a soul, a White Witch still has magic in her, but it's weak. Hester's recipes use physical ingredients to make up for that. I guess it works in its way, but every single spell that comes out of those factories is a pale imitation of a spell made using imagination, and wonder, and soul. See for yourself now.'

Double Eight completed the spell. Lara could tell he wasn't at all confident, but when Bernie took Double Eight's spell and fired it from her wand, the flare of light was so bright it filled Lara's vision, and she cowered back at the ferocity of it.

'Hell's teeth!' yelled Bernie, shaking the spell out. 'That's what I call a light spell!'

Double Eight stood gawping at the wand. He was trembling a little, and his breath was coming in short puffs of fog.

'*I* did that?'

'Yes, boy, you did that.'

He looked at Bernie, and smiled, and his eyes were bright and alive. 'Real wild magic. I always imagined . . . Can I do some more?'

'One step at a time,' said Bernie, and the way she looked at Double Eight, with satisfaction and curiosity and fondness, made Lara quite jealous.

'So what now?' she said. 'Will someone teach us how to be proper Witches? Do we get wands?'

'We'll get to Westerly Witch and take it from there.'

Lara imagined herself with her own wand and cauldron, creating powerful spells, and the thought of it was exciting and thrilling.

A wild, echoing call drifted down from high above.

'Look!'

Double Eight was pointing to the sky in the west, where six gigantic winged creatures of light were thundering eastward. They left trails of shimmering sparks behind them as they flew, and Lara became unaccountably emotional at the sight of them. Her eyes leaked tears and her chest rose and fell. The wondrous blazing shapes moved across the heavens at unimaginable speed, and the beat of their great wings was the sound of faraway thunder.

'Bernie?' Lara rushed to the old Witch's side, for she had weakened and was holding on to the side of the boat for support.

'It's the council,' Bernie's eyes followed the light. 'The High Witch is flying to face the Evernight.'

Lara saw that Bernie was crying too. She took her hand and squeezed as the three Witches stood at the bow of the ship and watched the souls of the Witch council disappear over the horizon.

THE BLACK BIRD

Coming to terms with the fact she was a Witch was not easy for Lara. The matter took up almost her every thought, and her mood swayed from excitement to happiness to fear and back again more times than she could count. Her mind was a bubbling stew of wonderings and apprehension, of magic and adventure and dread. Her whole life she'd been told that Hags were terrible creatures and heard about the dangers of their wild magic. She'd lived in uncomfortable awe of the White Witches in King's Haven. And here she was, a Witch all along.

She found the rocking movement of the boat calming as her mind went over recent events, and she spent a great deal of time out on deck. It was a strange thing, this Evernight. All sense of time had been lost very quickly, especially in the shining vastness of the Pewter Sea. The sky became so dappled with stars that it hurt Lara's eyes to look at them all. They made great streaks of milky light, and the sea was calm and smooth and reflected the stars and the moon so that it seemed at times there were two skies, one above and one below. Lara lay on the cold deck, staring up at those stars as the clockwork bird swooped and spun, the moonlight bouncing off his golden wings.

'That's what I'll call you,' she told him when he landed on her chest and settled down. 'Moonwing.'

She was curious, too, about Double Eight. He seemed so foreign and strange to her; he was timid and jumpy and softly-spoken, and she'd often catch him watching her, as if he wanted very much to come and speak to her but did not know how. For her part, Lara was still annoyed that his light spell had been better than hers, and she wondered if that would always be the way from now on, Double Eight being the star student and Lara forgotten.

Lara slept in *Dragonfly's* cargo hold that night, on a bed of straw and old sacks. It was warm, and the hum of the engines was comforting. Magnus Whitecrow explained that Westerly Witch was six days' sailing from King's Haven. Lara decided that she would go quite mad if she spent six whole days obsessing about Witches and magic, so she set about filling her time by exploring the boat. She didn't dare to go near the cabin, and tried to avoid Rob Nielsen, who watched her like a hawk. She played card games with the crew and had hoped to learn more spells, but Bernie had become a little distant after they'd seen the souls of the Witch council in the sky and Lara thought it best to leave her be.

As she stood out on the deck under the dark sky with the breeze on her face and the fresh salt air in her lungs, the feeling that someone was watching her made her quickly turn. Sure enough, there was Double Eight, hanging back by the cabin. He ducked back when he noticed she'd spotted him.

'Right. Come out here this instant.'

Double Eight broke away from the shadows of the cabin and approached like a naughty child.

'Why you spyin'?'

Double Eight looked scandalised. 'I'm not.'

'Well it seems like spyin' to me,' said Lara.

'I promise I'm not! I just . . . I've never seen anyone like you before.'

Lara stopped; she was not sure whether to be offended or pleased by this statement. 'How d'you mean?'

'You don't seem frightened by any of this,' said Double Eight. 'Not by the Evernight or leaving home or being a Witch—'

'Well, I am,' Lara cut him off. 'I am scared. I'll bet I'm just as frightened as you – and there's nothing wrong with that, nothing wrong with bein' scared. Fear kept me alive lots of times when I was down in the sewers.'

Double Eight shot her a puzzled look. 'The *sewers*?'

'Yeah. I was a tosher.'

'A *what*?'

'Tosher. It's someone who finds lost things down in the sewer tunnels and makes money from them. You have to be a little afraid down there, have to show the tunnels respect, or they'll chew you up.' For a moment the only sound was the lap of the waves on the hull. 'I never spoke to a White Witch before.'

Double Eight nodded. 'We're not known for our sparkling conversation.'

Lara smiled. She had never imagined a White Witch could have a sense of humour. 'Why did you run away? Why take the risk?'

Double Eight leaned on the side of the boat, watched Moonwing dip and spin above the water. 'I always felt I was different. The world was calling me, you know? Even when I was little and they'd teach us that White Witches had no place outside the city, that people hate us . . .'

'I don't hate you,' said Lara. She gave him a thoughtful glance. 'You know what? I've lived on the streets almost all my life. I watch people. And I reckon they mostly don't hate White Witches. I reckon they're scared of you.'

Double Eight looked puzzled. 'Scared? Why would they be scared?'

'Cos you're different,' said Lara with a shrug. 'When something is different, being scared of it is the easy thing to do. You know what I think?'

'What?'

'I think the Kingdom wants us all to be frightened of each other. Cos if people are frightened, they're easy to control.'

'I've been frightened every day of my life,' said Double Eight. 'Frightened that they'd find out I was different. Frightened of running away. Frightened of staying.'

Lara opened her mouth to speak, but the words jumbled up awkwardly. She tried again. 'What . . . um . . . how does it feel, to be separated from your soul? She's kept it, hasn't she, Mrs Hester?'

Double Eight nodded. 'You ever been hungry?' he asked. 'I mean really hungry?'

'Just every other day of my life.'

'Well, it's a little like that, I suppose. Only the hunger isn't in your belly. It's in some other part of you, deep in your chest, and you can't ever do anything to make it better.'

'That sounds awful.'

Double Eight shrugged. 'You get used to it. And I'm different, see.'

'Different?'

'Yeah. Mrs Hester . . . When I was a baby, she took my soul, but she didn't get all of it.' He pressed his hand to his chest and smiled. 'There's still a bit of me in there. That's what makes me different. That's why I always dreamed of escaping – because I *can* dream, see? When the Hags . . . sorry . . . when Bernie and the others found me, they gave me a spell, and now I can travel far away from the rest of my soul without it being unbearable.'

'Where does she keep the souls?' said Lara, remembering the strange cage Mrs Hester had held aloft in Reaper's Square and the shining, fluttering object inside it.

'Nobody knows but her.'

'Can't she do something to your soul? Hurt it?'

'Even Mrs Hester can't do that, Lara. She can lock a soul away, but never harm it.'

Lara found herself suddenly realising that she had more in common with this strange, brave boy than she could have ever imagined. They were both lost, in a way.

'How did you end up on the streets?' he asked, as if he'd read her thoughts.

Lara told him all about her parents and the night she'd been pulled from the rubble.

'And the spell is in your bird?' he asked, indicating Moonwing, who was still out above the waves.

'Maybe.'

'Aren't you terrified?'

'Course I am! Sometimes I'd give anything to be back in the sewers, plain old Lara the tosher.'

Double Eight nodded, seemingly searching for something in his head. 'Then maybe . . . maybe we can be terrified together?'

Lara smiled. 'Maybe.'

He twitched his head to one side, narrowing his eyes

like Lara was a puzzle and he was trying to figure her out. 'Did you *really* go down the sewers?'

Lara laughed. 'Yes.'

'And I thought I had it bad. White Witch children work as servants and cleaners, but the worst I had to do was scrub the toilets. You were actually knee-deep in—'

It was then, as Moonwing rose and fell with the rolling waves, that Lara spotted a dark shape arrowing down through the air.

'Moonwing!'

She watched in horror as the great black bird tore towards Moonwing. She covered her mouth and clung to the side of the boat as the tiny clockwork bird flashed out of the way at the last moment. The dark bird crashed into the sea. There was a moment of calm, Moonwing hovering above the peaks of the waves, and then the creature came bursting through the surface and made a grab for him. He spun away, up into the night, and Lara strained to see as the chase unfolded across the sky, catching glimpses of starlight reflecting on Moonwing's golden feathers.

'It's going to get him!' Double Eight was leaning over the side of the boat.

Lara had no time to reply, for Moonwing came ripping towards her and scrambled into her pocket. She stood on the deck, her hand hovering protectively over him as the large dark shape came swooping down. She ducked, fell to the deck, taking Double Eight with her as a raven the size of an eagle flashed past, and then seemed to vanish in the dark.

Lara waited for a while before she climbed back up and scouted around.

'I think it's gone,' she said, stroking Moonwing, who was trembling in her pocket. But she was wrong.

Light and Dark

The High Witch took the lead, ripping through the air at the tip of the golden arrow. The council had already passed over the northern tip of the Silver Kingdom, seen the blinking lamp light of King's Haven. Then they had moved south-east over the Pewter Sea, looking down upon a great fleet of near-invisible black ships bound, no doubt, for the Silver Kingdom's capital, carrying hordes of the Painted.

At last they reached the Midnight Lands, desert and forest and mountain streaking below, until a mass loomed on the horizon, a swirling, shifting column of unimaginably huge serpentine tendrils. They were made of something between solid mass and smoke, twining and slithering all over each other to form one massive being, lit from within by violent tongues of lightning that burst out and crackled in the sky in strobing flashes.

Leora Twigg, the High Witch, looked at the Evernight and knew that it was something from another time, from a place that would tear apart her mind if she tried to comprehend it.

Six dark serpents reached out of the column, miles long, coiling and twining, rearing up and striking at the Witches.

The Witch souls spun and dipped, avoiding the snakes, and plunged deep into the dark body of the Evernight, into the heart of the darkness, where time and space and magic seemed to stretch endlessly, and the skin of reality peeled away.

The snakes writhed and snapped, and thunder crashed, and lightning lit up the inside of the night demon. The Witches tore back out into the world and circled for another attack. More black snake branches shot from the Evernight, entwining and knotting, lashing out. This time they caught one of the Witches, Emmet Feather, biting down, injecting his soul with darkness and fear and evil, and the great beating wings of the soul became limp. Emmet Feather fell from the sky, down and down, and as his soul hit the Pewter Sea it scattered to nothingness.

Still the Witches swooped.

Again and again they came back, and the sky crackled lightning and thunderclaps, as the darkness fought the light.

One by one the Witch souls fell.

Each attack brought a greater number of serpents, until the heavens were crawling with them, and after a while Leora's comrades had all fallen and she was alone in the sky to face the evil. She spread her wings wide, climbed and climbed and climbed, so high the world curved beneath her. Then, with a spin, she tucked her wings to her side and began her dive.

Surely nothing in the world had ever travelled at such a speed. The very air around her burned as she dived. Between the snapping jaws of the great snakes she went, twisting and swooping, an arrow made of light.

Leora's soul plunged into the living darkness with such force that the world shook. A long moment later she came bursting back out of the ragged silk blackness and began to climb once more. One of the black, slashing tendrils caught her with a glancing blow, sending her spinning. The rest were on her in moments, biting, coiling, stabbing. She fought through, feeling the darkness, the evil, damaging her soul in a way she never imagined. Each strike made her light dim, and when she finally broke free the glow was as faint as a long-dead star. She climbed away from them, hurting, afraid she was going to go out like the others, and with no other choice she began the flight back to Westerly Witch – alone.

Cannon Fodder

'What do you mean we shouldn't stop it?' said the Silver King. He stood in Mrs Hester's spell room, towering over her. The look on his face was a mix of rage and disbelief. She sat calmly with her hands clasped on her desk. 'I have received a message telling me the Painted have taken the Weeping Isles and are now headed our way. And you want to do *nothing*?'

'Calm down, Your Majesty.'

'Calm down? *Calm down*, Mrs Hester? First the White Witches start to leave, then the Hags humiliate us in front of the city, and now this? Are you *trying* to ruin my hagging life?'

'I'm not saying we should do nothing, Your Majesty. I'm saying we are not quite in the position to do anything yet. But that might not be the worst thing. We could use this to our advantage.'

'You have lost your mind. What advantage can there be in letting the Evernight decimate my city?'

She smiled at him, her white teeth sparkling.

Your city? she thought. *It's never been* your *city.*

'The Evernight is not interested in the city,' she told him. 'It wants people.'

'People?'

'It needs an army, Your Majesty. Needs more bodies before it can go to Westerly Witch and wipe out the Hags.' She paused, went to the window, and looked towards the slums, which were mostly in complete darkness. 'How many people in the slums, do you think?'

The king shrugged impatiently. 'Don't know. Half a million at least.'

'Exactly. And what have they ever done for this city? What are they good for, besides spreading filth and disease and violence? Wouldn't it be grand, Your Majesty, to let the Evernight cleanse King's Haven of this infestation?'

The king's eyebrows knitted. She could see that he was putting the pieces together.

'You mean . . . let the Painted take people from the slums?'

'Exactly. Think about it, Your Majesty. We block off the slums, keep the rats in their cage. Then we evacuate the rest of the city, and we wait for the Evernight to empty the slums and take its new army to Westerly Witch and kill the Hags. Then, when the time is right, we stop and reverse the Evernight. When it's all over we won't have an enemy left in the world.'

She watched a smile dawn on his rubbery purple lips and spread across his fat, sweat-sheened face.

'You can do this?' he asked. 'You can control the Evernight?'

'Do you doubt me, Your Majesty?'

He raised an eyebrow.

'I have the means to stop this thing when we are ready, Your Majesty.'

He nodded. 'Make it happen.'

Mrs Hester returned the smile.

Good boy, she thought. *Good boy.*

Fireworks

Two days had passed since the attack on Moonwing, and the dark creature had not tried to get at him again. Rob Nielsen was pushing *Dragonfly's* engines to the limit, for there was still a huge distance to cover and none of them knew what awaited them in Westerly Witch. Had the Evernight already reached the Mother Tree? If it had not, could they beat it there?

Until now the sea had been kind and calm – hardly there at all unless you really thought about it, in fact. And Lara, being unfamiliar with the ways of seafaring, had come to believe that this was always the way of things.

Soon enough, she learned she was wrong.

Now, a thick wall of angry storm cloud gathered in the Evernight sky. The wind picked up, and the waves grew high and became frightening peaks. At first Lara tried to show the sea that she wasn't afraid, and stubbornly stood at her favourite spot at the bow. But the waves tossed the boat around like a toy, and when one of them crashed over and sent Lara careering across the deck, she picked herself up, soaked to the bone, her pride bruised, and decided that maybe it would be best to go below after all.

The sea grew angrier. Jagged mountains of water tossed the boat up and down, up and down. Lamps flickered, and the hum of the engine was drowned out by the constant wail of the wind and the thunder of the waves against the hull. Lara was terrified that one of the huge waves would punch a hole in the boat. It might fill with water and slowly sink, and she'd be thrown into the Pewter Sea and crushed and gobbled up by the creatures of the deep. Even the crew had retreated to the galley, though Lara took some comfort in the fact that none of these old seafaring Witches seemed too worried. They played card games, the playing cards fluttering around the room and bursting into flames. When Lara declined to join them they laughed and told her there was nothing to worry about, that the storm would pass and the old boat had survived much worse than this.

Moonwing seemed skittish too, refusing to leave Lara, sitting on her shoulder or nestling in her pocket as if something was greatly troubling him, and Double Eight became frightfully seasick.

Lara decided to go to bed and try to sleep through the storm in the hope it would be calm when she woke. She went to the cargo hold, climbed beneath the blankets and nestled in her bed of hay. The old boat creaked and moaned, and the wind whistled. Lara closed her eyes, and tossed and turned.

She must have fallen asleep at some point, because she woke with a start, and the feeling that something was very wrong clung to her.

'Double Eight? That you?'

When she looked around, she screamed.

There was a man in the hold. He was tall and dressed in a ragged black coat and top hat. His nose was sharp and his black eyes glistened. As far as she knew, Lara had never met him before, and yet the sight of him sent such a jolt of shock and dread through her that she gasped.

'I believe you have something which belongs to me,' he said, and as he moved closer to the lamp, Lara realised that he cast no shadow.

She heard Granny's voice, as clear as if she was standing beside her.

'Beware the man with no shadow.'

The Sewer Strangler. Lara twisted away and tried to run, but his hand was in her hair, pulling her back against him, and she struggled and breathed the scent of him, a smell like damp, dirty dog fur. His free hand was in her coat, feeling through the pockets. Before he could find it, the clockwork bird erupted from the folds, gold wings flashing in the lamplight, and attacked him, pecking at his face and eyes. He yelled in surprise, letting go of Lara for a moment, batting Moonwing away. A moment was all Lara needed. She dashed towards the door. Yet in a flash he intercepted her move. He dragged her up and clamped a hand over her mouth so that she could not scream again.

'Call the bird down here.'

Lara tried to squirm and fight and kick, but he was awesomely strong. A deep growl of unnatural power rumbled through him. Lara felt it in her bones. His grip tightened around her jaw, and she was sure he was going to crush her skull. But just then the door to the hold burst open. There was a sudden flash, and he let her go. Bernie, Magnus and the crew had poured into the hold, wands drawn, spells glowing in the revolver chambers.

They fired at the same time. Strands of brilliant light, fine as spider silk, shot from their wands, wrapping around the man in black, binding him tight. The stream of light from Bernie's wand faltered and crackled as he fought back.

'Go, Lara! Tell Rob Nielsen. Get off the boat!'

The shadowless man growled and shook off the bindings. He reached out and grabbed Lara by the hair again. But the Witches fired more spells, and he let go, and Lara ran in a blur of panic through the door to the passage. Moonwing stuck close as Lara snaked through the rocking boat. Around a corner she banged into Double Eight.

'What's happening? What's wrong?'

'There's someone on the boat . . . we need to get away. He's after Moonwing!'

The ship lurched as they climbed up and out to the

deck. As soon as the door opened, the roar of the wind smothered everything else, and Lara had to fight against the gale to move forward. The sky exploded here and there with great forks of lightning, and the flashes lit up the ocean too, towering mountains of water as far as the eye could see.

A wall of water came crashing over the boat, knocking Lara over, washing her across the deck. Up she staggered, Double Eight helping her, the wind and rain lashing at them, the spray hitting their faces like hail. The glow from the captain's cab flickered, and Lara stumbled towards it, clinging to ropes and poles as the boat climbed and fell and tilted. At last she threw open the door. Rob Nielsen was at the wheel, his huge hands gripping so tight they had turned the colour of bone.

'Captain! Captain, there's a man below deck!'

'I don't have time for your lies, street rat!' he thundered at her. 'I'm trying to keep us afloat. Go bother someone else.'

'But I swear it! There is a strange man on board! The others are fighting him! Bernie says I'm to get away with Moonwing, but I don't know how!'

'She's telling the truth!' screamed Double Eight.

An explosion shook the deck, and the cargo hold hatch blew open. Orange flames licked up through the gaping hole.

Rob Nielsen ripped his gaze from the angry sea, and there was a look of fury and disbelief on his face. He locked the wheel in place, stepping away from the controls.

'Hell's teeth! There's spells down there that could blow us to the Weeping Isles! Get to the lifeboat!'

Rob staggered across the sloping deck, loosening ropes, winding levers.

Something clubbed Lara on the side of the head. She saw spots of light, felt hot pain and fell to the floor. Now the shadowless man stood over her, drifting in and out of focus, his foot pinning her, squeezing. The tails of his coat were on fire. The storm roared, and the rain and sea spray whipped all around. Moonwing dived and swooped above the shadowless man, who grabbed at him as everything rolled and tilted sickeningly.

Double Eight pulled at the man's coat, and caught a blow just above the eye. He fell, his eyebrow bleeding.

Soon Bernie and the others were up on deck, firing spells. Double Eight got to his feet, grabbed Lara by the arm and helped her up. The pair of them tumbled into the lifeboat, which swung in the wind on its pulley. Lara tucked Moonwing safely in her coat and held on to the sides.

Back on the deck, Bernie made a desperate dash for the first of the pulley ropes, sawing at it with a knife. The rope frayed and snapped, and one end of the lifeboat dropped suddenly down. Lara screamed, hanging on, facing the swirling, angry water, and reached out a hand to stop Double Eight going overboard.

'Go, Bernie!' Lara heard Magnus Whitecrow scream

over the gale and the exploding spells. 'The girl must get to Westerly Witch!'

Bernie reloaded her wand. 'No! I won't leave you!'

'You must! Go, my love! Get Lara there safe!'

Bernie came flying into the lifeboat, staring up, eyes wide. Magnus's face appeared over the edge of the ship, the sky behind him flashing with lightning and spells. He smiled at Bernie and said, 'Be safe, my love.' Then he cut the remaining pulley rope.

Bernie called out as the lifeboat wrenched free and splashed into the Pewter Sea.

Immediately the waves grabbed hold of the smaller boat, tossing it around. No one could move, or set up the oars or think about anything other than not falling into the water. The waves raised them up and then threw them down again, corkscrewing the boat around, almost breaking it in half. As the current carried the three Witches further away, Lara tried to fix her gaze on the boat: smoke was coming from the deck, and there were flashes of light and figures darting around. But the waves were relentless, crashing over her, soaking her, battering her.

When *Dragonfly* blew up, the sound was thunderous, audible even over the scream of the wind and the crash of the waves. Lara fell back. Then she peered over the edge of the lifeboat at the fiery glow in the sky and the plume of smoke climbing towards the night. There, among the waves, the remains of Rob's boat were ablaze.

'No! No!' Bernie was wailing and clawing at the air, trying to climb over the edge of the lifeboat.

'Bernie! No! You'll drown!'

'I don't care! Magnus . . . I must help my Magnus!'

'Double Eight! Help me!'

Double Eight grabbed Bernie and helped Lara drag the older Witch back from the edge. Bernie crumpled to the floor and curled up and wailed. Lara grabbed the oars and tried to row, her heart filled with rage and fear. She had to do something to help Bernie, and Magnus, and Rob Nielsen and his crew – coves who'd risked everything for her, who'd *saved* her . . .

The storm was in no mood to go easy. A wave of grey water hammered down, snapping an oar clean in half, jarring her arm painfully. And then another great swell carried the boat up and up and up, almost tipping it over. When it came hurtling back down, they were being dragged further and further away from the wreckage of Rob's boat, and there was nothing they could do about it.

JOE LITTLEFOOT'S MISSION

'Joe? Joe . . . where are you, Joe?'

'I'm here, Granny. Don't you worry. I won't leave you.' Joe fetched another blanket, tossed it over the bed. The air had got so cold he had to wear all his clothes indoors, and his breath was an icy fog. A single candle burned beside the bed. Joe looked at it fearfully; it was their last candle, and there was little hope of finding another. The Kingdom had already taken command of all dragon breath in the city and was using it to keep the street lamps lit on the main roads and arteries. And now, by order of the king, they'd shut the slums off too, putting up roadblocks on every entrance and exit so the people here were left with no way out, and dwindling supplies.

'Coming . . . they're coming!'

'Who, Granny? Who's coming?'

Granny stared up at Joe with sunken, frightened old eyes. She looked so tiny and fragile he thought she might shatter if he touched her. She did not answer his question, because she did not hear it. The potion had worn off and her fever had come back worse than ever; she was thrashing around in the bed, shivering and sweating. Joe did not think she knew where she was any longer, and the best he could do was make her as comfortable as he could.

When Granny calmed down and closed her eyes, Joe sat on the edge of the bed with his head in his hands. She was dying. Granny was dying and there wasn't anything he could do to help. He'd spent every penny he had on medicines that didn't work.

Joe went to the little window. A scattering of flickering candles in the windows of tenements and houses reassured him that he and Granny were not alone in this vast sea of darkness. It had grown colder each day; blossoms of ice were creeping up the inside of the glass, and a cold, crisp wintry smell was everywhere. Granny kept window boxes filled with herbs for stew, and they were all dying with the cold and lack of sun. The streets were quiet; the darkness had brought a couple of days of chaos and looting and panic, and then the coppers had come and battered people into submission. Now the roadblocks penned them in; Joe had heard that some desperate, frightened coves were sometimes trying to force their way through, and when they did, the coppers were shooting them dead.

He pulled his coat tighter around his freezing body, looked to the Evernight sky, squeezing all the light and hope and happiness from the world. He wondered if it was possible to follow the dark back to the source, and what nightmarish thing might be lurking there.

Then he thought of Lara. *I wonder if she made it out the city. What were you thinkin', Lara, getting' mixed up with Hags, eh? What will become of you?*

He had heard about her run-in with Old Hans of course, could scarcely believe she'd tried to harm him, that she was a Hag. But something about her had been different the night the darkness came, when she'd shown up at his door . . .

A lightning-bright idea flashed in his head.

Old Hans! Of course! If anyone can get me a potion, it's him!

Old Hans had always been so good to toshers. Joe checked on Granny, tucking her blankets tight, kissing her sweat-slick forehead. She was sleeping deep.

'I'll be back soon.'

According to the church clock, it was just after ten in the morning, but it may as well have been midnight. Here and there Joe would find a store or pub open, but mostly the place was quiet, and without the streetlamps the slums were a dark maze. He'd heard some people had got out before the roadblocks went up around the slums, but most were trapped, cowering in their houses, praying for the sun to come back.

The cobbles glistened under a thick frost coat, and Joe's every step made a crunch. The darkness was so thick he was mostly navigating from memory. On Needle Street he tripped over something soft (he did not stop to think what it might have been) and fell in front of a stray flesh-and-blood horse, just managing to roll quickly away to avoid being crushed under its hooves.

When he reached Bone Alley, Joe was not surprised to find a warm glow coming from Old Hans' shop. Lara once told him that Old Hans had never missed a day's business, and that even if death came for Old Hans in the night, his ghost would be there at first light, throwing up the shutter.

Tingalingaling!

Old Hans was behind his counter. He looked up from his ledger, peered over his glasses, his head trembling up and down in a never-ending series of little nods.

'Why, Joe Littlefoot! It's good to see you, lad. Good to see you've recovered from that nasty business in the sewers.'

'Yeah,' said Joe. There was no time to waste, so he got right to the point. 'D'you have any potions, Old Hans?'

Old Hans stared at him, seemed almost to stare through him. 'Dealing in magic is illegal, boy.'

'I know that. I also know you can make a lot of money selling that stuff. Please, Old Hans. It's Granny – she's dying from fever. Will you help me?'

Old Hans continued to stare. He leaned closer over his counter. 'Even if I had such a thing, Joe Littlefoot, it wouldn't come cheap. How would you propose to pay for it?'

'I . . . I was hoping you'd treat it as a loan.'

'A loan?'

'I'd pay you back, Old Hans, I promise! I'd owe you . . .'

'You know perfectly well, Joe Littlefoot, I don't deal in loans. A promise isn't worth the air it takes to speak it.'

'What if I work for you?' said Joe, becoming desperate. 'I could be useful around here. And I could bring you everything I find in the tunnels until you get your money. Double your money!'

Old Hans took off his glasses, came out from behind the counter, locked the door of the shop and held up a finger. 'What I'm about to say don't leave this room, you understand, boy?'

Joe nodded. The hope in his chest made him feel like he was about to lift off the floor.

'I might . . . *might* have a potion such as the one you're after.'

'I knew you would! I knew it!'

Old Hans held his crooked finger up again. 'Maybe . . . yes, maybe you comin' here was meant to be, Joe Littlefoot. Something has recently come to my attention. I been doin' some digging around. Making use of my contacts – I got lots of 'em, you know. Turns out there's a certain object I want just as bad as you want this potion – maybe more. And to get it, I'll need a burglar.'

Joe's eyebrows shot up his forehead. 'Burglar? I don't know about *that* . . .'

'Well, that's the price, Joe, if you want the potion – and I think you do.'

'And just what am I supposed to steal?'

234

One side of Old Hans' mouth curled into a greedy smile. 'An urn. I want you to get me an urn.'

Joe relaxed a little. He had imagined Old Hans was going to want treasure, diamonds, jewels locked away in castles guarded by dragons. An urn sounded like it might be less trouble. 'Where is this urn?'

Old Hans licked his dry lips. 'It's in the palace.'

Joe's mouth opened. No words came out.

'In Mrs Hester's tower, I do believe,' added Old Hans.

'You want me,' said Joe, 'to steal from the most powerful Witch in the kingdom?'

'Well . . . she's got her *hands* full, hasn't she? White Witches runnin' off to Westerly Witch, the Evernight a-creeping across the world. And in any case, she won't be able to see you.'

'She won't?'

'No. On account of you being invisible.'

Joe's head was spinning.

'Invisible?'

Old Hans let out a wheezy chuckle. 'I got more than healing potions, boy.'

'You've got an invisibility potion?'

'I will have by tomorrow night,' said Old Hans. 'It's as simple as this: if you want that healing potion, if you want to save your old Granny, then you'll get me that urn.'

Old Hans offered Joe a hand. Joe hesitated, then shook it. 'Tell me, what's so important about an old urn anyway?'

'You let me worry about that, Joe Littlefoot,' said Old Hans, and there was a sparkle in his eyes Joe had never seen before. 'Just be here tomorrow night. Midnight. I'll be a-waitin'.'

NEL PEPPER

With only one oar, and no spells that could help in this situation, Lara, Bernie and Double Eight had been drifting aimlessly in their lifeboat for what seemed like a very long time. They had lost sight of the debris of *Dragonfly* hours ago. Now they sat there with empty bellies and a terrible thirst.

'It's so cold,' said Double Eight, hugging his knees. 'I'd wager the sea will turn to ice before long. People are going to freeze to death, and those who don't freeze will starve because the crops are sure to die.'

Lara rubbed her arms miserably. She felt hot tears welling in her eyes, spilling over, and she struggled to hide her sobs, but they burst out anyway. 'I'm sorry for what happened to Magnus,' she sniffed. 'And Rob and his crew. Oh, I'm sorry, Bernie. It's all my fault.'

Bernie had been almost silent since watching Rob's boat blow up, and Lara had been barely able to look at her. Now she moved to Lara's side, rocking the boat, and hugged her tight.

'Stop that at once, you hear? What happened wasn't down to you.'

'But it was! Magnus and Rob and the others would never have been in danger if it wasn't for me!'

'Look around you, child,' said Bernie. 'Everyone's in danger. Magnus and Rob chose to put themselves in danger every day of their lives, smuggling spells and freeing White Witches. It wasn't in their nature to do nothin'. What we have to do is finish the job.'

Lara sniffed, and wiped her nose with a soaking sleeve. 'I'll do my best, Bernie, I promise. For Magnus, and Rob, and the crew . . . whatever it takes.'

The cold grew unbearable. Lara huddled with Bernie and Double Eight, shivering, desperately trying to keep warm. She felt herself drifting in and out of sleep. There was frost on her eyelids, ice in her hair. She knew the cold would take her soon. She thought of King's Haven, of the sticky summer warmth, and she even longed for the sewer tunnels.

Double Eight shifted and sat up.

'What's that?'

'Hmm?'

'In the sky . . . what's that light?'

Lara opened her eyes, wiping away the frost. There was an object drifting among the scattered clouds, something large and twinkling with lamplight.

Bernie jerked forward, rubbing at her eyes to make sure

she was really seeing it. 'We're saved!' she said, and leaped to her feet, causing the little lifeboat to violently tip. She reached into her coat, brought out her wand, loaded a spell bottle and pointed the wand straight up. A jet of blinding red fired out of the wand and shot up into the sky, trailing a plume of reddish smoke.

A long moment later a red flare came from the object in the sky, answering Bernie's. The object turned and began to come nearer, growing, until Lara could clearly see the shape of it in the light of its lamps. Looming overhead was the hull of a large wooden boat, and above it, connected by many ropes and frames and cables, was an enormous balloon. A propeller spun in a blur at the back of the ship's body, and warm dragon-breath light spilled from the many windows and portholes.

'Ahoy down there!' came a voice, and Lara could see the shapes of people leaning over the side. 'Help is here! We'll have you up in no time!'

'Mother Earth was smiling on you,' said Nel Pepper, captain of the airship *Starchaser*. 'We were supposed to head home to Westerly Witch yesterday, but we decided at the last minute to have one more run. Otherwise we'd never have found you.' Nel was a big woman, with the darkest skin Lara had ever seen and a belly like the ship's balloon tucked into her chunky Witch's belt. They all sat at a round table in the captain's quarters. Nel Pepper had ordered the cook to bring up some fish stew, and Lara slurped it down into her empty belly, licking the bowl clean, even eating a fish eye, which she usually could not bear.

Lara found Nel enchanting; her charisma seemed to fill up all the empty space in a room. Lara hung on every word as Nel entertained them with stories of growing up in a Witch colony in a country called Dornia, of fighting the invading Argent Army, and of fleeing her home when Dornia became just another piece of the Silver Kingdom, swallowed up in the Southern Territories.

'So what are you doing out in this darkness?' asked Bernie as they finished eating.

'I could ask you the same,' replied Nel with a grin.

Bernie smiled.

'We've been trying to mine magic from the sky,' continued Nel. 'It gathers sometimes in clouds and mixes with moonlight. We need every whisper of it we can get. The Blossom on the Mother Tree won't survive the Evernight. But seriously, how did you come to be stranded in that little lifeboat?'

'The storm,' said Bernie, looking from Lara to Double Eight. 'It wrecked our boat. We smuggle spells and such in and out of King's Haven. We were on our way home.'

'Smuggling?' said Nel Pepper, raising her brows. 'Dangerous work, no?'

'Very.'

'Well, have no fear. We'll be back in Westerly Witch by

the morning.' She shook her head. 'Can't come soon enough for me. I can't wait to feel the sun on my skin again.'

Lara and the others exchanged startled looks.

'The sun? You mean the Evernight hasn't reached the Mother Tree yet?'

'Why, no. Hadn't you heard? The sky's still blue and the sun still shines. Though for how much longer is anyone's guess.'

Presently, a series of whoops and cheers drifted in from the deck of the airship.

'What's that?' said Lara.

Nel Pepper smiled. 'Go see for yourself. It's perfectly safe.'

Lara had never been on an airship. Until Nel and her crew had come swooping down to save them she had never even known such a thing existed.

Her exotic new surroundings helped distract her from her problems, and the food in her belly and warmth of the fire had lifted her spirits. She got up from the table and hurried away, Double Eight following closely behind.

Out on deck, Lara and Double Eight watched in wonder as Nel's crew hurried around the airship, yelling and singing, winding huge levers, pulling on ropes and chains. The chains ran through great metal holes in the ship's hull, and as the crew wound them in, Lara and Double Eight peered over the edge and saw that the links disappeared down into a cloud below the ship.

241

'Here she comes!'

'Pull, lads!'

The chains yanked a heavy shape from the cloud, a net, it seemed to Lara, made of shimmering gossamer strands. And inside the net . . .

'What *is* that?'

'Moonlight, Lara. It's moonlight mixed with magic.' Nel Pepper stood close to her.

'A single thread has the power to make many, many spells. But spell clouds are hard to find. Good job, lads!'

A cheer went up from the deck as the net was pulled on board. They opened a hatch in the deck, and the net opened, and the threads of moonlight spilled into the cargo hold. Lara and Double Eight peered down and saw that the threads were tangling and swirling around each other, and the sound from them was the sound of magic, of crystal music.

'Right, lads!' yelled Nel Pepper, running to the wheel, spinning it west. The *Starchaser* spun around in the sky, and the great engines roared, and they swooped through the stars. 'To Westerly Witch we go!'

Westerly Witch

'I never imagined I'd get the chance to do anything like this,' said Double Eight, as he and Lara stood on the deck of the airship and felt the wind rush against their faces. 'It's more than I dreamed.'

'Me too,' said Lara, her heart brimming with excitement . . . and sadness too. 'I wish my friend Joe were here. He'd have loved this. I don't know if I'll ever see him again.'

'Course you will.'

'But the Evernight . . . it's going to kill everything, you said so yourself.'

'We won't let it. I didn't escape a life of slavery to watch the world end. I'll fight and claw and bleed to stop it. I'll do anything. And I think you will too.'

They both fell silent then, because the sky was changing. Gradually, as the ship flew west, they left the Evernight behind, soaring into daylight. The crew gathered on deck. They cheered, standing in the sunlight with their eyes closed and soaking up the life-giving warmth of it. Lara had never felt anything so wonderful.

On the horizon, growing from the sea, was a tree as large as a mountain. The trunk of the great tree was a twisting tangle of bark, and as the airship swooped nearer, it was possible to see that the Witches had carved buildings and steps and alleyways into the countless cracks and nooks of the bark. Where it had not been possible to build directly onto the tree, they had constructed platforms and bridges and built upon those. Lara wondered if there was a single part of it that had not been modified or added to. Around the tree were a series of islands with bridges stretching from them to the trunk. Spell smoke and glowing auras drifted from chimneys in every colour of the spectrum. Lara had never seen anything like it, never imagined a place so fantastic was possible.

At the wheel of the airship, Nel Pepper let out a laugh. 'Home, lads! Home again!'

Bernie Whitecrow appeared too. She put her arms around Lara and Double Eight's shoulders.

'It's been a while,' she said, 'and I sure am glad to see that grand old tree.'

The airship descended towards one of the islands, and with a crash of spray came down into the Pewter Sea and sailed slowly into a harbour packed with boats and airships. As the ship docked, the crew were busy again, filled with the bouncing cheer of being home.

Nel Pepper came to see Lara and her friends off the ship.

'Hold up just a sec.' She reached into one of the many compartments in her big leather belt and brought out three spell bottles containing dancing tangles of fiercely-glowing thread. 'For all of you,' she said, handing the bottles over. They felt like icicles.

'That looks like . . .'

'Moonlight and magic. Strong enough to bind anything in the world. I hope it serves you well. Good luck with the rest of your journey. If it pleases Mother Earth, maybe we'll see each other again.'

'Thank you,' said Lara, tucking the spell away in her pocket. She shook Nel Pepper's hand and followed Bernie off the ship and through winding streets. A canopy of green leaves stretched across the heavens, and sunlight splinters fell through from the sky. The aroma of spell smoke was a strange and wonderful concoction: tree sap and wood and sea air, mixed with the scents of the spells themselves, the spice of the orange, the cool of the blue and the rich sweetness of the purple smoke.

There were horses on the streets, all flesh and blood, with no sign at all of the ironhearts or clockwork and magic-powered machinery that was so common in King's Haven. Lara thought that it was stunningly beautiful, and yet there was a sense of great loss in the air; Lara heard it in the crystalline call of the magic.

'Something's happened,' she said. 'It's not just the Evernight. Something else . . .'

'I feel it too,' said Bernie, looking grave.

'It's pressing down on me,' said Double Eight. 'Here.' He pointed to his chest.

They walked across a rope bridge that carried them high over the harbour to the base of the great Mother Tree, and as they touched down on one of the wooden platforms, a small bearded Witch in a long coat with a green hood approached them.

'Bernie? Bernie Whitecrow! They said it was you, but I didn't dare hope!' He grabbed her hand, shaking it vigorously. 'When Rob Nielsen told me what had happened . . .'

'Rob's *here*?' said Bernie, her face breaking into a smile. 'They made it? Magnus made it?'

The man's face crumpled. He looked at the floor.

'Bastien? Bastien Stone, what is the matter?'

Bastien Stone's lip trembled. 'I'm so sorry. Magnus didn't come home.'

Lara's breath became stuck in her throat. She grabbed Bernie's hand, squeezed tight. She felt the older Witch swaying slightly, and for a moment thought she might fall. But Bernie seemed to regain her strength. She sniffed. 'Well . . . thank you for telling me, Bastien. We'll talk about that later. Right now, we need to see the High Witch.'

Bastien stared at Bernie, his eyes flooding.

'What else? Tell me, Bastien. What has happened?'

'It's the High Witch, Bernie. Leora . . . She's not . . . I mean she isn't . . . she's been . . . well, you'd better come and see for yourself.'

INTO THE PALACE

Joe did not want to leave Granny on the night of the burglary. Her breathing came in short, shallow gasps, and where she had been restless she was now deathly still. Before he left, Joe dripped some water into her dry mouth and mopped her brow. The large candle had burned almost all the way down. It had become so cold in the flat, there was frost on the floor, and yet Granny's skin was still on fire with fever. He took her hand and kissed it, and then made his way through the streets of the slums.

The coppers had set up one of their many roadblocks near Bone Alley, and Joe glanced up the street to the place where a chain fence had been erected to stop people leaving. A crowd had gathered there, and on the other side of the fence, coppers stood with their pistols drawn, ready to shoot down anyone who tried to climb over.

'We'll freeze!'

'We need food!'

'We need coal and firewood!'

'Let us out! Don't lock us up like animals! It ain't right!'

Joe slipped into Bone Alley, approaching Old Hans' shop. He knocked gently on the door. It was almost midnight, but it could be any hour; the ever-present night sky played tricks with your mind, making time seem like something imaginary.

The door to Old Hans' shop creaked open, and his withered face peered out, his eyes magnified through his glasses. He motioned for Joe to enter and locked the door. He was wearing many layers of clothes, and a knitted hat, and gloves. Most everything in his shop was coated in ice crystals.

'You tell anyone about this?'

'Not a soul. Not even Granny.'

'Good lad. How is she?'

'Worse. I don't think she'll last much longer.'

'Then there's no time to lose, eh, boy?'

Old Hans brought out a small vial filled with purplish liquid.

'The invisibility potion.'

Joe held it up to the dim light of a single dragon-breath lamp. 'How do you know this is really an invisibility potion? How d'you know it won't turn me into a cat or somethin'?'

Old Hans shrugged. 'I don't, is the simple answer. I guess we'll have to trust the cove I bought it from, won't we? He's usually a good sort.' Old Hans cocked his head to the side. 'If you're havin' second thoughts, Joe Littlefoot, I'm sure I'll be able to find someone else . . .'

'No. No, I'll do it.'

'Good. Now, I don't know how long the effect of this potion will last, so you best not take it until you absolutely must.'

'Right,' said Joe.

'Good lad. Mrs Hester's tower is to the south-east of the palace. The urn you're a-lookin' for will be in there . . . it looks like this.' He gave Joe an old, tattered page ripped out of a book. On one side was a drawing of the object in question, a ceramic urn decorated with symbols. It didn't look particularly special.

Joe tucked the page in his pocket. 'Anything else?'

'Yes. Don't get caught.'

He would never say it out loud, but Joe fancied himself the second-best tosher in all King's Haven behind Lara. After all, she'd taught him all the tricks, the shortcuts and hidden corners, hadn't she? He knew, for instance, that the sewer leading under the palace was blocked by a grate. He also knew, thanks to Lara, that some clever tosher years ago had loosened some of the bricks beneath the grate so it was possible to remove them and slip under. Until tonight, he had never tried it; if you were caught beneath the palace you were likely to be shot on sight. But if you *had* to break into the palace, if the person you loved's life depended on it, then the sewers were the way to go.

Joe sloshed through the gently bubbling sewer stream,

guided by the warm light of his trusty lamp. When he passed under one of the roadblocks, he heard yelling and chanting, and he could picture the slum folk gathered there with their children, even at this late hour, begging and pushing to escape, and the coppers on the other side of the chain fence, pistols at the ready.

Perhaps it should have occurred to Joe that the coppers would be patrolling the sewers, looking to prevent escape from the slums that way. It never did. When he turned the corner and came face to face with a policeman, the man seemed for a moment to be as surprised as Joe. The copper reached for his pistol, but Joe was too quick: he pulled the crowbar from his toshing bag and smacked the copper's hand, making him drop the pistol in the stream. Then he swung again, this time knocking out the copper's lamp, and in the same movement he extinguished his own lamp, leaving the tunnel in complete darkness.

'Stop!' yelled the copper as Joe pushed past. The copper blew his whistle, and other whistles in the tunnels replied. Joe ran. Lara had taught him well. He knew every bend, every corner. It was like there was a map of the sewers in his head, and he ducked out of sight, avoiding coppers' lamps, changing direction at the sound of their footsteps, until at last he came to the tunnel leading to the palace. When he reached the grate, he fumbled on the bricks of the floor, found the loose ones and removed them carefully. The gap they left was tight, but toshers are generally a scrawny lot, and Joe squeezed through, submerging his head for a moment in the stinking water, coughing and heaving at the taste of it in the back of his throat. But he was in. On the other side of the gate he followed the tunnel to a larger chamber where he could see many smaller tunnels leading off towards different parts of the palace. All of these tunnels were too small – even for Joe – so he climbed the ladder towards the surface.

'Madness, that's what this is,' he muttered.

When he reached the top, he pushed up gently against the manhole cover, nudging it out of place. He had heard there were lots of outbuildings in the palace grounds, cottages and stables where many of the servants lived and worked – almost a village in itself – and this was exactly where the tunnel brought him out.

'Can't put it off any longer I suppose,' he said to himself, bringing the vial of purple liquid out from his pocket. Still in the open drain, he took the stopper out of the vial and touched it to his lips. He thought of Granny. 'Please don't let me turn to dust, or make me explode . . . or turn me into a hog . . .'

Joe closed his eyes and swallowed the potion.

The bitterness of it made him clench his teeth. It felt exactly like a cold wave had crashed over him. He gasped, clinging to the ladder, and when the feeling had passed he opened his eyes.

He held his hand up. He could see the sleeve of his

toshing coat, feel his skin, wriggle his fingers, but where the sleeve ended there seemed to be only air. He laughed under his breath.

'It worked!'

It took a moment for the exhilaration to fade, and for Joe to realise that while his *body* had become invisible, anyone with eyes could still see his clothes.

'Oh, you've got to be kidding . . .'

A minute later, Joe Littlefoot climbed out of the sewers, naked as the day he was born, swearing under his breath at the cold, and began his walk towards the palace.

THE MEETING

In the centre of the great tree the Witches had dug out a series of vertical shafts, fitted with platforms attached to pulleys. Great cogs and wheels raised and lowered the platforms, making it possible to travel between levels without having to climb for hours. Lara stood next to Bernie and Double Eight on one of these lifts, listening as the cogs turned and the ropes moaned and creaked. The platform climbed until the air thinned and ice crystals twinkled on every surface.

'The council is gone,' said Bastien Stone in a soft voice. 'They flew out to meet the Evernight. Only the High Witch came home . . . and she's in a bad way. The Mother Tree is keeping her alive, I think.'

'We saw them!' whispered Lara. 'Out on the boat we saw them fly across the sky.'

When the platform reached the top of the tree they walked out onto a junction in the trunk from which all the uppermost branches sprouted, and in the centre of this junction, growing from the tree itself, was the High Witch's palace. Every part of it, every tower and door and window was formed from intertwined vines and branches, as if the tree had decided that this was how a palace should be made. Glowing insects fluttered in the air around the palace, and flowers and fruit blossomed on the walls.

The guards at the main palace door stood aside as they approached. Inside, each room was formed from the same plant life; every piece of furniture and decoration grew from the Mother Tree. Cobweb curtains framed the windows and glowing bugs and insects filled the lamps with soft light.

The sound of magic here was so powerful and clear it seemed almost visible in the breeze, and it only intensified as they finally entered a room in which an enormous bed grew from the floor. In the centre of the bed lay a mass of vines and branches and leaves.

It shifted in the bed. Lara gasped: the mask of branches crept away, revealing the flesh-and-blood face of a youthful woman with curling red hair. She opened her huge eyes, and they were a dazzling, glowing green.

Double Eight hung back behind Bernie, his hand pressed to his chest, the remaining part of his soul overwhelmed by the strength of the gaze from the red-headed Witch.

'Bernie.'

'Leora Twigg,' said Bernie, dabbing her eyes, 'what foolish heroics have you been up to?'

'We flew, Bernie. We tried. But the Evernight was too strong. The others . . .'

'It's all right,' said Bernie. 'We'll fix this.'

Leora Twigg took a shallow breath. Her eyes shifted to Lara, and Lara felt that she might shrink away to nothing.

'This is Lara,' said Bernie. 'And this is Double Eight. Two special young Witches, ma'am.'

As Bernie spoke, Moonwing flapped out of Lara's pocket and landed on her shoulder. Leora's eyes closed for a moment, and a weak smile broke out on her lips.

'The Doomsday Spell? You've got it. But you're so young . . .'

Lara felt the buzz of her locket against her chest then, and she somehow knew what to do. She untucked the locket from her shirt, and let the High Witch see it. The engraving of the bird on the locket blazed bright, reflected in Leora's eyes, and she took a tiny, sharp breath.

'Will you leave us?' she asked Bernie. 'Just me and the girl . . . Lara.'

Lara looked to Bernie for reassurance, and she nodded and gave a half-smile.

It was then that Lara found, unbelievably, that she had an audience with the leader of all the free Witches in the world. She could feel the power crackling from the High Witch, feel her hair stand and her soul sing.

'Lara . . . come. Sit.'

Lara sat on the edge of the bed, looking at this strange,

powerful woman encased all in a shell of branches. 'Are you hurt?' she asked.

The High Witch smiled. 'That's not important, Lara. We're short on time. Where did you get your necklace?'

Lara's fingers found the chain. 'My mum, I think. She died when I was a baby. They said I was a miracle, after they scooped me out the rubble.'

'A miracle indeed,' said the High Witch.

'Did you know my parents, ma'am?'

'Sadly no, Lara. But I knew *of* them. I knew they were out there. Do you know what that necklace signifies?'

'Bernie said it's something to do with the Witches who've been keeping Moonwing safe.'

'Moonwing?'

'Oh. That's what I call him, ma'am. Suits him, don't you think?'

The High Witch smiled. 'I think it suits him very much. It really is amazing to see him, Lara. When Mrs Hester and her group brought civil war to Westerly Witch hundreds of years ago, they were after the power of the Doomsday Spell. But the High Witch of the time could not let that happen. The great Witches of the past left the Spell with us so that we'd have protection against the Evernight and other dangers left behind by the Gods. To protect Moonwing, the High Witch ordered the formation of a secret Coven – a group of brave Witches who'd go out into the world and keep him safe, always moving, never in one place too long.

Moonwing has been hidden all this time, even from me; no one even really knew if the Coven was still out there. But that locket of yours, Lara, is their sign.'

'So my mum was one of them? She was protecting the Spell?'

'I believe she must have been. It would have made sense, I think, that the Doomsday Coven passed their duty down to their children. Which means, Lara, your mother must have passed hers to you.'

Lara stared at the locket. She touched it, knowing that her mother had probably held it just like this.

'What am I supposed to do?'

'You are supposed to use the spell when it is needed,' said the High Witch. 'And I think it is very much needed now.'

'But how? I've only just found out I'm a Witch. I don't have the power . . . Double Eight has more magic than I do. I couldn't even make a decent light spell – and I've tried openin' the locket a thousand times, but I can't!'

The shell of branches that enveloped the High Witch twisted and snaked apart, revealing a pale, delicate arm. The High Witch reached out, opened her hand. When Lara took her hand, a great charge of magic rushed through her, making her dark hair vibrate.

'I feel the power in you,' said the High Witch. 'All you need is belief. Hold the locket in your hand. Know you are a Witch. Believe what's inside is meant for you.'

Lara took the locket in her open palm. She traced the

258

outline of the bird with her eyes, and the inscription of her name. Then she closed her eyes, heard the wonderful music of the magic in the air, and spoke to the necklace with her thoughts.

If this is meant to be . . . if I truly am supposed to play a part . . . then give me a sign. Open now. If you do that I'll believe. I'll know it's all true.

The locket vibrated and hummed. Lara looked down at it, and closed her hand around it. She felt a click and warmth spilled onto her flesh. The locket had opened in her hand. There was a tiny bottle inside.

Trembling, she took the bottle.

'What is it?'

'A message, I think.'

'From . . . from my mum?'

'Yes.'

Lara stared down at the bottle. Her head spun and her chest heaved and flooded with a great, aching desire.

My mum held this bottle, she thought. *My mum was the last person to touch it.*

It felt, in a strange way, that she was somehow touching her mother's hand. She looked at the High Witch, and tears began to fall down her face. 'I'm scared.'

The High Witch took her hand. 'Then let us do this together.'

Lara took a deep breath, unstoppered the bottle, and let out the spell.

A Spot of Bother

The first test of Joe's invisibility came soon enough.

He had reached the palace easily, keeping to the shadows and treading softly, and now he was walking around the base of the enormous building looking for a way in. It was then, as his eyes were busy scouting, that he turned a sharp corner and almost walked into a guard.

The guard was leaning against the wall, having a sly drag at his pipe, ghostly smoke drifting up into the night from his mouth. He must have heard Joe, because he stopped, became still, and stared at the spot which Joe stood upon, then right at Joe's face. Joe held his breath, hoping his heart was not really beating as terribly loud as it seemed. The guard stared for a long moment, and then he shrugged and went back to his pipe. Joe went weak at the knees with relief.

When the guard had finished, he made his way to a small side entrance, and Joe realised this was his chance. As the guard opened the door, Joe slipped past him. He was in.

The labyrinth of servants' tunnels and kitchens and storerooms reminded Joe of the sewers, and he was surprised to find that he felt quite at home as he wound up towards the main palace rooms. There was barely a soul around, and Joe's confidence was up, so he hurried faster and faster, out into a series of magnificent hallways and chambers. Everywhere he looked he saw treasures he imagined must be priceless: paintings and wall hangings and vases and crystal eggs. In one cavernous room he saw the perfectly preserved skeleton of a dragon, wings spread wide, teeth the size of his forearm shining in the golden lamp light.

South-east. Old Hans said Mrs Hester's tower was there . . .

Joe noticed a difference as he approached Mrs Hester's tower. It seemed the servants did not come here very often, for curtains of spider silk were draped on the walls and the windows and lamps, and there was no treasure on display. The freezing air seemed to grow even colder, making Joe tremble and curse the fact he'd had to ditch his clothes.

He came to the tower door and tried the handle. It opened.

Why would it be locked, I suppose? he thought to himself. *Who'd try to burgle the great Mrs Hester, Joe, apart from you? Nobody, that's who.*

Through the door he went, to the spiral staircase.

If I were keeping something valuable, he reasoned, *I'd put it at the top of the tower. So that's where I shall start.*

The climb was long. The tower seemed impossibly tall,

and the air grew ever colder with each step. By the time Joe reached the uppermost door his hands shook badly. He entered a large, comfortable room, and was glad to see a fire burning in the grate. He scurried to it, warmed his body, and looked around at the many shelves and cabinets holding books and jars filled with strange, dead-looking things in liquid. He could not see any sign of the urn Old Hans had shown him, so he went to the next room.

And became very still.

This was a bedroom. And in the bed slept Mrs Hester, the most powerful of all White Witches.

If she wakes up there's every chance she'll be able to see me somehow. And what then? She'll turn me inside out! Hell's teeth, you really are a fool, Joe Littlefoot, getting mixed up in a scheme like this. But Granny . . . it's all for Granny.

He went on looking around the room, wincing at his every move, waiting for Mrs Hester to wake up and set him ablaze with magic, but she slept on. Still no sign of the urn, so Joe moved to a third room, this one a study of sorts, with a desk and many books and ornaments.

Joe's heart gave a jump.

There, on a shelf among a great number of treasures, was the urn. It had to be. He moved quickly, tucking it under his arm, and had turned to head away when a sound made him stop. It was a sorrowful noise, and it drew him in, made him walk to the last room, the fourth chamber, where he found a full-length mirror standing on the bare floor.

There were two sides to the mirror, and it sat in an ornate wooden frame carved in the shapes of many birds. As Joe approached, he saw the reflection of the urn tucked under his invisible arm as if floating. The surface of the mirror rippled like a pond in the breeze, and when it became still the reflection was gone. Now the mirror had become a window, or a door, to another room.

Joe knew that he should turn and run, knew that he was in great danger in this tower, and yet he was being called. He stepped towards the mirror, reached out a hand, and . . .

His hand passed through the glass. Joe pushed through, stepping into the other side, and stared around at an unimaginably large room filled with towering cabinets. On the shelves of these cabinets Joe saw many thousands of what looked like bird cages made from a shimmering material. Beautiful winged creatures made of light flapped around inside those cages. They called out to Joe, and their calls were so filled with sadness and longing that it made his heart ache.

A distant echo from Mrs Hester's chambers brought Joe back to his senses, and he hurried through the mirror to the tower. Mrs Hester was still asleep, but she was yelling out, dreaming . . .

'The Spell. Bring me the Spell! The bird! Kill her . . . kill the girl . . .'

Joe crept past, out to the staircase, hurrying, almost tripping in his haste, the urn tucked under his arm. Through the shining palace he went, navigating the winding maze of servants' passageways and out into the night. Then across the palace grounds to the outbuildings and the manhole cover back to the sewers.

He'd hidden his crowbar in a rosebush, and he retrieved it and began to manoeuvre the cover out of place. As he worked, there was a heart-stopping moment where he saw a flash of the flesh of his hand. Then his foot. He held his hand up, filling with horror. The potion was wearing off. Joe was becoming visible again.

Panic knotting his guts, he pushed and pulled on the cover, and it popped out of place and dropped with a loud *CLANG!*

'Here, what was that? Who's there?'

Joe slid the cover out of the way, desperately clambering into the manhole. He was almost in, just reaching for the urn, when he looked along the alley and saw a guard catch sight of him. The man's eyes grew wide and he stared at Joe, seemingly dumbfounded.

'Oi! You there!'

Joe ducked into the manhole, half climbing, half falling down the ladder. When he got to the bottom he could hear the guard's boots on the rungs above. He grabbed his clothes, wrapped the urn in them, and hurried along to the grate. He dropped down, slipping under.

He was almost there when a strong hand grabbed hold of his ankle.

'Gotcha!'

The guard was dragging him back. Joe kicked out, felt something bony crack as his foot made contact. The guard gave a nasal cry and let go, and Joe knew he'd broken the man's nose. He scrambled all the way under the bars, crawling and wriggling for his life. On the other side he gathered his things and ran. The guard cursed down the sewer at him, but Joe knew it was over. He'd soon disappear into the tunnels beneath the city. It was time to go home.

Message in a
Bottle

The smoke from the spell bottle in Lara's locket rolled and twined and tumbled in the air above the High Witch's bed. It glowed deep inside, and there were flashes, and the sound of crackling. For a while Lara was scared that something had gone wrong with the spell, that she had damaged it somehow without knowing. She was about to call out to the High Witch when shapes began appearing in the smoke: what might have been hands, fingers, the folds of clothing.

And a face.

Lara watched, frozen, bewitched, as the spell swirled and assumed the shape of a person. A woman. Her face took form, the nose and mouth and eyes, all familiar to Lara, because looking at this woman, even though her features were made of spell smoke, was in some ways like looking at herself. Her skin was deep brown, and the shape of her face was very similar, with a pointed chin and large dark eyes. Her hair was identical to Lara's, black and sprouting in every direction in tight curls.

Echoes began to fill the room, banging, clattering, yelling; the sounds of a struggle. The image of the woman held up her wand and said something that almost stopped Lara's heart.

'Lara.'

She was frozen, unable to do anything but stare.

'Lara . . .'

'I'm here. I'm here, Mum . . .'

Another bang came from somewhere behind the image of her mother.

'Lara, I don't have much time. It's coming.'

Lara made to say something, but there was another flash, and a bang, and the smoking image flickered and repeated.

'Lara, I don't have much time. It's coming.'

And that was the moment Lara realised that what she was seeing was a memory. An echo. This message travelled only one way, and her mother could not see her as well.

She dabbed her eyes, brushed away the tears that were obscuring her view. 'I see you, Mum. I'm here.'

'I know you're going to wonder about us, Moonshine. I wonder about you, too. Since you were born I've dreamed of what you'll become, what you'll look like. I'm sorry, my beautiful girl, that I won't be there to see it. There's so much to say. So much to tell you—'

A gunshot interrupted her, and she turned away for a moment.

'Hurry!' came another voice, a man's, and Lara peered into the smoke, trying to see, realising that she had probably just heard her father.

When her mother turned back to face her, she was shaking. 'You are a Witch, Larabelle Fox. And a Witch is a fine thing to be. More than that, you have inherited a sacred duty – my duty. The Doomsday Coven.' Lara's mother took the locket off and held it towards Lara. 'When it's time, your magic will wake up and you will become the Witch you are destined to be.'

Lara heard an unexpected sound then, the gurgling of a baby, and she realised that she was seeing these events through her own eyes, as she'd seen them when she was an infant. Then there was another noise, a man calling out in pain, and then falling silent. Lara's mother crouched low, kissed her baby and put the locket round its neck.

'You are loved, Lara. Remember that. We will love you, wherever you are. Always and for ever.'

Lara reached out a hand, and her fingers passed through the spell. It was cold.

'I love you,' she whispered.

The echo of Lara's mum raised her wand, and a spell lit up in its chamber, drifting out of the wand and surrounding baby Lara with light. 'I won't let him get you tonight, Lara. Not while I'm alive. But if you are watching this message in the future, my dear, I can't keep you safe. The shadowless man will come for you one day. I wish I didn't have to bring you into this . . . but it's our duty. The Coven must protect the spell, must give our lives to keep it safe.'

Someone shouted something unintelligible, and Lara's mother hunched over her baby.

'We don't have long. The spell, Lara. What's left of the Coven will protect it. He'll hunt them too. I pray it never comes to you. But if it does, if one day you must use the Doomsday Spell to push back the dark, then you must be prepared' – she swallowed hard – 'must be prepared for a journey from which you might not return. Your soul, Lara. Your soul is the key. You must give it—'

A bright flash, and Lara's mother let out a cry. Lara leaned forward, reaching out, unable to see anything through the spell her mother had cast. 'What's happening? Mum?'

The sound of a great explosion, and the smoke scattered, leaving Lara and the High Witch alone once more.

Through her tears, Lara could see the High Witch staring at her. Moonwing pecked affectionately at her ear, and she stroked his cool golden wing feathers.

'You should be very proud,' said the High Witch. 'Your mother was a brave woman.'

'Who was coming for her?' said Lara. 'Who killed her?'

The High Witch shook her head. 'I don't know for sure. Mrs Hester has been hunting for that Spell for centuries.'

'I hate her,' said Lara, meaning it, feeling her blood boil with fury. 'I'll get her.'

A trickle of bright red blood ran from the High Witch's

ear. 'Don't waste time on hate, Lara. It'll only make you empty.' She coughed, and the branches encasing her twisted tighter. She gasped. 'Bernie. Get Bernie.'

Lara ran for the door to bring Bernie back into the room. Bernie took the High Witch's hand. 'Leora. Oh, Leora!'

'Teach her, Bernie. Give her a wand. Don't let Hester win.'

'I won't,' said Bernie. 'I promise.'

'You are the last . . . the last remaining member of my council, Bernie. I have no children. You must . . . you must be the one to lead.'

'Lead, ma'am. I don't—'

A crown of branches broke off from the High Witch's head, rising up in the air. The crown touched down upon Bernie's head, and her eyes were wide and frightened. 'Leora?'

'Long live the High Witch,' said Leora, and she closed her eyes and let the branches grow and twist and encase her face then her whole head. After a few moments the shell broke apart and turned to dust. There was no trace of anyone inside.

Bastien Stone raced into the room, and when he saw the bed was empty he goggled at it. Bastien spotted the crown on Bernie's head, and he dropped to one knee. Double Eight crept into the chamber. Lara nodded to him and they fell to one knee too.

'Long live the High Witch!'

DON'T TRUST
ANYBODY

Tap tap tap.

The door to Old Hans' shop cracked open a little, and there he was, peering out like an old owl. When he saw it was Joe, he took a sharp breath and his wild eyebrows jumped inquisitively. 'Well? You get it?'

Joe brought the urn out from under his coat.

Old Hans almost fell back in excitement. He unlocked the door, motioning for Joe to enter the shop. 'Well done, boy! Well done!'

Joe handed the urn to Old Hans, who placed it on the counter with a great deal of reverence. 'Beautiful. Just look at it.' He chuckled to himself and rubbed his hands together. 'Oh, Joe Littlefoot, the things I'm going to be able to do!'

'Right,' said Joe. 'Good. Now, about that healing potion . . .'

'I never imagined I'd have this chance,' said Old Hans, ignoring Joe, shining the urn with his sleeve. 'I mean. I *mean.*'

'Old Hans.'

'I can do whatever I want!' said Old Hans. 'And not even Mrs Hester can stop me!'

'Old Hans!'

Joe's voice finally brought the old man back to the here and now. He raised an eyebrow.

'The potion?' said Joe, holding out an open hand. 'My payment.'

Old Hans walked behind the counter, he rested his elbows either side of the urn. He looked at Joe with a great deal of curiosity. 'First rule of business, boy: grab every chance you get.'

'I don't understand.' But now a horrible sickness was swirling in Joe's stomach.

'There *is* no healing potion,' said Old Hans. 'I'm not a Hag.'

'What? But . . . you said!'

'I said what you wanted to hear so you'd do what I wanted you to do,' said Old Hans, rolling his eyes in their sunken sockets as if he was explaining the simplest thing in the world. 'Now look here, Joe, consider this a lesson, right? Everybody in this world will use you for somethin' if you let 'em. I used you tonight, but I'm not a monster. I'll pay you.' He brought out a single gold coin, placed it on the counter, slid it towards Joe.

Joe stared at it. 'That's not enough.' Fury was beginning to stoke a fire in his chest. 'I'd need much more to buy a potion on the black market. You know that!'

Old Hans chewed on the inside of his cheek. 'Final offer,' he said, placing a silver coin on top of the gold one.

'Still not enough!' Joe's eyes were watering, burning. He stared at Old Hans, and then at the urn.

Slowly, very slowly, Old Hans reached beneath the counter and brought out a knife. 'Don't do anythin' daft, Joe.'

Joe's insides were ablaze with anger. He made a foolish grab for the urn, but Old Hans cracked him on the shoulder with the handle of the knife and Joe stumbled back, crashing hard into a display cabinet. First it rocked back, almost fell over, then it rocked forwards, gathering momentum, sending Joe ducking out of the way.

'No!' Old Hans threw himself over the urn as the cabinet came crashing down on top of him with the sounds of smashing plates and snapping wood and a short, sharp cry of pain. Then nothing.

'Old Hans?' Joe snuck forward, peering beneath the cabinet. Old Hans was slumped and unconscious, and the sight of him caused a stab of fear in Joe's chest. Was he dead? The thought of that made Joe feel sick. It had been an accident! He reached in, pressed his fingers to Old Hans' neck, and felt for a pulse. Alive! The old git was alive, thank Lady Light! Putting every muscle on his wiry little frame to work, Joe tipped the cabinet off the old man, who groaned and started to stir. Then Joe grabbed the urn, tucked it in his coat and ran out of the shop.

THE WAND GROVE

When word of the High Witch's passing spread around the city of Westerly Witch, black smoke began to breathe from every chimney, shrouding the Mother Tree and surrounding islands in a fog of sadness.

Bernie Whitecrow, now dressed all in black in mourning for the High Witch and her beloved husband, wasted no time in following her predecessor's final orders – to ensure that Lara had a wand to begin her training.

'Double Eight too,' she said, leading them out of the palace and down level after level of the Mother Tree, towards the base. Everywhere they went, people dropped to their knees in reverence. 'I wish they'd stop bowing. Will everyone just stop bowing!'

'What should we call you?' asked Double Eight, giving Lara a sly wink. 'I've never met a queen before.'

'Well, what a question! Call me Bernie, same as always.'

'Where are we going?'

'To the Wand Grove.'

'The what?'

'You'll see.'

Through carved streets and over rickety platforms and round wooden towers they went. It was a city, just like King's Haven; there was the same buzz of life and activity, but here the people wore long Witch coats and the shops sold potions and strange and wonderful spells. There were jars of pickled creatures in many of the windows, and powders and glowing crystals. Witch paper messages flew overhead constantly. Strange creeping vines grew over many of the buildings, and flocks of birds would fly in and perch on the vines to eat their purple fruit. It occurred to Lara that the Mother Tree was not just something upon which a city was built. It *was* the city, a living, breathing thing, connected to every soul who lived upon it. Even after only a day here she could begin to feel that strong connection, that tether to the Mother Tree and her magical Blossom.

They came to one of the rope bridges connecting the Mother Tree to the surrounding islands, and as they crossed, the Pewter Sea lapping far below, Lara could see someone waiting at the halfway point. When they were close enough, Bernie burst into a wide smile.

'Rob! Rob Nielsen!'

He came striding towards them, his eyes sparkling and a smile spreading beneath his huge beard. Bernie threw her arms around him, and he looked both surprised and uneasy.

'Hell's teeth, Bernie. I don't think a common old sea

dog like me should be hugging Your Majesty the High Witch.'

'Oh, don't you start, Rob Nielsen!'

Rob turned very serious. 'I'm awful sorry about Magnus. I feel . . .' he looked at his big feet. 'I'm the only one who made it. I clung to some driftwood and I tried to get to him in the water, but the tide . . . the storm was too much. I should have been braver. I should have swum out and . . .'

Bernie swallowed, taking a deep breath. 'And then you'd both be dead, Rob, and what good could you do then? My Magnus . . . I love him with everything I am, but he died fighting for something he believed in, for freedom, and he'd be happy with that. I will mourn him, Rob, but right now I can hear him yelling at us to finish the damned job, so that's what we must do. We must make sure he didn't die for nothing.'

Rob walked with them across the remainder of the bridge.

'Have you thought about electing a new council?'

'I have. And I will soon enough. I'd like you to be on it, Rob.'

Rob's hands clasped over his heart. 'I'd . . . why, I'd be honoured, Bernie. Thank you.'

Off the bridge now, they came upon a huge, church-like structure. Inside was a great hall, filled with the statues of many past High Witches, mostly standing with their wands drawn. Little flames burned at the tips.

'You ready?' asked Bernie, coming to a grand set of doors at the back of the hall.

'For what?' said Lara.

Bernie threw open the doors, revealing a sprawling woodland carpeted with fallen leaves. The trees were tall and wide, their branches long, hanging fingers. The fruits of the trees were small and round, like berries, and they glowed every colour Lara had ever seen. The sound of magic tinkled in the air, and the scent of frost and sap made Lara think of winter. The effect of the place was startling. A warmth spread through her every thought. As if answering the call of the magic, Moonwing came out from Lara's pocket and swooped around the trees.

'You feel that?' Lara asked.

Double Eight looked back at her, his dark straggly hair standing up in the charged air. 'What is it?'

'It's the trees,' said Rob Nielsen. 'They're talking to you. Callin' to you. Listen to 'em. Let 'em guide you.'

Double Eight looked puzzled. 'I already have a wand. The White Witches gave me one.'

Bernie Whitecrow snorted. 'A wand? Don't make me laugh, boy! The White Witches don't know how to make proper wands. They don't have trees like these. That wand you had might have been fine for makin' White Witch spells, but you wait, Double Eight, till you have a real, wild wand in your hand. Now go on, the pair of you. Choose a branch.' Bernie shooed them away, and they walked among the trees, staring up at the branches and their glowing orbs of fruit. Lara let the branches brush her hair, and she felt sparks of magic run through her.

'There're so many!' said Double Eight. 'I want all of them. How do we choose?'

One branch sent a wave of magic so strongly through Lara she almost fell over. 'This one!' She reached up and snapped the branch from the tree, and when she held it in her hand the sound of magic rose to a chorus of crystal voices.

Double Eight picked his wand from a tree further across the grove, and when he came back a huge smile was breaking across his face. He waved the branch this way and that.

'Good,' said Bernie. 'I'll get them to the wandsmith tonight. Congratulations, Lara, Double Eight. You're real Witches now.'

Jack's Back

Lara was given a room in the palace atop the Mother Tree. That night, after a meal of freshly baked bread and fried fish with herbs and butter, she retired to her chamber, her head filled with so many thoughts and wonderings she thought they might begin to leak from her ears.

A knock on the door. Lara let Bernie Whitecrow and Double Eight into the room.

'Thought we'd see how you're settling,' said Bernie.

'Hey. Your room is bigger than mine!' said Double Eight.

'I'm fine I guess,' said Lara, though she could tell Bernie was watching her closely, as if she was trying to see inside her head. 'I mean . . . I think I'm fine. So much has happened. The High Witch, and getting my own wand . . . and . . . and the message from my mum . . .'

Bernie went to the balcony of Lara's room, lit a cigar, and they stood together and looked out from the top of the great tree over a night sky that was natural.

'The Evernight won't stay back for ever, will it?' said Lara.

'No, love. When it's strong enough it'll come for us.'

'You think the Painted are at King's Haven yet?'

'I honestly don't know.'

'I keep thinkin' about Joe and Granny and . . . and all the poor people there. I want to help them.'

'You think you can?' said Double Eight.

Moonwing came down from somewhere high in the branches, landing on her shoulder. Lara stroked him, and with her other hand she held the locket.

'Mum was in the Doomsday Coven. It was her duty to protect Moonwing, to use the Spell if it was ever needed. And she passed that duty to me.'

Bernie took a deep breath, letting it out slowly. 'We're all right beside you, Lara.'

'But I don't know what to do!'

'Well that's why you have friends, Lara. To help you.'

Lara felt hot tears spill from her eyes. 'I'm frightened. Mum said something. She said . . . she said something about using my soul to make the spell work.'

Something else was bothering her too, eating into every thought. Mum had said that if Lara ever did use the spell, she might not come back. What did that mean? Was she going to die? Did she have to give up her soul for ever? As troubled as she was, Lara could not tell Bernie or Double Eight about this, because there was enough to

280

worry about, wasn't there? And Bernie had lost so much already . . .

There was a long silence.

'If I was to guess,' said Bernie, 'I'd say that the Coven were all connected to Moonwing through their souls. That must be why he only comes to life when you're around. It's genius, really. It means nobody outside the Coven can ever use it while any member of the Coven is still alive. That's why they were hunted, I'm afraid: to send their souls to the next life and break the connection with the spell. And it's why you're in danger.'

They stood in silence, watching the milky band of stars twinkle across the sky.

'I'm sorry about Magnus,' said Lara.

'Me too,' said Double Eight.

Bernie's lips trembled. 'First time I ever met him he told me he was going to marry me. We were in the south, helping a group of Witches holed up in a dusty little town to escape the oncoming Argent Army. I laughed in his face that day. But I reckon I knew it was true even then.' She wiped her eyes. 'I'm sorry about your mum, Lara. I'm sorry you got dragged into all this.'

They hugged, the three friends, and cried beneath the stars.

Bernie said, 'It's our job to honour them now. To be strong and finish what they started. Get some sleep, my dears. Tomorrow is another day, eh? And you've a wand to get.'

Lara watched the old Witch leave, but Double Eight hung back.

'You all right?' Lara asked him.

'Yeah.' He looked a little embarrassed. 'Um . . . I didn't know my parents either. White Witches are taken away as soon as we're born. I've probably walked past my mum in the street and never even knew it.'

'That's awful,' said Lara.

'I just want to tell you that I understand how you feel. What it's like to grow up not knowing who you are. But we're not alone any more. And we can be whoever we want to be.'

Lara walked to Double Eight and hugged him tight. 'Thank you.'

She stayed on the balcony for a while after he left, wrapped up warm, breathing the night air. Moonwing spun swiftly through the branches, the gold of his wings catching the light, and Lara chuckled at his antics as he played, until tiredness weighed heavy on her and she went inside.

Time for bed. Tomorrow she'd get her wand, and—

The sound of silk wings, of something heavy landing on the balcony.

Lara spun around and saw the shadowless man come towards her. Before she could scream, before she could do anything, he cracked his fist on the side of her head, and down she went, the room splitting into many fractured shards.

'No,' she managed to say, reaching out, realising he held Moonwing tight in his hand. He kicked her hand away, put his foot on her throat, and she gasped and choked as he pressed down.

'No more running,' he told her. 'Shadow Jack's here and it's time to end this. Don't struggle, girl.'

Something nightmarish happened then; the shadowless man opened his jaw so wide it seemed his face would tear in two. In the vast dark cave of his mouth there were rows and rows of needle-sharp teeth. He made a hungry, slurping sound, and Lara felt a terrible pain in her chest, felt part of herself ripping away, coming loose. She tried to scream, but she could not gather the air. There was a hollow, empty ache deep in her chest, and she knew, with a moment of terrifying clarity, that he was taking her soul . . .

It began to leave her, to break through her flesh; she could see it, the glow of it, and staring into his dark mouth was like staring into a place beyond time, beyond the world she knew . . .

A Parting

'Joe! Joe!'

Joe Littlefoot heard Granny's calls from halfway up the stairs, and he dashed the rest of the way two steps at a time and burst through the tenement door. The candle was out. The flat was in pitch darkness. Joe fumbled to the bed, banging his shin, cursing, and found Granny sitting up in bed, clawing at the air as if trying to fend off a fire wasp.

'Granny!'

'Joe! My Joe! Where is he?'

Joe tried to calm her. Her skin was burning up, her eyes wild with confusion and fever. He scrabbled around for his toshing lamp – there was a tiny bit of dragon breath left in it and he lit that. As his eyes adjusted to the gloom, he saw a slow trickle of blood running from Granny's nose.

'It's me, Granny,' he said, holding her tight. 'Look. It's your Joe.'

She looked like she might strike him, but then she seemed to calm, and her eyes rested on the urn, which had dropped onto the bed from Joe's coat. When she saw it the most remarkable thing happened: Granny shut her eyes tight, and when she opened them again she was lucid.

'She's in trouble, Joe. You have to help her!'

'Who, Granny?'

'The Witch-girl!'

'The W— Lara? You mean Lara?'

Granny's entire body suddenly jerked and stiffened.

Joe leaned over her, holding her rigid hand. She was trying to say something, trying to speak in a stuttering whisper.

'U-u-ur-urn.'

'Urn?'

'O-op-p-pen.'

'Open . . . open the urn?'

Granny squeezed his hand so tight he thought his fingers might snap.

'Granny!'

'Now! Open it NOW!'

Not knowing what else to do, Joe grabbed for the urn. He tried to pull the lid off, but it was stuck.

'The shapes. Follow the shapes, Joe . . .'

He examined the urn, his heart pounding, his guts squirming and writhing. He used a finger to trace over the markings on the ceramic, and he heard a click from the lid. Joe reached for the lid of the urn and pulled it open . . .

*

. . . In Westerly Witch Shadow Jack's eyes grew wide, not with pleasure at eating Lara's soul, but something else. His foot left her throat, and she felt clean cold air rush into her lungs. He straightened up, and closed his mouth, and the terrible ripping, tearing feeling inside her chest faded.

Shadow Jack stared at his hands, looking from one to the other. Moonwing flapped and struggled, but Shadow Jack managed to stuff him in his pocket and fasten the button. Then the edges of him blurred, falling away like sand in an hourglass. More of him disintegrated into a strange dust, which swirled in a column, a dry wind stinging Lara's eyes. She tried to scramble away on her back, watching in fear and confusion as Shadow Jack turned all to dust, which scattered to the night.

Shadow Jack, somehow, was gone.

And so was Moonwing.

Joe's little tenement filled with harsh flashes of light, and in the middle of the room a swirl of black sand appeared, spinning so fast the wind from it shook the rickety windows. The black column of sand spun and spun, until it became a shape, the shape of a tall man. The sand fell away, and the wind died.

Joe stared disbelievingly at the man in black now standing in his dim flat. He remembered his crowbar and grabbed it from his toshing bag. The man in black stared back at Joe, and to Joe's astonishment the man bowed his head and dropped to one knee as if Joe was the Silver King himself.

'Holder of the urn, I live to serve you.'

Joe noticed that the man in black did not have a shadow, and at once he was back in the sewers, frightened for his life, and he knew this was the Sewer Strangler.

'It's you!' Joe rushed at him, swung the bar, but the man simply turned to shadow and reappeared behind him.

'I was serving another master.'

Joe took another swing at him. 'Mrs Hester, you mean?'

'Yes.' He pointed to the urn. 'But now you are my master. I am Shadow Jack, and it's my duty – my curse – to serve you to the end of the world and beyond, until the day you tell me I am free.'

Joe was about to swing again when a soft moan turned his attention back to the bed. Granny held out a trembling hand, and Joe grabbed it.

'You did it, Joe. You saved her.' The old woman's eyes rolled forward, and fixed on her grandson, and she smiled. 'It's so dark . . . but you can help Lara fix it, you know. It's in you to do that. You have the power now. Free their souls, Joe. Let 'em fly. You were always a good boy. Always good. They're in the mirror, Joe. Smash the mirror . . .'

And then, holding Joe's hand, Granny closed her eyes for the last time.

ARRIVAL

All over the slums of King's Haven, where the roadblocks had been set up to cage the poor, there were terrible signs of growing desperation. The piles of bodies around the fences grew as starving, freezing people tried to climb them and were cut down by bullets from coppers' pistols. The coppers themselves had been threatened with death by the Silver King if they were to let a single soul through, and so they stood firm.

The morning after Granny died and Joe became Shadow Jack's master, the stars began to go out in King's Haven. As is often the case with important things, the children noticed first. It was as if the stars were candles, and someone was going around the heavens snuffing them out one by one. When only the moon remained, the people of the slums – abandoned by their king – stood in the streets and begged their Gods, Lady Light, Mother Earth and whoever else might be listening, to help them. Their Gods were not listening.

The moon blinked once, twice, faded, and was gone. The sky was nothing but a vast, empty blackness, a hole that seemed to reach down and swallow everything. Clinging to each other, to the few lamps and candles they had left, the people of the slums began to scream.

The coppers at the roadblock fences took one look at the blackness above and abandoned their positions.

Nobody noticed the armada of black ships sailing, unlit, into the harbour. With their eyes turned to the sky, the slum folk only saw the Painted when it was too late.

The Painted swarmed through the slums, carving their dark spells into the flesh of the poor who dwelt there, deleting their memories, connecting them with the hive mind, so that their only thoughts were of the Evernight.

Tens of thousands bottlenecked at the alleys and roads. And the panic spread . . .

The palace was mostly empty. Only the king, Mrs Hester and a handful of servants had remained when the others had evacuated. Now the king stared up at the smothering black sky, starless, moonless, his fat hands grabbing at the walls to steady himself. The sight of it had made him weak. His shrivelled heart shrunk further in his chest.

A hand rested on his shoulder, and he jumped.

'Time for you to go, Your Majesty,' said Mrs Hester. 'The Painted have reached the slums.'

The king nodded. 'Yes. Yes, I think you are right. Give

the order. Evacuate the rest of the palace.' He went to the door, stopped, and looked back at her. 'Do you think we have made a mistake?'

Mrs Hester smiled.

'No, Your Majesty. We've played this just right.'

'And you're sure you can control this thing when it's done what we need it to do?'

'Yes, Your Majesty.'

If you only knew, she thought.

Joe Littlefoot had wrapped Granny's body in clean sheets and now he stood by the bed, his head bowed.

'I'm sorry for your loss, master,' said Shadow Jack.

'Don't call me that. I'm nobody's master.'

'You hold the urn,' said Shadow Jack. 'Whoever holds the urn is my master – until the day my master sets me free.' He scoffed, as if he knew that this would never happen, and his eyes became dark pools of sorrow. Joe was about to ask him to elaborate, but he stopped, and tilted his head, listening.

Through the window, the eerie, freezing quiet of the slums had given way to the sound of a mob.

Joe went to the window, threw it open and looked up at the sky. 'The stars are gone!'

'The Painted are coming, master,' said Shadow Jack. 'You should leave. I can take you anywhere.'

Joe stared out at the city; most of the streetlamps were

out now, and King's Haven was a collection of towering shadows. 'Is it over? Are we finished?'

Shadow Jack reached into his pocket and brought out a splendid clockwork bird, made of gold and wood and brass. It lay still in his palm, shining and gleaming in the light of the dimming toshing lamp. Joe reached out to touch the cold, fine metal of the bird's wings. 'What is it?'

'It's a way to stop the Evernight,' said Shadow Jack. 'A spell. Mrs Hester sent me to get it. It was part of her plan.'

'Plan?'

'She is the one who brought the Evernight back.'

'Why would she do that?'

'To kill the Hags. And to become the saviour of the world.'

Joe stared at Shadow Jack's bone-coloured face. 'She's mad.'

'Yes. She is. But I no longer serve her.'

'And we can sort this? That bird can help, that's what you said . . .'

'Yes. But it hasn't moved since I took it away from the last member of the secret Coven charged with protecting it. Until she dies, and her soul leaves this existence, the Fox girl is the only person who can use the spell.'

Joe gasped. 'Lara? Do you mean Larabelle Fox? I can't believe it!' He stared around. 'You need to take it to her.'

Shadow Jack gave an ironic smile. An hour ago he had been about to kill Larabelle Fox, and now he was going to have to find her all over again and, this time, probably protect her. He wondered if he'd ever be free. 'Very well.'

'Wait! Before you go . . .' Granny's last words were still ringing in his ears. *Smash the mirror.* 'Mrs Hester . . . she has a mirror in her tower, right?'

'Yes.'

'Only it's not just a mirror, is it? There's a room inside it. I've seen it. She keeps things in there, glowing things in cages.'

'Souls,' said Shadow Jack. 'White Witch souls. It's how she controls them.'

Joe nodded, staring up towards the palace. He opened his toshing bag. Inside was Shadow Jack's urn. Joe held it up. 'Can you get me to that mirror?'

'Of course.'

'And after that take the bird back to Lara?'

'Anything you wish.'

'Right. Good.' Joe turned the small urn in his hands. 'Nobody should belong to someone else. It's not right. I need your help, but when this is done, I'll set you free. That's a promise.'

THE WITCH GATE

When Lara opened her eyes, the first thing she wondered was why there was such pain in the side of her face. The second thing she wondered was why she had gone to sleep on the floor. Then her brain fizzed into life, and the memories came back. *Shadow Jack!* He'd been squeezing the life out of her before he vanished. She must have lost consciousness.

She jumped to her feet, holding her swollen cheek. 'Moonwing?' Dashing to the balcony, she looked around frantically. 'Moonwing! Moonwing!' It felt like her heart had frozen. Dizzy, Lara ran for the door, exploding out into the passageway. 'Bernie! Bernie!'

Double Eight came rushing out of a nearby room. 'Lara? What's happened to your face?'

'Bernie! I need to see Bernie! He's gone.'

'Who?'

'He's gone, Double Eight! Bernie!'

Bernie came hurrying up the passageway, and when she

saw Lara's bruised, swollen face she inhaled sharply. 'Lara, love!'

Lara ran to her, throwing her arms around her. 'Bernie! Oh, Bernie I'm so sorry. I tried to stop him, but I couldn't. He's gone!'

'Mother Earth's flaming nostrils, child! Who? Who is gone?'

'Moonwing!'

Lara felt the old Witch take a sharp breath. Then Bernie gently broke from Lara's grip, placing a hand on her shoulder, looking her right in the eye. 'Calm down, love. Breathe. That's it. Now tell me, what happened?'

Lara recounted the events of the previous night.

'He came here? To Westerly Witch? How dare he!'

'I'm so sorry.'

Bernie shook her head. 'I'm the one that's sorry. I never should have left you alone. But I never thought . . . I never *dreamed* you wouldn't be safe here.'

'What do we do?' Double Eight asked.

Hurrying footsteps approached, and Bastien Stone came rushing up the hall, puffing and panting. 'Bernie. You must come quick!'

'What now?'

'The Painted. The Evernight. They've reached King's Haven, Bernie. They're raising an army!'

Bernie's face lost what was left of its colour. 'You sure?'

He nodded.

Bernie Whitecrow buried her face in her hands. 'Right,' she said, pointing at Bastien. 'Find Rob Nielsen. Tell him to meet us at the wandsmith's.'

The wandsmith worked down in the bowels of the Mother Tree, his workshop nestled and entangled among the great roots. His name was Eli Wolfback, and he was a short but powerfully-built red-haired Witch with a button nose and small black eyes.

'It ain't usual,' he said, scowling at Bernie, 'to turn around a wand as quick as this.'

'I know that, Eli,' said Bernie. 'But you must.'

Eli scoffed, looked from Lara to Double Eight as if it was their fault that he was being so inconvenienced. It occurred to Lara that Eli Wolfback was the sort of person who thought his work was the most important thing in all the world. She wondered if he even knew about the Evernight.

Eli Wolfback disappeared for a moment behind rows of great shelves stacked with branches and wands at all different stages of completion. When he came back he was holding two branches of similar length and thickness, stripped of their bark and lacquered and fitted with handles made of bone. The end of one handle had been roughly carved in the shape of a fox's head, and the other a lion.

'They're beautiful,' said Lara.

'They're half-done is what they are,' mumbled Eli.

'Well then let's get 'em finished,' said Bernie, and Eli gave her such an indignant look Lara would have laughed in other circumstances.

He took the wands to a work bench and, one at a time, began the process of hollowing them out. His big freckled hands worked so delicately, so quickly, that Lara was bewitched. The tool for hollowing the wands was very thin and fragile-looking. When both wands were ready, Eli Wolfback went away and returned with two revolver chambers made of shining silvery metal. He fitted the chambers to each wand, lining them up precisely so that when they spun, the spell in the top chamber would fit perfectly in the barrel of the wand. Finally, he took both wands to the furnace and opened the door. Inside, white flames licked and leaped, and a baking, searing heat made Lara shield her face. Eli Wolfback did not seem to feel the scorch, though. He slid the wands into this oven, closed the door, and folded his arms, tapping his foot on the floor and waiting in silence.

Next he slipped a pair of big padded gloves on, opened the door and grabbed the wands. Then he tossed them into a barrel of cold water, where they hissed and steamed. At last, Eli Wolfback brought the wands out of the water, examined them, and shrugged.

'Not my best work, but what do you expect in such a hurry?'

He handed the wand with the fox handle to Lara, and

the lion to Double Eight. The heat of the magical furnace had made the bone handles smooth, and the wooden barrels of the wands had hardened and dried out. Lara took the wand – her wand – in her hands and smiled down at it. The feel of it was warm and good and right.

'It's simple enough to fire,' said Eli. He brought out two spell bottles, loading one into a chamber on each wand. 'Right . . . hold the wand natural-like in your hand. Good. Now, to spin the chamber, twist your wrist to the right.'

Lara and Double Eight did as he asked. Sure enough, the revolver chamber clicked around one notch with every twist of the wrist.

'You'll find a button on the handle, under your fingers. Yes?'

Lara and Double Eight nodded.

'Good. The button is to load the spell into the chamber. Once you've done that it's live. Try it.'

Lara felt for the button, pressed it, felt a heavy click. The spell flared bright in the revolver chamber and locked up into the barrel.

'To fire,' said Eli Wolfback, 'aim your wand and press the trigger. Got it?'

'What should we aim at?' asked Lara.

'Each other,' said Eli.

Lara and Double Eight exchanged doubtful looks, and then raised their wands and pulled the triggers.

Jets of cold water shot out of the wand tips, splashing them in the face.

'Hell's teeth!' yelled Lara, covering her face with a sleeve.

'Ha!' Double Eight brandished the wand, his water jet growing more powerful.

'Oi!' Lara spat. 'Enough!'

'To stop the spell, just let go of the trigger,' said Eli. 'The bottle will stop glowing when the spell is spent.'

Lara stopped the flow of water, wrung out her hair and stared at the wand in her hand with hushed disbelief. In all her life she had never imagined she'd ever be involved in the world of Witches and magic. Now here she was, in Westerly Witch, holding her very own wand.

'It's far more powerful than a White Witch wand,' said Double Eight, blinking away water and looking quite amazed. 'You can feel the magic buzzing through it, just waiting to get out.'

'Oh, Mother Earth we're in trouble now!' Rob Nielsen stood in the doorway, hands on hips, smiling at the sight of the two young Witches with their new wands.

'It's good to see you, Rob,' said Bernie. 'But there isn't much time. You've heard that the Painted are in King's Haven?'

'Yes, I was coming to speak to you about it.'

He glanced at Lara and Double Eight, unsure whether to carry on speaking in front of them.

'It's all right, Rob,' Bernie reassured him. 'Tell me what you wanted to say.'

'They're rampaging through the slums, destroying minds with their dark magic, building an army to wipe us out. I've had word from a friend at the docks – it's carnage.'

Lara tugged at Bernie's sleeve. 'We need to do something! My friend Joe's there! We need to stop them somehow. We must beat the Evernight.'

Bernie gave Lara a grave look. 'My dear, you're right. But without Moonwing I'm not sure how we can.'

'I've seen what Mrs Hester can do,' said Double Eight, his face colourless. 'If she's got Moonwing, she'll work out a way to use him. What if she ends up in control of the Evernight? She'd be unstoppable.'

'I've no doubt she's arrogant enough to try it,' said Bernie, 'but I've been reading everything I can find about the Doomsday Spell all night and I don't think she can. Not while Lara still lives. It needs a member of the Coven. It needs *you*, Lara. We need to return to King's Haven and retrieve the spell.'

'Aye,' said Rob.

'Rob,' said Bernie, 'I've called on you many a time to smuggle me in and out and protect me in the city. Can I count on you once more?'

'Do you even have to ask?' he said.

'Thank you. Lara, you may be young and inexperienced, but Hell's teeth, girl, you're brave and resourceful and I need you. Will you join us?'

Lara forced a smile, and felt terrified and honoured all at the same time. They were going after the Spell, and it would be up to her to use it. Did that mean giving up her soul? And if it did, would Lara ever be coming back?

'What about me?' asked Double Eight.

Bernie raised an eyebrow.

'Yes, me! I want to come too.'

'It's too dangerous, Double Eight. Lara wouldn't be coming if it wasn't for her connection to the Spell. Stay here, where it's safe.'

'If you fail then this place isn't safe either. You risked so much to save me, Bernie. You lost so much too. I want to pay you back . . . you and Magnus.' He scratched at his face, searching for the right words. 'Look . . . I'm a White Witch, I've served Mrs Hester, I might be able to help. You saved me so I could make my own choices. Let me make this one.'

'It's a good point,' said Rob.

Double Eight shot him a grateful look.

'I'd feel better if he was with us,' said Lara.

Bernie looked Double Eight dead in the eye. 'Don't make me regret this.'

'Oh, I won't, Bernie. Thank you!'

'I'm certain,' Bernie went on, 'Hester sent Shadow Jack to get Moonwing. If we find her, we find the spell. It'll be dangerous, my loves, and we might not all come back, but we must think of those who have died to get us this far – your mum, Lara, and my Magnus, and all the others. We must finish it so no one else has to make the sacrifice our friends did. Are you with me?'

Lara thought of her mum, of the message she'd left behind. Of her duty. *We might not all come back.* Could Bernie sense what was coming? Did she have an idea that Lara might have to give up her life? Lara looked at Double Eight, and he set his wiry jaw and nodded.

'Of course we're with you, Bernie.'

'You know I'm with you,' said Rob Nielsen.

Bernie smiled around at them.

'Well then,' she said, 'there's work to do. Let's get to the gate.'

Before they'd left the wandsmith's workshop, Eli Wolfback had given them each a thick leather belt with a place to tuck the wand and many compartments in which to keep spells. As they walked, Lara and Double Eight practised drawing their wands and firing.

'I wish there was time to give you both more training,' said Bernie. 'But I'm afraid the situation is so dire we'll have to make do. Just stick close.'

Off the bridge now, onto the little island. As they climbed to the highest point a circle of standing stones came into view. Dragon-breath lamps stood around the stones, and beside them sat the statue of a creature larger than an ironheart, with the body and tail of a lion and the head and wings of an eagle. When they were almost upon it, the statue stood up with a rumble and fixed them with its eagle eyes.

'It's all right, Griff,' said Bernie gently. 'It's just me. Just old Bernie.'

'What *is* that thing?' asked Lara.

'He guards the gate, don't you, Griff?' Bernie took another step towards the stone griffin, and she reached out slowly and began to stroke his head and beak. Griff rubbed against her hand and let out a deep, stony rumble. 'We need to get to King's Haven, Griff. You can see my thoughts. You know how important it is.'

The great beast looked deep in Bernie's eyes and then moved towards the stone circle. With its beak it touched each of the seven stones as it passed. When the seventh stone had been touched, the island shook, and the ground in the middle of the circle gave way, revealing a deep hole. A strange, warm wind came from the hole in the earth, and distant, jumbled sounds – voices, maybe, and thunder, and magic . . .

'It's a one-way trip,' said Bernie, 'unless you're going somewhere with stones on the other side, which we're not. You ready?'

'No,' said Lara.

'Not in the slightest,' said Double Eight.

Bernie took their hands, and walked forward, to the edge of the gate; the noise was rumbling and thunderous, and Lara looked down to see a swirling darkness. Rob

Nielsen stepped forward first, falling down into the gate and spinning out of sight.

Bernie's grip tightened, and over the roar she yelled, 'On three? Right! One . . . two . . . THREE!'

Together, they jumped.

HESTER'S TOWER

When Shadow Jack had become a great raven, Joe had steadfastly refused to fly. So the shadowless man had instead transformed into a huge black dog, and carried Joe first through the panic and chaos of the slums, and then the eerie quiet of the rest of the city. He had taken the palace wall in a single leap, and walked through the solid door to Hester's tower, unlocking it from the inside for Joe to enter.

The palace was deserted. Mrs Hester was not in her rooms. Joe went to the window and saw buildings on fire. As Shadow Jack had carried him, he had caught glimpses in the darkness of the Painted, huge and long-armed, stalking the streets. Distant screams and yells drifted up to the tower. He broke away from the window and went through to the next chamber. There, in the centre of the room, was Hester's mirror. He approached it, reached out and touched the surface. This time the glass stayed solid, and he could hear no sounds from the other side. Turning to Shadow Jack, he brought the toshing bag down from his shoulder and took the urn out.

Shadow Jack stared hungrily at it.

'You just have to take the bird to Lara,' said Joe. 'After that, you're free. I promise.'

Mrs Hester moved quickly through the deserted palace towards her tower. She had seen the king off safely, and despite his insistence that she go with him to the south, she had wanted to stay in King's Haven a little longer. She wished to see for herself if the Painted were as terrible as the legends said. And she had hoped that Shadow Jack would have arrived with the Doomsday Spell by now.

Something else had gone wrong. She could feel it. For the first time she allowed true fear into her body, let herself really think about what might happen if she didn't secure the Spell.

She closed her eyes, breathed deep. No. She wasn't going to lose. Things would work out. It was just taking a little longer than she'd prefer. For now it was time to leave. When he had the Spell, Shadow Jack would have to find her wherever she was.

Up the stairs of the tower she went, ready to collect her belongings, to leave the palace and the city. Up to the highest door. She reached for the handle, opened the door, and . . .

*

. . . Joe stared disbelievingly as the urn floated out of his hands. He turned to look at Shadow Jack, but Shadow Jack was not looking back at him; he was staring at the door, where Mrs Hester was pointing her wand at the urn, a mad look of joy on her face. Slowly, the urn floated into her waiting hands. She turned her head to Shadow Jack, and Joe saw the man's shoulders slump.

Shadow Jack dropped to one knee in front of her.

'No,' said Joe. 'He was going to be free!'

Mrs Hester laughed coldly. 'Free? Oh, my dear little sewer rat! He's never going to be free!' She flicked her wand at Joe, and a spell blazed bright. A rope of red fire wrapped around him, tossing him whiplike across the room. He landed on his back, the wind all knocked out of his chest.

Gasping on the floor, Joe watched as Shadow Jack reached into his pocket and pulled out the bird made of clockwork and gold and wood. 'No!' He tried to scramble up, but Mrs Hester hit him with another spell. She approached the bird as if it was the most wondrous object she'd ever seen. She took it from Shadow Jack with gentle hands and examined every gleaming part of it. Her eyes narrowed, and she poked at it as if trying to wake it up.

'Why is it not moving?'

Shadow Jack paused. He looked at Joe. 'I was . . . interrupted before I could finish the girl.'

Mrs Hester rubbed her eyes wearily. 'She's still *alive*?'

'Yes.'

Hester slapped Shadow Jack across the face. For a moment it seemed as if he was going to lose his cool, that he would strike back. But the fire in his eyes died.

'I'm sorry,' was all he said.

'You will be.' Hester made to slap him again, but she stopped when she saw the look on his face. 'What is it?'

Shadow Jack began to sniff at the air like a dog. He had caught a scent, and his nose led him past Joe, to the window. He turned back, and said with a puzzled frown, 'She's here.'

'*What?*'

'The girl. She's back in the city.'

Hester approached him, standing face to face, and poked his chest with a long finger. 'You sure?'

'I am.'

'Then take me to her. This time I'll finish the job myself.'

'What about the boy?' said Shadow Jack.

Mrs Hester stared at Joe, who was once again on his feet, thinking of Lara, wanting to protect her as she had protected him for so long.

'We could let him go,' said Shadow Jack. 'He's harmless.'

'We could,' said Mrs Hester. 'We *could* do that.' She moved towards Joe, and quick as a blink, she pulled a small knife from her coat and stabbed him in the gut.

Joe folded in half, pain coursing through him, and

crumpled to the floor. He reached out a desperate, shaking hand to Shadow Jack. 'Help . . .'

Shadow Jack looked down at him, and his face was blank.

'Come,' said Mrs Hester. 'Take me to the girl.'

BACK TO THE SEWERS

As the world reformed around Lara, an arrow flew past her face. The air from it brushed her cheek. The first few moments after travelling through a Witch Gate were full of confusion and bewilderment, and the wall of noise that met her, the screams and thunderous bangs, the smells of gunpowder and fire, only compounded this.

A hand grabbed Lara by the elbow, spinning her around, and she looked up into the face of Rob Nielsen. Behind him, Bernie Whitecrow was shaking the confusion away, and Double Eight was tilting his head to one side as if trying to empty his ear of water.

Rob Nielsen seemed the most aware of the surrounding danger; he shepherded everyone to the shadows. 'We all safe and well?'

'Safe?' said Bernie. 'Safe? Look around you, man!'

The fog in Lara's mind had evaporated. The Witch Gate had brought them out in the slums. Everywhere she looked she saw the flickering light of the Painted's lamps falling upon bodies on the ground, and upon the nightmarish Painted themselves, carving marks on the flesh of poor slum folk, turning them, to Lara's horror, into mad creatures that bit and scratched and slashed at anything that was not a Painted. Those who had not yet been marked grabbed anything they could find to use as weapons. Some had pistols, or knives, or even swords, while others were swinging garden forks and table legs and hammers. When Lara looked up at the sky and saw that the stars were gone, she felt her heart shrivel.

A crowd of cursed slum folk spotted them and came running at Lara and the others, foaming at the mouths, teeth flashing like animals. Bernie loaded her wand quick, sent a spell out at them, a web that pinned them to a wall. The commotion attracted the attention of more marked folk, and of the Painted.

'Here!' said Bernie, tossing Lara and Double Eight spell bottles. 'Load 'em in your chambers. They'll shoot bullets of sunlight at the Painted.' She fired her own as Lara and Double Eight loaded their wands with shaking hands. A burning blade of light erupted from the end of Rob Nielsen's wand, and he swung it, cutting the head off one of the Painted's shoulders.

Bernie led the way down an alleyway. As Lara ran, she heard footsteps closing behind. Remembering the wandsmith's instructions, she turned and shot a blazing bullet of sunlight at a chasing Painted. It was a wild shot, but it hit him in the leg, turning it to ash, and he fell.

Down an alleyway they ran, trapping more enchanted slum folk with magical webs, twisting this way and that through the streets, until it seemed they had a few moments' respite.

'The sewer!' said Lara, remembering suddenly that this was *her* city. 'We can use the sewers. I'll get us to the palace that way.'

Bernie brought an angry-looking orange spell out of her big coat, loaded it into the revolver chamber of her wand, and shot the spell at the nearest drain cover. It exploded, leaving a ragged hole in the street.

'Go!' Lara told Double Eight. 'You'll be fine, I promise.'

Double Eight stared down at the black hole and gave Lara a doubtful look.

'I'll be right behind you. I've spent most of my life down there . . .'

'And didn't *you* turn out just fine,' said Double Eight. He climbed awkwardly into the sewer. Lara was next. Just as she was about to duck her head under, Rob yelled a warning to Bernie. A wave of Painted came flooding into the alley. Bernie spun around, tossing a spell to Lara.

'Light spell. It'll help in the tunnels.'

'But . . . come with us!'

'No time,' said Bernie. 'Go, Lara. I'll seal the entrance behind you.'

'Bernie . . .'

'GO, GIRL! Find that bird. And don't you fail me now!'

Lara looked into Bernie's blazing eyes and dared not argue. She ducked into the manhole and climbed down the ladder as quick as she could. As her feet touched the floor, an explosion rocked the alleyway above, and dust and pieces of brick came raining down. It took a few moments for her to catch her breath, to calm herself enough to think. She loaded the spell, pressed the trigger, and a blaze of warm light appeared at the tip of her wand. Muffled sounds reached down from the street: Bernie's shouts. Rob Nielsen's replies. Spellfire.

A spluttering cough brought Lara round. Double Eight was drenched from head to foot in sewer water. He stared at Lara with a look of intense disgust and held his hands away from his face like they were chunks of rotten meat. 'The smell. Oh, the smell!'

Lara breathed in. Yes. The smell. It wasn't pleasant, was it? It seemed like a lifetime since she'd been here. She was someone else now, and she could never go back to that life. The light from her wand glistened on the surface of the stream and reflected on the smooth bricks. She gathered her senses, went to the place in her head where Lara the tosher still lived: she could see every street, every tunnel, and she knew the way to anywhere in the city.

Above was Fishtail Alley. That meant the palace was

north-west from here. She could see the route unfolding in her mind.

'You get used to it,' she told Double Eight. 'Just breathe through your mouth. Come on.'

As they walked, Lara realised that there had been a time, not too long ago in fact, when she might have taken the chance to hide away down here, to let the world get on with tearing itself apart while she looked after herself. But not now. There were friends to help. Promises to keep. There was the duty Mum had passed to her.

With these thoughts in her head, and Double Eight beside her, the sewer tunnels did not feel a lonely place any more. How could she be alone when so many people were on her side, willing her on? How could she ever be alone when she knew her mother was always with her?

'Be brave, Double Eight,' she said, taking his hand. 'We're almost there. It'll be over soon.'

'You're right,' said a voice that was not Double Eight's. 'It *will* be over soon.'

Footsteps.

Coming closer.

Fwoosh.

Fwoosh.

Fwoosh.

Fwoosh.

The light from her spell only travelled so far into the darkness of the waiting tunnel. And from that darkness came a man. A man Lara recognised at once when he stepped into the light.

'Hello, girl,' said Shadow Jack. He reached into his coat and brought out a knife, and the look in his eyes was as sharp as any blade. 'Welcome home.'

FACE TO FACE

It happened so quickly.

Double Eight gave a roar and fired one of the sunlight spells from his wand at Shadow Jack. In a tangle of darkness, Shadow Jack became a raven, avoiding the blazing spell, arrowing through the tunnel towards them. Before he could fire another spell, the raven snatched the wand from Double Eight's hand. Lara spun around, her wand raised, trying to see what was going on, only to find the raven swooping down on her, taking her wand too. The light spell went out, and thick, inky blackness pushed in on them.

'Lara!'

'Double Eight! You hurt?'

'No . . .'

The sewer stream gurgled over their soaking feet in the dark.

Fwoosh.

Fwoosh.

Fwoosh.

Double Eight let out a cry.

'Don't move, girl,' said Shadow Jack's voice from the blackness. 'I have a knife at your friend's throat. Ordinarily I would finish the job here and now, but Mrs Hester wants to do it herself this time. So you climb to the surface like a good girl, eh? Don't try to run. Don't try anything smart. If you do, I'll bleed him dry. Now: move.'

Lara began to walk. Her mind raced, filled with a hundred different possibilities, ways she could try to escape, try to throw him off. But every option put Double Eight in danger, and she would not have that. She did as he asked. She found a ladder and began to climb to the surface, and when she pushed the manhole cover up and broke out into the freezing Evernight air, she found that some of the streetlamps here were still burning. The streets were deserted. The chaos had not yet found its way here.

'Move,' said Shadow Jack again, his knife still pressed to Double Eight's throat. 'To the church up the hill.'

Over the icy cobbles they went, to the old church at the corner of Cinnamon Lane. Shadow Jack directed them around the crumbling, ancient building, to the graveyard around the back. It was an overgrown, mostly forgotten place, and the church itself had fallen into disrepair. Lara pushed through trees and bushes, tripping over fallen headstones, until they came to a clearing where the stars would usually have shone. But there were no stars.

Mrs Hester waited among the graves, the light from her

wand falling upon the headstones, all jutting and broken like rotting teeth. Shadow Jack threw Double Eight down, then went to Mrs Hester's side and handed her the wands he'd taken.

Mrs Hester examined them under the light of her own wand. 'Pretty things. Hags always did have an eye for wand-making. Such a shame you'll never get to use them for anything great.' She tossed the wands to the ground, then approached Lara. 'You, my dear, have caused me more trouble than I care to admit. But not to worry. It'll be over soon enough.' As she was talking, Mrs Hester was fishing in her pockets, and she brought out a spell of darkest red, with a core that looked like a black spider. She loaded the spell into her wand, and it lit up in the chamber. 'My own version of a death spell. I've had a long time to get it right. Lots of practice. You'll feel pain before you go, I promise you that.' She smiled and fished in another pocket. This time when she brought out her hand Lara saw Moonwing in her palm, still and dead.

'What have you done to him?' She lunged forward, but Shadow Jack kicked her away.

'I want you to know,' said Mrs Hester, 'that you failed, girl. You are the last of the Doomsday Coven, and you are the one who has lost. You are the one who has given me the Spell. All their efforts, all this time, were for nothing. What would your mother think?'

Lara stared up, clenching her teeth. 'Don't you talk about my mother!'

'Oh, but she'd be so disappointed, wouldn't she? After all, she died so you could live. She protected you from Shadow Jack, and for what, eh?'

Lara's eyes flicked to Shadow Jack, standing still beside Hester. 'You . . . you killed my parents? It was . . . it was *you*, coming to get her?'

He stared down at her, emotionless.

'She suffered, you know,' said Mrs Hester, obviously enjoying herself. 'Greatly. He ate her soul. It's what he does.'

Lara thought she would vomit on the frozen grass.

'As for you,' Hester said to Double Eight, 'well, what shall we do with you, eh? I'm going to make sure every second of the rest of your life is agony, boy. You will pray for every breath to be the last. But I'll keep you alive. I'll dream up new ways to make you suffer.'

Something caught Lara's eye; did she see . . . had there been a twinkle of light in Moonwing's sapphire eyes?

Hester pointed her wand at Lara.

The death spell flared.

Lara closed her eyes, hoped, prayed.

Please. Please let it work.

'Moonwing. Now!'

Mrs Hester paused. She lowered her wand. She looked at her other hand, where Moonwing was now sitting up in her palm, his shining head twitching to one side, sapphire eyes fixed on her.

'It's awake!'

318

Moonwing exploded upwards at her face, his sharp beak piercing her right eye. She screamed, and staggered back, clawing at her face, blood gushing from the half-empty eye socket. Lara dived forward, grabbed the two wands on the ground, tossed Double Eight his, and rolled to her feet.

Double Eight jumped up and fired a sunlight spell straight at Mrs Hester. It hit her in the chest, sending her flying back, crashing through a crumbling headstone. Her wand went spinning across the graveyard.

Shadow Jack took a step towards Lara. And another.

Lara raised her wand, knowing that the magic would not stop him. 'Stay back. I'm warning you!' He took another step, getting closer now, too close. Lara tripped on a root and fell back.

Somewhere in Lara's mind, a memory lit up.

Nel Pepper had given her a spell.

A thread of pure moonlight from the clouds.

It'll bind anything . . .

She rolled across the grass, reached into her coat, brought out the bottle and loaded it into the chamber. Then, with barely a moment to spare, she raised the wand and, as Shadow Jack's hand came down on her shoulder, she fired.

A thread of moonlight erupted from the wand, wrapping around Shadow Jack again and again, the way a spider might wrap its prey in web. He yelled and screamed and fought, but the moonlight held firm. Lara felt the wand shake with the power of the spell, the heat of it on her face.

The smell of it was hot metal, and the wind that came from it blew her hair wildly around her head. She curled her lip in a hateful sneer, enjoying the pain she was causing him. 'Is this what it was like for my mum?' she asked. 'Is this the sort of pain she felt? Is it?' She moved the wand, and the binding grew tighter, squeezed him, so that his eyes popped wide and black veins stuck out on his face, his neck. Still she squeezed. Lara had waited a lifetime for this, to finally take all her frustration, her suffering, her loneliness out on someone . . . anyone . . .

She walked forward, the spell pushing him against an old oak tree, the heat of it making the bark smoke, and in her mind there was no doubt.

She was going to kill him.

Across the graveyard, Double Eight gave Mrs Hester a kick. She did not respond. She lay awkwardly on her side, her head buried in the crook of an arm, the other arm flailing out wide behind her. Double Eight gave her another kick. Nothing.

A shape in the folds of her coat caught his eye, and he reached down and found that she'd been carrying, in one of those impossible pockets, a small, ancient-looking urn. Double Eight turned it in his hands.

A moment's distraction was all Mrs Hester needed.

She lunged at him. Double Eight dropped his wand as she dragged him to the ground and began clawing and tearing at his face with her long nails. He tried to protect himself, to keep his hands up, but she was strong, and angry. Her white-blonde hair was dyed red with blood, and her right eye mostly gone. She screamed incomprehensible things at him, spitting on him, ripping at his flesh.

He could not fight her off.

SHATTERED

Joe Littlefoot knew he was dying. He lay frightened and alone in a spreading pool of blood on the floor of Mrs Hester's rooms, far from home. The pain where she had stuck him with the knife was burning, yet the rest of him felt icy cold as his life leaked out.

Joe's eyes were heavy, his lips dry. He looked around the room, thinking that this would be the last place he'd ever see.

His eyes found the mirror.

Smash the mirror, Joe.

'I can't, Granny. I'm hurt.'

You have it in you to do it, Joe. Set them free. Smash the mirror.

Joe slowly managed to get to his knees. Shaking badly, spattering blood from his side onto the cold floor, he crawled to the mirror. Gathering everything he had, he reared back and brought his fist down on the shining surface.

The glass did not break.

Joe's head fell forward, his chin resting on his chest. Eyes blurring in and out of focus, he spotted a glass paperweight on Mrs Hester's desk, and he reached up, moaning in pain, grabbed it, and hammered against the glass.

Still it did not smash.

To his great surprise, Joe found that he was laughing. It was a desperate, angry laugh, and when he next managed to raise his heavy head, the open window came into focus.

Joe looked at the window.

He looked at the mirror.

'Nothin's ever easy.'

Using the table as support, he pulled himself agonisingly to his feet and then began the torturous task of dragging the mirror to the window. Each time the mirror's feet scuffed the floor the sound was a scraping scream.

Blood from his wound dripped on the floor, and after each effort he had to stop and gather his strength. Eventually he made it, knowing what came next would be the real effort. Joe dropped to his knees and grabbed the mirror's chunky feet. He took a deep breath, tried to lift the mirror, and screamed in pain.

Oh no. I didn't drag it all the way over here to give up now. Come on, Joe. Come. ON!

He grabbed the feet, lifted, screamed in pain again, only this time he fought through, pushed and pushed, felt the mirror lift, and lift some more, and teeter on the window ledge. Then, with a final, triumphant roar he sent the mirror spinning down the side of the palace. Joe leaned out, half-hanging from the window, watching the mirror fall. Far, far below, it hit the ground.

Finally, Mrs Hester's mirror smashed.

When the mirror hit the ground, it exploded with such force that the sound could be heard across the city. In the graveyard, Mrs Hester let out a shrieking scream. She stopped scratching and biting and clawing at Double Eight, and he watched in puzzled horror as her skin began to melt and run like candle wax. Her hair turned dirty grey and fell out, leaving her mostly bald. Her bones grew hunched and twisted. Mrs Hester looked at her swollen, gnarled hands, and her one remaining eye widened in shock and disgust and terror.

She screamed. Then, mad with fear, she went scuttling off into the night.

Lara still had Shadow Jack pressed against the tree, bound in moonlight, but even she glanced over to the palace, where thousands of glowing creatures were soaring and spinning around the highest tower, lighting the inky blackness that had been pressing down from the sky.

'Is that . . . ?'

'Souls!' gasped Double Eight from the other side of the graveyard. 'It's White Witch souls, Lara! They're free!'

*

Up in the tower, golden souls streamed through the window and enveloped Joe Littlefoot.

They surrounded him, flew through him, through his body, his veins and the wound Mrs Hester had caused, repairing the damage. They lifted him up. His heart began to beat once more. His lungs sucked in air and his eyes cracked open.

The souls carried him out of the window, flew him across the city, and gently deposited him on the frozen grass of an overgrown graveyard.

When the souls were gone, Joe stood up and blinked. He felt like he had just awakened from a very long sleep. He touched the place the wound had been, found that it was gone. Then he looked around the dimness of the graveyard, and the first thing he saw was a familiar object lying in the grass nearby. An urn. As Joe picked it up he heard a scream. He came out from behind a tree, and he saw his best friend in all the world . . . 'Lara?'

Sweat poured down Lara's brow. Her wand hand shook terribly with the effort of controlling the spell. Still she squeezed the trigger.

I'll split him open, that's what I'll do. Watch his guts spill out on the grass!

'Lara!'

She blinked. 'Joe?'

'It's me, Lara.' Joe moved slowly towards her. 'What are you doing?'

Lara turned her head back to Shadow Jack. The black veins on his face were multiplying. 'I'm killing him, Joe. Just like he killed my mum and dad.'

Joe moved closer, palms out, open. 'He did terrible things, Lara. I know he did. But he didn't have a choice. He's a Djinni. Mrs Hester was controlling him.'

'It doesn't make it right!'

'I know it don't,' said Joe, holding his hands out. 'But Lara . . . if you kill him, you're no better than him. No better than Mrs Hester.'

She was crying. 'I *want* to hurt him!'

'It looks like you've done a good job. Come on, Lara. This isn't you. This isn't the Lara I know. Don't let hate win, Lara. If hate wins, what's the point in anything?'

Lara looked to the blank heavens with tear-filled eyes, up at the Evernight, and the golden White Witch souls. The locket buzzed against her chest.

Lara lowered her wand.

The spell fizzed away to nothing, letting Shadow Jack collapse on the grass.

'Thank you,' he said, gasping.

'You don't get to speak,' Joe told him. 'You don't get to be here anymore.' He held the urn up over his head. 'It's over. Get out of here. I set you free, Shadow Jack. Leave this world, and don't you ever come back.'

Joe threw the urn. It tumbled through the graveyard, hit a headstone and shattered into countless shards and pieces.

Shadow Jack stood up and looked at Joe. His eyes were sparkling with tears. He opened his mouth to speak, but before he could say anything, the souls of the Witches he'd eaten, the power that had fuelled him in his human form, drifted out of his mouth, back into the world.

Lara's own mouth dropped open, and she wiped her eyes and reached out as she watched the souls floating away towards the next life, fading, knowing in her heart that her parents were among them.

'Goodbye,' she whispered.

When the last soul was gone, Shadow Jack turned to dust and went with the wind to find his brothers and sisters.

Moonwing's Flight

Lara's locket continued to buzz. As she gripped it tight, Moonwing fluttered around her, landing on her, pecking at her. A feeling hatched deep in her chest . . . deeper even than that. It was like a part of her she had not known was even there had awakened. And she knew.

'It's time, isn't it?'

Moonwing pecked at her ear.

'But what do I do?' She searched her feelings. 'My soul is the key. That's what Mum said. My soul is the key . . .'

It occurred to Lara then that souls were the key to everything. Mrs Hester with White Witch souls. Shadow Jack eating souls to stay alive. The High Witch and her council flying their souls out across the world to face the darkness. But what *was* a soul? If you could take all the best bits of a person, the love, the happiness, the good things they'd done, the mark they left on the world, the part of them that lived on in other people's hearts and memories even long after they'd gone . . . that was the soul, wasn't it?

She opened her hand, let Moonwing sit on her palm, and with the other hand she clutched the locket, thought of her mother, of the joy of seeing her face, and the sacrifice she'd made for her daughter. And now it was Lara's turn.

At once Moonwing's clockwork sped up, and his eyes blazed brighter blue. Still it was not enough. Lara kept the picture of her mum in her head, and she also thought of the friends she'd made, of how she'd once been alone in the world, how others had opened their hearts to her. First little Joe and Granny. Then Magnus and Bernie. And dear Double Eight. If anyone knew the power of a soul, it was him. For the first time in her life, Lara understood what love really was. Love lived in those people, made the world worth fighting for. Worth dying for.

Moonwing glowed brighter, and brighter still. A golden light began to burst from his chest, from the spinning clockwork there, and the warmth of it felt like summer on Lara's skin.

'Take it,' Lara said, her eyes brimming with warm tears. 'Take my soul, Moonwing.'

The etching of the bird on her locket came suddenly to life, lighting up. The gears in Moonwing's chest quickened to such a rate that they were blurring as they turned, the heat growing so intense that it almost burned Lara's fingers. The light from his eyes was warm as the sun, expanding outward, so that Lara was standing in the centre of a sphere of light, every cell in her body alive with magic and power.

The spell was flowing from the bird into her, through her veins and back again, like they were one. He was a part of her, and she of him. The glow became so bright it seemed like the world melted away, and there was only Lara and Moonwing, and nothing else.

A flash of blinding gold, and Moonwing was the size of a great eagle, and Lara was upon his back.

Another echo from the past came to her then. Granny's voice, something she'd said to Lara as she'd read her fortune.

'I see you flying . . . on blazing wings, my love! Wings the colour of the sun!'

'Fly,' said Lara. 'Fly, Moonwing.'

The cogs in him clicked, and he spread his golden wings, and carried her into the sky.

What Goes Up . . .

Bernie Whitecrow was bleeding heavily from the hand, staggering through the streets among the scores of surviving slum folk. Nearby in the crowd, Rob Nielsen crouched down, clutching at an arrow lodged in his leg. The Painted came from every street, every alleyway, flanked by their enchanted servants. They drew their bows, and aimed.

Bernie closed her eyes.

'I'm coming, Magnus.'

Suddenly everything stopped. One by one, they looked up, the Painted and the Witches and the people of King's Haven, at the golden streak in the sky.

Bernie smiled through her tears. 'Lara!'

The wind was in Lara's hair as Moonwing arrowed through the dark. She clung to him, looking down upon the city. For so long that place had been her world, and now it seemed so small.

Up and up and up they went, towards the Evernight, the demon in the sky.

Still they climbed, until the air became frighteningly thin. But Lara was not scared. Whatever happened, wherever she ended up, she had known love and friendship, and those things burned bright in her heart. She clung on as Moonwing rocketed unstoppably onwards, into a darkness so vast and ancient that Lara could not comprehend it.

'I'm coming, Mum.'

The darkness enveloped them.

Everything became nothing.

Moonwing opened out his wings, and let out a long, musical call.

A great explosion of light. Where Moonwing had been there was only light. Everything was light.

Lara began to fall.

They watched. Bernie and Rob watched the streak of gold climb impossibly high, disappearing into the Evernight. When it exploded, the flash was blinding, and they shielded their eyes.

'Lara!'

'Oh, Lara!'

She was falling. They could see her, tumbling through the heavens, head over feet, encased in a sphere of gold. The White Witch souls were trying to protect her. It looked like a star was falling.

Down.

Down.

Down.

She hit the ground a few streets away, in the slums, and there were gasps and cries as the boom rang through the city. Smoke and dust billowed into the air.

Then, quiet.

The White Witch souls streaked out across the lightening sky, flashing over King's Haven, over the entire Kingdom, each one hungry to reunite with its body.

On the frozen grass of the overgrown graveyard on Cinnamon Lane, Joe Littlefoot was helping Double Eight to his feet when the darkness of the clearing erupted with golden warmth. Frightened, awed, Joe held Double Eight steady as his soul approached. Bloodied and beaten, Double Eight reached disbelievingly out, like he thought he was imagining it. But the soul came closer, and closer still, until it touched Double Eight's chest, pushed through and became a part of him for the first time since the day he was born.

Double Eight's head shot back, and he sucked air into his lungs. Tears were flowing as he touched his chest, and a strange, wonderful feeling swelled in him.

The feeling of being whole.

Daybreak

'Look there! At the sky!'

'Something's happening to the dark!'

'It's crackin' open! Like an egg!'

This was an apt description. After the explosion of light, cracks began to creep and trace across the sky, and through the cracks daylight shone.

The cracks grew bigger, joining up, and the Evernight sky dissolved.

Daylight returned to the world.

The Painted shielded their eyes, cried out in pain and fell to the ground, their skin bubbling and hissing. They burned, the Painted, until they were nothing but dark stains on the streets. At first the survivors were too stunned, too relieved and exhausted to do anything but stare. But soon the cheers began, the yells of victory, and those cheers spread through the streets the way the sunlight had spread across the sky.

*

Out in Bad Mouth Bay, on one of the dark ships, as the Painted yelled and tried to turn their boats around, those who had been marked and bewitched began to wake up.

A fishing boat captain remembered who she was. She remembered her childhood, her brothers, her father. She remembered her boat, her crew, the day the Evernight had come, had taken her, placing her under a dark spell.

She looked around, as if waking from a dream, dazzled by the light, and saw the Painted in panic, their skin burning in the sun. She took the wheel from a screaming, burning Painted, spun it around so that the ship was pointing towards another of the black ships, and steered a straight course at it.

As one ship crashed into the other, she jumped into the Pewter Sea, and began swimming for the shore.

The first thing Agata remembered was her son Joshua's blond hair. Then the rest of her life came back to her. She remembered the night the Painted had arrived, the Painted who'd carved the curse on her forehead and taken her life from her. Now, as she scanned the boat, she saw Painted on the deck, some dead, others writhing in pain. The strongest of them were still on their feet, trying to steer their ships away, to follow the receding darkness. Agata picked up a bow from a fallen body, a handful of arrows, and she aimed, loosing arrow after arrow. Then, when there were no more arrows, she climbed to the edge of the ship, and closed her eyes, and jumped to freedom as the last of the Painted's black ships drifted dead in the bay or sank burning to the bottom of the Pewter Sea.

The first thing Lara heard was the familiar gurgle of the stream. The water splashed and sprayed her, and she breathed in the smells of the sewers, the sweet stench of rot and filth, and felt that she was home.

Her eyes cracked open.

How weird.

She was lying in the tunnels, and yet she was also looking at the sky.

The sky was blue, and bright.

'Outta the way! Let me through!'

'Where is she?'

'Move!'

High above, Bernie Whitecrow's face appeared over the edge of the hole in the street, and then Rob Nielsen and Double Eight, and Joe.

'Hello,' said Lara. 'Am I alive? Lovely to see you.'

And then she passed out.

PAYBACK

Two days had passed since the sun returned and still the festivities showed no sign of slowing. The streets were alive with celebration, with singing and dancing, with fire whisky and food and laughter.

Among all of this, Lara and her friends cut through the crowds, heads down, trying not to be recognised. Lara was not smiling.

These streets were familiar to her, of course. She had grown up on them, and they had been a part of her, running through her blood, for so long. But now she felt like a stranger in the city.

She had been among the crowds when the Silver King had addressed his people yesterday, and Lara had shaken her head that he could be so bombastic and arrogant. He had claimed victory over the Evernight for himself, and made out that the Silver Kingdom and Mrs Hester's White Witches were responsible for pushing back the darkness. Mrs Hester had been strangely absent. Lara wondered what had become of her. Was she still out there, hiding in the shadows, licking her wounds?

In most of the city, the Silver King's announcement that anyone who had been marked by the Painted should be immediately arrested and made to stand trial was popular. The coppers had already begun arresting and trying those who'd been cursed. They were easy to spot, with the scars on their foreheads. Easy to blame too, Lara realised. Some of them had already been hanged! These were people with families, people who had done nothing wrong except be in the wrong place at the wrong time.

Because of this, unrest was beginning to creep around the slums.

Many of the slum folk had been bewitched or lost loved ones in the fight. Anger towards the king, disgust that he had been willing to leave the poor trapped in the city to face the Evernight alone, was growing, and Lara sensed that this was the start of something bigger, the first cracks, maybe, in the armour of the Silver Kingdom.

She pushed through a crowd of drinkers, down Needle Street and into Bone Alley.

Tingalingaling!

Old Hans was not known for his lovely complexion, but when he looked up from his counter and saw Lara and her friends standing in his shop, he turned a shade of green unhealthy even by his own standards.

'Don't say a word,' Lara told him. 'Don't scream for

help or try to attract attention, otherwise you'll have a shop full of very angry Witches. You hear?'

Old Hans nodded fearfully. 'What you want, Lara?'

She stared at him, and she felt tall and powerful. 'You've heard what they're doin'? To them that the Painted cursed?'

Old Hans nodded. 'Can't be too careful, can we? I *mean*, who's to say they won't turn bad again at the drop of a hat, eh? Who's to say the Hags can't now use 'em for their own means?'

'That's not how it works. It could have been you, Old Hans. Would you feel differently then?'

He shrugged, stuck out his chin.

Lara leaned on the counter. 'This is what is going to happen. I'm goin' to smuggle as many of those poor marked folks out of this city as I can. To do that I need a boat. And to get a boat, I need coins.'

Old Hans stared blankly at her. 'That's generally how it works, yes.'

'I want you to give me that money.'

Old Hans laughed, right in her face. 'I ain't in the habit of doin' business with Hags.' He spat on his own shop floor, at Lara's feet.

Rob Nielsen burst forward, dragging Old Hans across the counter and pinning him against a wall. 'You listen here, you worthless old fart. If it wasn't for Lara you'd still be cowerin' in the dark. She saved your city, your precious, stinkin' little shop. And you will show her respect!'

A bead of sweat rolled down Old Hans' crooked nose. 'Let him go, Rob.'

Lara stood face to face with Old Hans. 'I think I'm a fair person. I don't want everythin' you got. But I know you got a safe back there, filled with all the treasure you've swindled from toshers like me and Joe over the years.'

'That's right,' said Joe, who'd stuck closely to Lara ever since the events of the night in the graveyard. 'We're here to collect what we're owed for our hard work. We reckon that should just about cover the cost of a boat. So you run along, Old Hans, and fetch what we're due.'

Old Hans stared around the shop, from Lara to Bernie, Rob to Double Eight to Joe, and his shoulders slumped. He disappeared into the back. When he returned, he dropped a pile of gold onto the counter and glared at Lara. 'Don't you ever come back.'

Lara stared at him, at the old man she had once believed to be her friend. 'That I can promise.'

ONWARD

Lara stood at the bow of her new boat, closed her eyes and felt the wind flowing through her dark curls. The sunlight was warm on her skin, and it glittered on the peaks of the waves, and on Lara's locket. She wore it on the outside of her shirt now, no longer wishing to hide it away.

They had been three days at sea, still a fair sail yet to Westerly Witch. The boat was laden with slum-folk, as many of the cursed and their families as could fit safely. They looked so frightened, and Lara could understand why: Hags were strange, dangerous creatures to these coves, and they had placed their faith in Lara and her friends – in Hags – because the only other choice was to face trial and probably be hanged. There would be more trips to come, more boatloads of terrified people forced to leave their homes. Lara heard lots of them muttering about the king with hate in their voices.

'He's made a mistake,' said Bernie, joining Lara. 'He's underestimated the power of ordinary folk. Things are goin' to get interesting, girl, you mark my words.'

'Is the Evernight gone for good?' said Lara.

'The Doomsday Spell has it under control,' said Bernie. 'And I think that's the best we can hope for.'

'Bernie . . . what'll happen to all these poor people?'

'Well, we'll take care of 'em till it's safe for 'em to go home.'

Double Eight and Joe came striding over the deck, pointing up to the blue sky.

'What a sight for sore eyes that is,' said Joe. 'I thought I'd never see the sun again.'

'I wish I could have been there for you, Joe,' said Lara. 'When Granny passed.'

He stared out towards the horizon. 'She loved you, Lara. You know that, right?'

Lara felt the urge to hug him, and she could not fight it.

'Hell's teeth!' Joe exclaimed. 'You'll pop my ribs.'

'Thank you, Joe. For everything you did. If it hadn't been for you . . .'

'I'd be dead, for one thing,' said Double Eight.

'How's the soul settling in?' Lara asked him with a smile.

Double Eight tapped his chest. 'Just fine.'

'No more hunger?'

'No. No more hunger, Lara.'

Lara tilted her head. 'But?'

Double Eight shrugged. 'But . . . well, I *wanted* to run away, Lara. And I've got you and the others to help me get

342

used to my new life. It might sound mad to you, but there are an awful lot of White Witches out there who have never even considered what it means to be free, and whole, and able to think and question and wonder. What are they feeling now? What'll happen to them? They're all alone.'

Lara took his hand. 'I don't think anything will ever be the same,' she said, 'for any of us. And I don't think anyone knows what's going to happen next. But we made it through, didn't we? We survived. And so will those White Witches who want to be free.'

He nodded, and Lara turned back to the sea. So much had changed. She did not recognise the girl from the sewers any more. Her old life seemed like it had happened to someone else. She had spent her entire existence wondering who she was, where she belonged, and now that she'd found out, it felt almost as if she'd lost as much as she'd gained.

She could never return to those simple days. But she'd look forward, not back, and she'd embrace the person she was meant to be, the Witch she could become, as frightening as that still seemed. There was so much to learn, such a long journey to come, and the thought of it made her feel small.

As she watched the sun-gilded waves tumble and roll beneath the boat, her hands went to her pockets, and she remembered the feeling of Moonwing there, fluttering and twitching. He had been a wondrous object, the most magical thing she would ever encounter, and she was going to miss him dearly. But there was so much more magic out there, an entire world of it waiting to be discovered.

So Larabelle Fox smiled, and felt the sea spray on her face, and sailed towards tomorrow.

Acknowledgements

One of the joys of being an author is to work with, and learn from, so many talented and passionate people.

From the moment I first spoke to Charlie Sheppard, my wonderful editor, I hoped that Andersen would become my home. Charlie, thank you for your wisdom and guidance. Thank you for the unflinching belief you've shown in Lara and her story. I promise we're just getting started.

Everyone at Andersen has made me feel so welcome. I hope this book makes you proud.

Thanks as always to Stephanie Thwaites, super-agent, guardian angel, for guiding me through the unpredictable wonderland of publishing. I couldn't imagine making the journey with anyone else.

Thank you, Isobel Gahan, for the magic you added to the manuscript along the way.

Without my family I might never have worked up the courage to write down the stories in my head. Mum and Dad, thank you for always telling me that anything is possible. Selina and Mollie, my heart fills with wonder when I imagine what you might grow up to be. I can't wait to find out. And Aileen. Wife. Bestie. Partner in crime. Thank you for everything.